MW00567874

Marlene Streeruwitz

SEDUCTIONS.

Part 3
Women's Years.

TRANSLATED FROM THE GERMAN
BY KATHARINA ROUT

OOLICHAN BOOKS
LANTZVILLE, BRITISH COLUMBIA, CANADA
1998

Translation Copyright © 1998 by Katharina Rout. ALL RIGHTS RE-
SERVED. No part of this publication may be reproduced, stored in a
retrieval system, or transmitted, in any form or by any means, without
prior written permission of the publisher, except by a reviewer who
may quote brief passages in a review to be printed in a newspaper or
magazine or broadcast on radio or television; or, in the case of photo-
copying or other reprographic copying, a licence from CANCOPY (Canadian Copyright Licensing Agency), 6 Adelaide Street East, Suite 900,
Toronto, Ontario M5C 1H6.

Originally published by Suhrkamp Verlag, Frankfurt am Main,
Germany, under the title *VERFÜHRUNGEN*: © 1996 by Suhrkamp
Verlag.

Canadian Cataloguing in Publication Data

Streeruwitz, Marlene.

   Seductions

Translation of: Verfuhrungen

ISBN 0-88982-174-7

   I. Title.

PT2681.T6916V4713 1998   833'.914   C98-910904-6

Cover photo and design by Jonathan Rout

The Publisher gratefully acknowledges the financial support of the Government of Canada through the Book Publishing Industry Development Program
for our publishing activities, and the Austrian Chancellor's Office.

Published by
Oolichan Books
P.O. Box 10, Lantzville
British Columbia, Canada
V0R 2H0

Printed in Canada by
Morriss Printing Company
Victoria, British Columbia

Translator's Acknowledgments

I would like to express my gratitude to Marlene Streeruwitz for all the help and support she gave me with this translation and for the delightful conversations we had about her novel, about language, women, men, and Sachertorte.

I would also like to thank the Austrian Chancellor's Office and the Canadian government's Book Publishing Development Program for their generous financial assistance for the translation and publication of the novel, and Malaspina University-College for granting me the time.

Last but not least, I would like to Ron Smith of Oolichan Books for his encouragement and his editing of the text; Barbara, Hanna, Michael, Stefan and my father for their support; and my husband Jonathan for sharing our life with Helene and her children, for being always willing to discuss the words and sentences of the book, and for shooting the photo and designing the cover.

Errington, Canada   *Katharina Rout*

Seductions.

The phone rang at 3 a.m. It was Püppi. Helene must come. Right away. Urgently. Or did she have better things to do than take care of her friend. Was she busy. With a Swede perhaps? Helene got dressed. She put notes on her bed and outside Grandmother's apartment next door. On these notes Helene wrote Püppi's phone number, in case one of the children woke up and looked for her. Püppi lived in the Karolinengasse. In the fourth district. Near the Belvedere. Helene drove along the Franz Joseph's Quay and the Ringstrasse to the Prinz Eugen Strasse. Close to the center, the streets were busy. But in the nineteenth and then in the fourth district nobody was on the streets. A police cruiser was parked in front of the Turkish Embassy, at the corner of Karolinengasse and Prinz Eugen Strasse. The police watched as Helene drove past. Helene wondered what she might find this time. Püppi had sounded calm. Mysterious. Reproachful. But coherent. The heater had only started to warm the car by the time she'd reached the Schwedenplatz. Chilled right through, Helene ran up the stairs of 9 Karolinengasse. She had a key to the front door, for situations like this one. There was no intercom. Not even door bells. If you wanted to see Püppi, you had to phone first.

Or be skilled enough to throw a pebble at the windows on the fifth floor. The door to the apartment was ajar, the door to Sophie's room wide open. Helene went in. The Thai nanny sat in the corner behind Sophie's bed. Crouched on the floor, the young woman stared at Ebner. Karl Ebner, art dealer, stood by the child's bed and looked down at Sophie. The bedside lamp was on, and Sophie's blond baby hair shone in the light. The child was asleep. Ebner swayed slightly. The Thai woman watched him anxiously. Relieved, she smiled at Helene and stood up. Helene laid her finger on her lips. And took Ebner's hand. Ebner was grunting to himself. Helene turned the light off, shoved the nanny out of the room and closed the door. Ebner wanted to go back into the child's room. But Helene held his hand tight and led him down the hallway. The Thai woman slipped into her own room. Ebner wanted to go after the young woman. Helene held him tight. With Ebner in her grip, she went on a search for Püppi. They found her in the bathroom. Püppi sat in the bathtub, bubbles piled all around her. Steaming hot water ran into the tub. Püppi was on the phone and scrubbing her back. Ebner began to undress. Awkwardly. He put his clothes on a little stool. He folded everything neatly, swaying while doing it. Naked, he squeezed himself into the tub, facing Püppi. Püppi was on the phone. She waved to Helene with the brush. Helene went into the kitchen and sat down at the table. She could see through the kitchen window into the light well. All other windows were dark. Helene would have liked some coffee. Anything warm to drink. She went back into the bathroom. Ebner had fallen asleep in the tub. His head had dropped forward into the bubbles. Püppi was on the phone. Plastic animals were lying around. Everything in the bathroom had animal motifs on it. Towels, soap bars, tooth brushes, glasses, face cloths, combs, brushes, tiles. Everywhere Mickey Mouses,

Donald Ducks, Houies, Louies and Douies. Elephants.
Ducks. Monkeys. All for Sophie. Helene asked Püppi if she
knew. Ebner had been in her daughter's room. The Thai
woman had woken up. Fortunately. Didn't she think? Püppi
said on the phone, "I'll pass you on to somebody now who
can confirm that he isn't here." She held out the receiver to
Helene. Helene took the receiver which was wet and covered with bubbles. "What's up?" she asked. "I know he's
there. I know it. I. Know it. I can feel it. I feel it. Now you
don't know what to do. The two of you. Know nothing.
Not any longer. But. There'll be other stuff. A whole lot of
other stuff is going to happen. You'll see sooner or later.
Sooner or later you'll see. I'm telling you. Both of you. No
way you're taking Jack away from me. Not the two of you.
Not anybody. You may as well . . ." The woman spoke fast,
without emphasis, as if prompting herself. "What's it about?
What's going on?" Püppi continued to scrub her back.
Helene held the receiver far away from her ear. "It's that
lunatic from Salzburg," Püppi said. "It's about Jack." "The
Sophie?" Helene asked. "Yes. The one who went nuts."
Helene spoke into the receiver. "But. Alex. Isn't Alex there.
Isn't he there anymore?" For a moment the receiver was
silent, then the voice started screeching. Cracked. Screamed.
"Just piss off with Alex. Fuck off. I wish he'd bugger off.
Finally. Piss off, all of you . . ." Helene held the receiver up
in the air. Püppi beamed at her radiantly. From the receiver
you could hear, "Jack. Jack. I need you, Jack. If you don't
come! I'll do it. I'll just do it . . ." Püppi's bedroom door
opened. A tall ash-blonde man came in. Püppi's Chinese
gown barely reached his thigh. He was cleaning his fingernails with a hunting knife. He took the receiver from
Helene. "Shhh. Pussy," he said. Calm. Friendly. "Be nice.
Otherwise. When I get home." The voice from the receiver
cracked. Sobbed. Screamed. The man put the receiver on

the floor. He looked at Helene and grinned. The receiver remained on the floor. They could hear the screeching. Feeble. The man pulled Püppi up from the tub. Bubbles stuck to her. He embraced her. Looking back over his shoulder at Helene he asked, "Is she going to join in?" And Püppi said, "Helene, may I introduce Herr Niemeyer to you?" She laughed. "Jack. Called Jack. Like the Ripper." She sounded happy. She climbed onto the edge of the bathtub. The man lifted her up. He flung the knife into the light-colored wood paneling behind the bathtub where it remained stuck in the wood. Above Ebner's head. The man looked at the knife. Then he picked up Püppi. Kissing, the two disappeared into the bedroom. Ebner slowly slid down into the tub. Helene pulled the plug and turned off the water. She left. Nothing could be heard from the receiver. She carefully locked the doors and drove home. She hadn't been away much more than an hour.

Alex phoned on Sunday. After lunch, Helene lay down on the bed to read and fell asleep. At first she didn't realize who was on the phone. "Hey. It's me," Alex said. "The little green man." The children had called Alex the little green man because he'd always worn green Trachtenjanker, traditional Austrian jackets, when he'd picked up Helene. Yes. He'd been thinking they should see each other. He'd already tried the day before, but nobody had been at home. "We'd gone for a walk," Helene said. And yes. Why not. Why shouldn't they see each other. But today? Helene hesitated. The office. She should sleep. But she let herself be persuaded. At 8 o'clock. Yes. He should ring the bell downstairs. She'd come down.

The Swede phoned at 4 o'clock. Would she be free in the evening. Helene turned him down. She had to sleep. The office. Yes? "That's a pity," he said. By then he'd be back in Milan. "Yes. Have a good trip then," Helene said. "What do you mean?" asked the Swede. Yes. The trip to Milan. That was a trip, wasn't it? "Oh well. Yes. Of course!" he laughed.

Helene prepared supper for the children and supervised the teeth brushing and bathing. In the meantime she wondered whether to wash her hair. What did Alex want. They hadn't talked since their phone calls in August. Helene washed her hair and put on her only decent dress. An aunt had given her the Balmain dress at Christmas as a gift for her 30th birthday. It's time to be elegant, Aunt Adele had said. Helene would have preferred the money. She didn't even have shoes to match the dress. Once more, she lay down on the bed. The children were romping in their room. The grandmother sat in the living room and watched TV. Helene had carefully rolled her hair up and lay back on her pillow. The hair on her neck still felt damp. She pressed her head into the pillow. So that no cool air could get to her wet hair. For a moment, she felt a great fatigue flow into her body. She thought she wouldn't be able to get up again. And for a moment she didn't care. Rest. She thought. Keep resting. Just rest. Then Alex rang the bell, and she jumped up. Shook her hair into place and got her coat. Kissed them all good-bye. Made them all promise to go to bed soon. And left.

Alex was waiting at the front door. Suddenly Helene didn't know how to greet him. They stood facing each other. "You have a new car?" Helene asked. Alex explained the advantages of his new Subaru to her. Then they laughed and fell into each other's arms. Laughed about this stupid dialog. Laughed as if the phone calls in August had never happened. Nor the months Helene had been waiting for his call. They went to the Stony Owl for a meal. Alex ordered the food and the wine. Alex had always chosen the food and the wine. Helene asked what he'd been up to. Why he was in Vienna. Didn't he live in Salzburg anymore? Alex had things to do in Vienna. And he didn't live in Salzburg anymore. And what was she doing with herself. Did she have a lover? Had she finally gotten her divorce? Helene ate and drank automatically. Didn't taste a thing. Briefly she thought of the children. Should she call home? After dessert she would ask Alex. Alex had ordered the house specialty. Nougat parfait. Helene looked at her plate and picked a little cube off her ice cream. She couldn't think of a beginning for the question. No word. No sentence. And she worried her voice would shake too much. Or would sound hoarse. She looked up. Alex watched her. They looked into each other's eyes. "I can't tell you either. I don't really know why myself," Alex said. "And I regret it. Believe me." Alex ordered two Grappa. "Do you still like this dreadful yellow stuff?" he asked. Helene felt like crying. Quietly and softly. And at the same time she felt light and separated from it all. She drank her Grappa. Alex paid. They left the restaurant. Helene got into the car with Alex. She sat next to him. Silent. Didn't ask where he was going. In front of a house on the Prinz Eugen Strasse, way up, almost at the South Station, Alex parked the car. Helene let him help her out of the car. A small bronze sign saying "Pension Monopol" hung next to the entrance. Alex rang the bell and said something into the intercom. Helene thought Püppi should have a chance to see her now. Going into a seedy hotel. As if she were doing this every day. A man opened the door and sized them up. Helene tried to look as natural as possible. Alex slipped some bills into the man's hand. In the hallway with its marble panels and wooden pavement a chambermaid appeared. She wore a black dress, black shoes and stockings, a small white apron and a white lace cap. She was old and fat. The woman led them into a room. Everything was white. The walls, the wall panels, the bed, the vanity, the concealed door to the bathroom. "Towels are in the bathroom," the woman said and opened the bathroom door. And would the lady and gentleman like anything else. There was no minibar. Alex turned to Helene. "I guess Champagne is in order, isn't it?" Helene asked. "But. I'd like orange juice." The woman shrugged. Alex ordered orange juice as well, and the woman left. Helene sat on the bed. "Do we have to wait for the juice now?" Alex flung her back on the bed and leaned over her. "The woman wouldn't care one bit," he whispered. But when the orange juice was delivered, Helene sat up anyway and straightened her hair. The woman put the orange juice on the vanity. "That's 200 schillings, Sir." Alex fished money out of his pocket and locked the door behind the woman. Suddenly Helene felt weepy. It made her laugh. Then everything was quite easy, as if the calendar had been turned back to last July. Or June. May. As usual, Alex didn't give her any chance to pretend. He kept sucking her until nothing was possible but an orgasm. Then he pulled her onto himself and came while she rode him. He held her for a long time, just as he had before. Helene was roused from a deep sleep. It was 3 a.m. Alex was asleep. Helene began to dress. Alex woke up as she searched for her underwear under the covers. Half asleep he asked who she'd gone to bed with in the meantime. She had changed somehow. She was more intense. Then he started to dress. Helene carried on in silence. She wanted her own bed. She didn't want to hear what he'd asked her. She didn't want to think about it. She said nothing. They left the room. Didn't see anybody. But then Helen couldn't hold back her tears. She sat in the car and felt the tears roll down her cheeks and dry on her neck. In front of the house, Alex wanted to say something, but Helene quickly got out and went to the front door. Alex actually got out and was about to call something after her. She closed the door as fast as possible. And ran up to the apartment. The children were asleep. Everything's all right, a note from Grandmother said. Without undressing Helene threw herself on the bed.

Püppi called Helene at the office. Could they have lunch. They met in Café Prückl. Püppi was just in jeans and sweater. She was alone. She had ordered sparkling wine. "You have to congratulate me," she said. "I'm getting married." Helene stared at Püppi. "Who?" "Jack. Of course." The waiter brought Helene's coffee, a Melange. Püppi was smoking. She kept pouring little sips of Henckell Trocken from the Piccolo bottle into her glass and emptying it right away. She looked at Helene. In triumph. Her eyes were not made up and seemed to dissolve behind her glasses. Helene said nothing. She knew she should say something enthusiastic. Words that showed she shared in her joy. But it only occurred to her how Püppi had advised her against men and marriage. It had been Püppi who'd appealed to her conscience. When Alex had proposed they look for an apartment together. Move in together. Püppi had asked, "What about the kids? And your freedom? Now when you finally have it." Helene asked Püppi the same questions. "What about Sophie? And your freedom?" Püppi poured herself a few more drops of sparkling wine. She smiled into her glass. "Well. Püppi," Helene said, "just see that you become happy." Püppi continued to smile into her glass. Helene leaned back. They were sitting at one of the window tables facing the Ring. Beyond the naked branches of the chestnut trees the sky was leaden. In the café, the great chandeliers from the 50's were lit. All the tables were occupied.

The checkroom attendant made her rounds to collect the coats, but Helene told her she'd be leaving soon. Helene immediately felt guilty having deprived the woman of her five-schilling fee. But she had only a half hour lunch break. "Could you take care of Sophie today?" Püppi asked. "The Thai woman's walked out on me." "When?" Helene asked. She didn't want to. "Only this once." Püppi was twisting her glass. "You don't have any other plans anyway." Helene could have lied to Püppi, but Püppi always knew what was true and what wasn't. Helene was no good at lying. Even Frau Sprecher in the office could tell by her face when she was using excuses. "Why don't you stay home?" Helene asked. Püppi looked at her with surprise. "But. Helene. I ask you a favor. Just once. And what do I get!" Helene agreed. She could be at the Karolinengasse at 9. She wouldn't be free any earlier. On the other hand, Püppi could drop Sophie off at her place. The child could sleep there. That way, her own children wouldn't be alone. "Helene. You've got the Grandma, haven't you," Püppi said. "I have nobody. You know what it means. And you know perfectly well. Sophie doesn't sleep when she's elsewhere." "All right then." Helene put 40 schillings next to her empty cup. She kissed Püppi on the cheek. Püppi let her bend all the way over. Straight away Püppi poured herself a few more drops of sparkling wine. On her way to Ferdinandstrasse, to the office, Helene bought a bunch of tulips in the flower shop on the Ring. She gave the flowers to Frau Sprecher. They were for her. Frau Sprecher was surprised. "By the way, Frau Gebhardt," she said to Helene, "somebody asked for you. A Herr Ericsen. Or Ericson. I told him you were out." Helene sat down at her desk. Herr Nadolny wasn't in. The door to his office was open. She got herself some coffee from the kitchen. The Swede had phoned here. She must ask him how he got the number. It meant he'd phoned from

Milan. Helene began to finish some letters. When Herr Nadolny came back from one of his protracted lunches, the file for his signatures lay on his desk. Nadolny wasn't in a good mood. He immediately demanded coffee. And Helene had to get a little bottle of Underberg from the Greislerei around the corner on Czerningasse. This was a bad sign. Normally, the little bottle of herb bitters was not needed until 5 p.m. Helene wasn't allowed to stock up. She had to get each bottle separately from the store. She had a few bottles on her shelf in the wardrobe. She took one and for fifteen minutes sat down on the staircase outside the office. She could see the Ferris wheel. Nobody used the stairs. They all took the elevator. After fifteen minutes, she went back into the office. She put the bottle of Underberg with a glass of water on a tray. "Prost," she said when she put it on the desk for Herr Nadolny.

Helene prepared a hot supper for the children. Fresh mashed potatoes and a schnitzel in butter for Barbara. Katharina didn't eat meat. Helene had gone shopping on her way home from work. At the Meinl on Gymnasiumstrasse a sick man had stood by the exit. The man had a grayish-yellow face. Sweat ran down his face and dripped on his neck. His neck was shiny. The man swallowed. His Adam's apple kept bobbing. Incessantly. In between, he gasped for air. He leaned against the wall. His hands pressed against the wall. He slid down the wall. Then propped himself against it higher up again. His hands left dark stains on the dirty white wall next to the checkout. Helene asked the cashier what was the matter. Could they do anything? The cashier shrugged. Mumbled something like "Could have found himself somewhere else to do it." She continued to punch in the prices of Helene's groceries. Totally focused on her work. Reproachful, as if offended. Helene went over to the sick man and asked if he might like to lie down. Could she get him a blanket. There had to be a stretcher somewhere. After all, the store had more than 10 employees. Workers Compensation required a stretcher in workplaces of this size. The manager showed up. His name tag said Kurt Binder. "Help is on the way," he said. An older woman in a light track suit, sneakers and parka joined them and asked if she could help. No. The man didn't want to lie down. Couldn't. Shook his head. Gasped for air. Propped himself against the wall. Slid down. Sweat dripped off the tip of his nose. Helene left. She carried the two big bags of groceries to her car. She had parked on Sternwartestrasse. She heard the ambulance siren. As usual, hearing the siren almost made her cry. A sob pushed against her throat. In the car on the short way to Lannerstrasse she suddenly realized why the man had pressed himself so tight against the wall. And had refused to lie down. He had filled his pants. For a long time Helene remained in the car in front of her house. The sobbing pushed against the inside of her breastbone. As if she had swallowed too big a piece of apple.

After dinner Helene let the children sit on her bed and she read to them. They had asked to be read to from The Treasure Hunting Trip. As always, they had to take a long pause at the spot where the little lion and the little tiger are far away from home and where the world is so empty. They talked about the misery of the little lion and the little tiger. Knowing the happy ending, they conjured up the cruelest blows of fate for the two little animals. And what would happen if the little tiger and the little lion were to be separated. Helene allowed the children to sleep in her bed. Grandma would come later and check on them. The children could phone her. Why was she going to Sophie's? And why didn't Sophie simply come to them? "But, Barbara," said Helene, "you know, don't you. Sophie is so much younger than you. And she's had to move so often in the last 2 years. First to England. Then from England to Vienna. And in Vienna she's already lived in 4 different apartments. Her dad isn't there anymore." "We don't have a dad anymore either," said Katharina. "Yes. But we have Grandma. Sophie only has her mom. And their new nanny's left again. No, I don't know why. But she was from far away and never learned our language. Maybe she was homesick or didn't get along with Aunt Püppi. I don't know. But now it's time to sleep. You have school tomorrow. You have to sleep now, my pussycats. I'll phone you. Okay? Do you want me to phone? All right. I'll phone when I get there. You can go to sleep then. And I'll be back soon. Okay?" Helene kissed the girls. She went to the grandmother and asked if everything was all right. She wanted to thank her for baby-sitting the children. The old woman had cried. Gregor had phoned. She had asked him what was going on. Where he lived. She'd wanted to know where he lived. She'd plucked up courage, finally. She, his mother, had the right to know where he lived, didn't she? After all, she was old. You never know what's going to happen. And how could they reach him? But Gregor had hung up. In the middle of her talking. His own mother. Just hung up. The old woman began crying again. Helene could have told her how badly she'd spoiled her son. Picked up his underwear from the floor and answered to his beck and call. And adored him. How could it ever occur to this man that he might not be a model of perfection. And might not be entitled to everything under the sun. But Helene was too tired to argue. The old woman wouldn't have understood her anyway. Helene kissed the old woman's cheek and left. On her drive to Karolinengasse rage and a sense of powerlessness washed over her. She didn't know where Gregor lived either. Püppi had recommended following him around. She'd have helped. It'd be quite easy. Nobody expected to be followed. Helene hadn't wanted to know where he lived. If he didn't want her to know, why should she care.

Püppi was already done up when Helene arrived. Sophie sat in her pajamas on Püppi's bed. She was playing with Püppi's jewelry. Püppi stood in front of the mirror with the gilded frame and dabbed rouge on her cheeks. She wore the Missoni dress. Had put her contacts in and done her hair up artfully. She called out to Sophie to find her the three rings with the green stones. Helene phoned the children and promised to be back soon. Sophie rummaged through the tangle she had created out of necklaces, brooches and belt buckles. "Sophie," Püppi called. "Mommy's got to go. Green. Green stones. You know what green looks like, don't you." Sophie laughed and rummaged. Helene sat down with the child. She started to put the jewelry back in its case. She mentioned the colors of the stones, and Sophie repeated them after her. "Hey Püppi. There aren't any rings here," Helene said. "That can't be," Püppi sighed. "In that case, they must be somewhere in the bed." Helene put Sophie into an easy chair and began to search the double bed. It was strewn with pillows and blankets. Helene picked them up one at a time. Shook them, felt inside the seams, and piled everything on the floor. Sophie dug herself into the mountain of pillows and squealed with glee. Helene shook out the blankets. The sheet was stained. There was nowhere in the mattress for the rings to hide. Püppi had turned pale. She threw herself on the floor and crawled under the bed. She groped and rooted under the bed. At the same time, she scolded Sophie. After all she'd done for her. This was the gratitude she got. Her emerald rings. The only precious things she'd inherited from her father. And her last valuables at that. What did the child think they were going to live on for the next months. One of her reasons for going out had been to get an estimate for the rings. From a friend of some friends, a jeweler from Graz. The rings weren't under the bed either. Sophie had started to cry. Helene picked up the child. Sophie screamed. Püppi came out from under the bed, yelled at Sophie and yanked the child's mouth open. Did she have the rings in her mouth. Had she swallowed them. Sophie didn't want to stay with Helene. She wanted to be with Püppi. Püppi tore open drawers. Dashed into the bathroom. Dust balls stuck to her dress. Her hair had come down. Scolding and shouting, Püppi put her hair up again. Helene brushed the dust off her. Then Püppi rushed off. As a farewell she shouted at Sophie that she never wanted to see her again. Then she ran back to the child. Embraced her violently and hurried off. Helene took Sophie into her room. For hours, Sophie cried to herself. When Helene tried to leave the room, the crying would rise to a screaming. Helene couldn't calm Sophie down. She was close to hitting the child. Unnerved, she sat down in the kitchen. She had a vodka. Sometime later Sophie got tired. The phone rang. A female voice asked, "Who's speaking, please?" Helene hung up. Again Sophie began to cry for her mother. The woman on the phone was the Sophie from Salzburg. Helene was sure. She should have asked her about Alex. What it had really been like with him. By now the little Sophie was sobbing quietly to herself. Helene sat down again with her. The child let her hold her hand. Sophie wanted a Coke. Helene didn't think Coke was a suitable drink for a four-year old at 11 p.m. But she got her a Coke. She diluted it with mineral water. She was glad to see the child drink and to be able to talk to her again. Sophie was hot and jittery. But then fell asleep. In the dark, Helene sat down at the living-room window. She looked into the street.

It wasn't that cold anymore. She opened the window and leaned out. Hardly a car passed. People walked home. An old woman across the street was also leaning out of a window. At some point, Helene lay down on the sofa. She dozed. Püppi came home after 1 o'clock. She brought company with her, a theater critic and his wife. Helene knew them vaguely. And two more couples. Helene could hear the group in the hallway. She knew they'd realize she'd been asleep. She didn't want to be seen this way. The group came into the room. Püppi told the others that she was the baby-sitter. And what would they like to drink. Helene left and went into Sophie's room. She had left the night light on. The child was asleep. Helene waited till everybody was in the living room. Then she left. From the hallway, she could hear the theater critic's wife commenting on the decor. The woman thought the price of the apartment too high. Helene held on to the door until it clicked shut behind her. She went to her car. Helene was furious. Felt humiliated. Püppi had let that jerk steal her emerald rings. Then had yelled at her child. Left the child behind in hysterics. Left it for her to look after. And then, "that's the baby-sitter." Püppi hadn't even asked if she might like a drink. Helene cranked up the car radio. She let herself be chased by the disco beat. At home, the phone rang. She pulled the plug and went to bed. She pushed Barbara to the middle of the double bed. She lay down next to the children. They smelled of baby soap and cocoa. Grandma must have made it for them. She was sure the children hadn't brushed their teeth afterwards. She'd have to remind the old woman. As she drifted off to sleep, Helene remembered. She hadn't heard from Alex.

Next morning, Helene had a headache and ached all over as if she were getting the flu. The scales in the bathroom showed she'd lost two pounds. The children were noisy.

They jumped up and down on the double bed. Squealed. Helene barked at them. Hurry up and get dressed. She prepared soft-boiled eggs and soldiers. As if for a Sunday breakfast. As an apology. Helene felt dizzy. During breakfast, Barbara said that Grandma wanted the phone bill paid. "Why didn't she tell me? I was only just over there. Only yesterday." The grandmother always paid the phone bill. That was her contribution to the young household, she used to say. She'd do anything for them. And she'd even given up half her apartment. And now she had to come and go through the service entrance. But anything for the young people, she used to say. Since Gregor was no longer living there, she'd begun to demand that the phone bill be paid. She wanted the money from Gregor. "Yes. We are so expensive, says Grandma. Since Dad left." Barbara drank her cocoa. Satisfied. Helene felt her heart beat faster and her blood violently pulsing behind her temples. Her headache had turned into a migraine. "Wash your hands and faces. We have to get to school." Helene locked herself in the bathroom and found a Cafergot PB. While she was inserting the suppository, she looked in the mirror. Looked into her eyes. Saw her pupils widen for a moment as the suppository slid in. Then she closed her eyes and leaned her forehead against the mirror. She told herself things were only the way they were because of her period. Her period was due in 2 days. She sat down on the edge of the tub and put her head on the edge of the sink. The cold porcelain against her forehead. Then the children banged against the bathroom door. To wash their hands and faces. Helene took the children to school. The Cafergot PB began to work. In front of the school she kissed the children and waited till they disappeared through the entrance.

The Swede phoned the office. "A Herr Ericson," Frau Sprecher said. "He says he's calling from Milan." Would Helene be free on Saturday. Yes? He'd be back in Vienna. At 8 p.m. Café Sacher. He was looking forward to it. At this time, the café would be completely empty and they could have a nice chat. And then go for dinner. The call from Milan had impressed Frau Sprecher. Helene stayed at the reception and listened to how the tomcat Georgie had again been tortured by the vet. Finally, in spite of herself, Frau Sprecher asked who the gentleman from Milan was. "A musician," Helene said. She went back to her room. Sat down. Sat there. Alex wouldn't call this late.

The dishwasher was broken. Helene had turned it on before she left. After work she found the kitchen flooded. Dirty gray water covered the kitchen floor. Helene stood in the kitchen door. She couldn't see the floor under the foaming slick. She closed the kitchen door and went in the bedroom. Lay on the bed. She knew, could already see, how she'd be mopping up. Sop up the water with rags. Wring the rags into buckets. Wipe the floor dry. Rinse with clean water. How the next day she'd phone the Miele service department. She'd go to Frau Bamberger in the flat below and ask if there was any damage. Contact the insurance agent. But before all this would unwind, Helene would lie down. Then she'd do things. Everything she'd do. Then. But first, lie down. On the bed. Helene stared at the blanket. She asked herself. When would she collapse into the emptiness inside her. When would her ribs cave in and she be flat like paper, unable to breathe. Helene lay there. She waited for fatigue. For the fatigue that would rise when she got back to where she could end it all. In the beginning she'd wanted to hang herself. Or shoot herself. Or slash her belly with knives and watch her innards come out. Like the young soldiers in the cockpit in M.A.S.H. Now she only wanted last breaths. Sleep away. Stay in bed and sink away. Lie stretched out. Leave everything behind. Gently. Now she would have cleaned up first. Before. In the very beginning she'd thrown crockery. She had hurled piece after piece of Grandmother's Wedgwood to the kitchen floor. She had searched the basement for the ax and imagined how the Biedermeier secretaire would splinter. What should happen to the children was less clear now. On her worst days, she would have given them sleeping pills. The package of Mogadon had been in the top drawer of the Biedermeier secretaire, too high for the children to reach. She would have taken the children in her arms. Barbara on her right because she was heavier. Katharina on her left. And then she'd have jumped. Somewhere deep down. And the last thing she'd have known would have been the feeling of the two little warm bodies. But there was no way out. She would have had no right. To her children. And therefore she had no right to herself. Helene felt pressed into life. She knew why everything was the way it was and who was acting which part. What she wasn't supposed to think or believe and what she had to think but not hope. It didn't help. She'd have to go to the kitchen and sop up dirty, cold, greasy water with rags. Smelly, stinking water. Wring out the rags and pour the water down the toilet. She went into the living room and had a sip of bourbon straight from the bottle. Against the nausea.

Helene took the Balmain dress to Stross' One-Hour Cleaners in the Prater Hauptstrasse. She had seen a pair of shoes to match the dress at Bruno Magli on the Stephansplatz. Buying them was out of the question. Easter was coming and she hadn't bought a present for the children yet. On her way from the cleaners back to the office she wondered again how to talk to Gregor. About the money. In early January she'd meant to pick up her bank card. As always, she'd gone to the Credit Union in the Schottengasse and lined up in front of a clerk she knew casually. The woman checked a binder and then told her that there was no card for her. How was that possible, Helene had asked. And smiled. With understanding. Because files aren't always right and anybody can make a mistake. And this card. She was entitled to it, wasn't she. It was, after all, for their joint account. "Yes. You get one if the account owner signs a form. But your husband hasn't signed one." Helene had said nothing after that. Had bolted out of the bank. All the way to the Freyung, she'd felt her face burning. Remembering how the clerk had looked down at her and how she'd been unable to keep her composure. Remembering this, Helene felt she had to turn aside and walk away. Helene hadn't mentioned it to Gregor. Hadn't been able to. She was afraid Gregor would tell her to her face that she had no right. No right to anything. She had thought at least he'd think of the children. But Gregor had done nothing. And her debts grew. The small paycheck from Nadolny didn't go anywhere. Gregor didn't seem to care what happened to them. And of course he knew she'd do anything. And she'd do it right. With the children she did everything right. He said. But that's what Gregor had to say. Because otherwise he'd have to take care of them himself. She should have seen a lawyer long ago. Helene didn't understand why she hadn't.

Café Sacher was empty. Helene was on time. She took a Neue Züricher off the rack at the entrance and sat down under the portrait of Empress Sisi. She ordered a Campari Orange, began to leaf through the paper and waited. She thought she looked good. The dress helped. Aunt Adele had always been right about these things. She had married two rich men and advised Helene to do the same. A bell-boy with a cap that read Hotel Sacher in bronze letters walked around with a slate. He showed it to the only other guest, who sat in the corner near the entrance. The guest made a remark. The boy blushed and grinned. He came up to Helene. "Frau Gebhardt" was written on his slate with chalk. Helene read the name and looked at the boy. Then she understood. That was her name. "Yes?" she asked. "That's me." "Please, a call for you, Ma'am." Helene fol-lowed the boy. He led her out of the café into a hallway to the right and then to the right again. He opened the door to a phone box. She would only have to pick up the re-ceiver. Helene sat on the little red velvet covered seat and lifted the receiver. The bellboy had closed the door. She couldn't hear anything from outside. "Yes, please," Helene said. "Helene, is that you?" Helene confirmed. She didn't recognize the voice right away. And she and the Swede weren't on first-name terms. "Who's speaking?" Helene asked. She knew it could only be the Swede. Nobody else knew where she was. And while she was still asking her question, she realized the Swede was backing out. For a moment she couldn't breathe. The man began to explain that he couldn't make it. He was sure she'd understand. After all, she was a caring person. He'd had a dizzy spell. He was in bed in his hotel. He was unable to leave the ho-tel. Helene felt her strength drain out of her. She felt her shoulders droop and rested her elbows on the little table. She sat hunched over the phone. Hang up, she thought, hang up and leave. Just hang up and go. Go home to bed. The children would be happy. The grandmother surprised. She could say she had gotten a headache and had to lie down. But then she got furious. Why the excuses, she asked the man. It was nice of him of course to come up with such complicated reasons. But. He could simply say he had no time. "No," he interrupted her. "No, don't you get it. I am in a terrible mess. I am suffering!" Helene paused. "Shall I come?" she asked. "And, you have to eat something. If you feel weak, you have to eat." "Yes," he replied. Yes. She should come. He was staying in the Hotel Elisabeth in the Weihburggasse. In the Emperor's Suite. He'd let the reception know. See you soon. Sure. Helene hung up. For a moment she remained sitting in the little sound-proof booth. She had imagined a different evening. She was exhausted. Why didn't she go home. She should go home. Put her dress in her closet, read to the children about the little tiger and the little lion, and go to bed. Helene grabbed her purse. Went back. Paid for the Campari. Got her coat. She didn't give a big enough tip. The checkroom attendant didn't help her with her coat.

It had rained while Helene had been waiting in the café. The lights were reflected in the wet asphalt in front of the hotel. Shone on the wet pavement of the Kärntner Strasse. Helene turned up her collar and dug her hands into her pockets. She was relieved to be wearing black stockings. Helene couldn't go anywhere when it was wet without splashing the backs of her legs. Black stockings didn't show the stains. She tried to change her balance by leaning forward to avoid the splashing. It didn't help. She felt her calves getting damp. She walked fast. Hardly anybody was on the street. She saw her reflection walk past the shop windows. Stop briefly in front of a children's fashion store. The children needed new clothes for the spring. Barbara had grown. And Katharina was never able to wear Barbara's clothes. She was much more delicate. In the Weihburggasse, Helene first had to look for the hotel. She'd never been there. Then she found it at the top of the street, across from the 3 Hussars. An old man sat at the reception. He told her how to get to the Emperor's Suite. Was she the lady that was expected? Helene took the elevator to the 4th floor. At first she walked in the wrong direction. Then she found the room number at the end of a long corridor. The room was on the left. She knocked. Nobody answered. Helene knocked again. Her heart began to beat faster. She listened at the door but couldn't hear anything. Only the pulsing of the blood in her ears. Should she simply go in. Or go back downstairs. Or phone. Or leave. Standing in front of the big white door, she suddenly no longer knew why she was there. Or what she was looking for. She pushed down the handle. The door wasn't locked. She opened the door and put her head in the room. There was a coffee table with easy chairs. Golden scroll-work. Flowery. Fake. To the right, a curtain in front of a doorway. "Henryk?" Helene asked. "Yes. Come in." His voice sounded weak. Through the arched doorway Helene went into the bedroom. Henryk lay on the left side of the double bed. The right bedside lamp was on and Henryk rested in its shadow. He lay stretched out, with his arms on the blanket. Motionless. Didn't even turn his head towards her. Helene quietly walked to the bed and looked down at him. He gave her a wan smile. "Nothing is working out for me right now," he said. Helene sat down on the edge of the bed. What's wrong with him? Headache? Stomachache? Backache? Cramps? Indigestion? Stomach? Head? Blood pressure? The Swede smiled. He was familiar with his condition. It was perfectly normal, for him. The problem was nerves. Not to worry. He was a musician, and that's just the way it was. Helene looked at him. The room was too dim for her to see him clearly. If it wasn't an illness but just a condition. That was good news. But. Shouldn't he eat something in that case? Particularly if he was feeling weak. "Yes, that would be good," the man sighed. But surely she realized how weak he was. He could hardly move, and his blood pressure would play up. She knew the problem, she said. And eating something was vital. Was there a restaurant in the hotel? It turned out to be impossible to get a warm meal. Or any meal. Helene thought about getting something from one of the pubs or restaurants in the neighborhood. If worse came to worse, from the 3 Hussars. The man hadn't had a decent meal for 2 days. And the foehn weather to top it off. It was easy to get sick. She'd been suffering too, Helene told him, from a migraine attack. She always took the strongest medicine for it right away. At that moment she realized her period had not started. She sat in her coat on the edge of the Swede's bed. The man was very handsome in his dark blue satin pajamas with their thin white piping. Helene wasn't sure if she should just leave him alone. He was sick, that was all. Then again, maybe it had something to do with her. He had gotten sick instead of going out with her. She would have to think about this. But the evening had become important. She couldn't imagine postponing everything. Her concern for his well-being was really a ruse to lure him out of bed. And to have the evening she had imagined. Helene felt incapable of getting up and wishing the man to get better soon. And leaving. It was impossible. Helene didn't want to be pushed to the side by someone's condition. She didn't want to wait. Be patient. Sympathetic. She wanted to sit with this man at a table and talk and eat. Helene got up and looked down at him. "I am going to sit in the other room. And you get dressed. Then we'll go for a meal. Near here, really close. And then I'll bring you back. Okay? Half an hour. The exercise will do you good. The more you give in, the worse it gets." Helene smiled down at him. Turned around and went into the other room. She went to the window. She looked down into the

Weihburggasse. The wind had picked up. Pedestrians leaned into the wind. Or were propelled by it. The Swede had said nothing. She heard the bed creak. "You all right?" Helene called. She got no answer. She heard the bathroom door shut. Then running water. Helene sat on the sofa. Could it have happened with Alex? She counted the days. The Sunday when she and Alex. That had been the 24th day. It was impossible. But what if? Helene calculated again. She took her pocket calendar out of her purse and counted off the days with her finger. 2 days late. It meant nothing. Just relax, she thought. You can't do anything right now anyway. From the bathroom she heard banging. Then the door. The man walked around in the room next door. Closets were opened. Cloth rustled. Coat hangers were moved. Helene leaned back and stared at the ceiling. On the opposite wall was another portrait of Empress Sisi. On this one it seemed as if the Empress had a mustache or a harelip. The shadow under her nose was painted too dark. The Swede suddenly stood in front of her, fully dressed. His shoulders were drooping. But otherwise he seemed normal. They left the hotel. Slowly. They turned into the Singerstrasse and went to the 3 Hooks. On the way, Helene wished she'd left him. He leaned on her heavily and dragged his feet. But she was suddenly in a good mood. She felt light and could have skipped. At the 3 Hooks, they found a table right next to the door. They ate marinated fillet of beef, Tafelspitz, with spinach, and drank Grüner Veltliner. They laughed about the crappy wine and mixed it with soda water. They were having a good time. Henryk moved next to Helene on the bench. They laughed about everybody who came. Or left. About the waiters. About the food. About the table cloth and the menu. About Vienna. They shared a Kaiserschmarren pancake for dessert, and Helene felt victorious as if she'd won a competition. She laughed. Then she took the Swede back to his hotel. She'd had to pay the bill. Henryk hadn't been able to get any money changed. Because of his dizzy spell. He offered Lire. No, Helene said, it was quite all right. On the way to the hotel the Swede wanted to slip into the Santo Spirito, just for a moment. Helene had to remind him of his suffering. Shouldn't he take it easy. She didn't want to go to this bar. She was afraid Püppi or somebody else might be there and see her with the Swede. She didn't want to be watched. With him. Or anybody. Püppi would ask her immediately how the Swede was in bed and then tell her that she had tried him, too. And Helene never knew what was true or when Püppi was lying. In front of the hotel Helene said good-bye. The Swede was half a head taller than she was. She looked up at him and said, "Good night." She left. At the corner to the Kärntner Strasse she turned around. He was still standing in front of the hotel entrance. He waved. Helene waved back. She hurried to her car. She had parked in the Goethegasse. She let the wind blow into her unbuttoned coat. The wind had warmed up. Her long hair slapped against her cheeks. When she got home, her period had started. She immediately took a Buscopan. So as not to feel the cramps during the night.

The next day Helene drove with the children to the Helenen Valley. To go for a walk. As a child, she had often been sent to an aunt in Baden. The slopes of the Vienna Woods there. Covered with foliage. Golden brown under the gray trunks of the beech trees. The white lime cliffs that sprang abruptly from the ground. The pine trees that spread their black umbrellas on the cliffs. The ruins of the two castles at the entrance to the Helenen Valley. Helene and the children turned off the road at the Hotel Sacher and parked the car. They crossed the Schwechat river. A pathetic trickle in its wide bed. Behind the Jammerpeppi Helene looked for the path to the ruins of Merkenstein castle. They followed the narrow path. It was lunch time. Hardly anybody yet on their Sunday afternoon walk. With long loops, the path wound up the side of a valley. Dark brown leaves lay between the silver gray trunks. The naked branches formed a black web against a cloudless light-blue sky. Where roots had broken through the soil, liverwort bloomed, hidden among the leaves. Helene pointed out each flower to the children. The blossoms, pale violet with white stamens, disturbed her. She could have cried. The children ran ahead. Barbara climbed on every rock. Katharina looked at the rocks and began to suck her thumb. Helene pulled the thumb gently out of her mouth and took the child by the hand. The little wet hand and the way the child pressed against her made Helene even sadder. Only the foundations of Merkenstein castle were left. In many places grass had grown over them. Helene sat down on the remains of the wall that must have been the keep. From here she could overlook the valley. The slope fell steeply down to the river. Thinking of robber knights spying on their victims from this spot and of what happened afterwards brought her close to tears again. The children had started to play house. Helene heard them assign rooms. "That's my room. You're not allowed in." Helene looked at the sky. On the opposite slope, cliffs rose up between the trees. The cliffs were barely higher than the trees. They glistened white in the sunlight. Pine trees stood out black against them. Helene's chest felt like bursting. Narrow. Crushing her. Helene had to sit up straight and breathe deeply. She would have liked to remain sitting. The sky was blue. Blue as a feather. The birds sang. The air was warm. The sun made everything glitter. She would have liked never to move again. To remain sitting. The children were tired of playing house. They wanted to go down to the river. Play with stones in the water. "But only if you prom-

[34]

ise not to get your shoes wet." The shoes got wet, and Helene took the children back to Vienna. On the way home they should have visited her parents in Hietzing. The wet shoes were a good reason not to. At home Helene let the children watch TV. She lay down on her bed. To think. But she didn't think anything. She wished. Hoped. But she didn't think. When their program ended, the children romped all over the place, leaping over her. Helene went to bed at the same time as the children. Her period was particularly heavy. She felt the blood run out of her in a small stream. Helene took a Valium.

On Monday, Herr Nadolny called Helene into his office. He wanted her to bring him a coffee. And one for herself. Helene put the sugar bowl and the little milk jug on the tray. Her hands began to tremble. She had to focus all her attention on pouring the coffee without spilling it. She was absolutely sure Nadolny was going to tell her that he didn't need her any longer. She had seen it coming. She should have preempted him. She'd been there now for 2 months. She'd never felt she was doing anything that only she could have done. That sort of thing didn't exist anyway. She could look nice. She was able to write letters without taking dictation. She didn't know shorthand. Had studied art history. And not finished her degree. Helene took the coffee into the office and sat down in front of Nadolny's desk. She didn't know whether she'd worked long enough to be entitled to unemployment money. She should talk with somebody about what to do now. And talk with Gregor about the money. And she should tell her parents how things were with Gregor and ask them for help. The butterflies in her stomach turned into a flagstone in her chest. As if her heartbeat pressed against a wall, slowed down and then stopped. Helene sat very straight. She didn't pick up her cup. The trembling would have been too noticeable. She hoped she wouldn't start crying until later. Nadolny had finished his coffee in silence and looked at her. Helene looked at her knees. Then Nadolny started. He looked out the window while speaking. She'd been with him for a while now. And she was employed as a secretary, really. But. She had to admit. Surely she was capable of more. Helene was surprised how politely Nadolny set about firing her. She felt even more weighed down. He. Nadolny continued. He had a series of projects that took all his time right now. He'd reached his limit. For a start, she could try a project herself. Do some research. And write copy. First a report. Surely she could do that. A company producing sunscreens needed help. Because of the tanning salons. And because of the new dangers of tanning. There was a list of people to talk to. The address. She should start right away. She'd be free all week to work on it. By then she should have a report. And some suggestion as to how the company might present itself in future. He realized she wasn't being paid for that. But wasn't it a good opportunity for her. Wouldn't she be interested? And they could talk about money later. First she'd be like an apprentice, kind of. Right? Nadolny laughed at his joke. Helene merely nodded. Then Nadolny left. He wouldn't be back today, he said. Cheerfully. Helene took the cups back to the kitchen. She tipped her coffee out and poured herself a fresh one. Frau Sprecher stopped her on her way to her office. What was going on. Helene only told her that Nadolny had left for the day. Frau Sprecher rolled her eyes and quickly went to get herself a coffee. Helene got the documents from Nadolny's office. She started to read. She made appointments and was pleased to see her appointment book filled. She told Frau Sprecher where she'd be at what time. She felt important.

Helene had to go to school. Katharina's Phys Ed teacher
had summoned her. Helene was glad to be able to hide this
appointment with the school among her other appointments. So nobody would find out. Katharina hadn't been
able really to explain why Helene was to go to school. At
breakfast, she'd stared at her plate. The teacher was stupid,
was all she said. Helene had phoned immediately. The
teacher had been very friendly. She said it was about a more
general problem. She'd appreciate it if both parents would
come. But for God's sake, she shouldn't worry. Helene
hadn't told Gregor of this summons. He'd immediately
blame her. And go on about the teacher's incompetence.
And Helene should spare him her home-made psychology.
In the elementary school in the Cottagegasse Helene sat on
a children's bench in the hallway. On the wall were children's drawings. Snowmen stared from the sheets. Each
snowman had a carrot nose. Each carrot pointed to the left.
Helene remembered how as a little girl in kindergarten she'd
drawn the sun in the middle of her pictures. She could still
see the finger on her picture as the nun showed her to draw
the sun in the corner. From then on, she'd squeezed the
sun into the upper left corner of her pictures. The sun since
then would only shine diagonally from the left. She had
wanted to get it right. The teacher was on time. They stood
at a window in the hallway. The school yard was a concrete
square, surrounded by narrow flower beds. Tulips had been
planted. Their shoots had already come up quite a bit. Some
had been stepped on. They could see shoe prints on the
beds. The sun shone on the asphalt where the water in the
cracks in the ground reflected the light. The teacher was in
her 50s. She was small and delicate, with dark hair. She
wore a gray suit. Her name was Zöchling, and she was re-
sponsible for Phys Ed. And that's where the problem lay.
Why was the father not present. She'd thought it impor-

tant. After all, they were dealing with a deep-seated disorder. In her opinion at least. It went far beyond your ordinary troubles at school. Helene got scared. Immediately she felt guilty. It sounded really serious. She felt damned for all eternity. Never another happy moment. She felt like she had during her pregnancies when she imagined what it would be like with a sick child. A disabled child. Helene no longer looked at the woman. She looked at the floor. Fought against the moist film in her eyes. She stared through the dirty window panes at the tulip shoots. Everything was very far away. The teacher was silent. She was waiting for an explanation. Why the father wasn't there. With as much anger as she could muster against her growing panic, Helene demanded to hear finally what disorder they were dealing with. What the problem was. "Well, all right," the teacher said. Katharina was of course a good student. But that didn't disprove the pattern. On the contrary. And that's why she'd suggest therapy. She'd already consulted the school psychologist. Yes. Well. Katharina. That's how it had started. The child had refused to hold her legs above her head when swinging in the rings. And then keep swinging in this position. Later she'd stopped swinging in the rings altogether. Yes. Not even touched the rings. And recently, she'd been sitting in a corner and had done nothing at all. Had crouched in the fetal position and refused all cooperation. The teacher looked at Helene. Triumphant. "And that's it?" Helene exclaimed. She could have run into the classroom and clutched her child in her arms. Grabbed her and not ever let her out off sight again. Katharina. A little warm bundle that pressed itself against her, full of trust. How lonely she must have felt in those moments. And how all the others must have laughed at the little coward. And felt so much superior themselves, more courageous, stronger. "Well. Don't you see what it means," said the teacher. "This child is fundamentally . . ." "Don't you think you're exaggerating?" Helene asked. She had to try hard not to begin stuttering with fury. "If you can't get the children to participate voluntarily in your classes. It's your problem. For me, fear is a sign of intelligence. I wouldn't force either of my children to do things they are frightened of. Swinging in the rings. It's not exactly a question of survival, is it? I mean, we're not in the jungle. If you think you have to resort to therapy to get rid of fear and make all children behave the same, you'd better stay away from my child. If you make the slightest attempt to put my child into therapy, I'll sue you." Helene was out of breath. She turned and left. The teacher called after her that she'd known it was a more general problem. Helene dashed from the school. She drove home and locked herself in. She hated the teacher. Called her a gym fascist. But maybe things were somehow her fault. If she'd been a bit more like what Gregor had imagined, would he have stayed? And would everything be fine? And would Katharina be swinging in the rings? With her legs above her head. A humiliating position at that, Helene thought. And would the child not cower in a corner? Sucking her thumb and crouched like a fetus. Helene cooked spaghetti sauce. The children's favorite. When she had regained her control more or less, she phoned Gregor. She told him the story. Was even able to laugh about it. She left it to him to phone the principal. Gregor agreed with her. Helene was proud of herself. Gregor would have a reasonable talk with the principal. And the problem would vanish from the earth. Overreaction, he'd say. On all sides. My wife is very emotional. But was it necessary to terrify first graders that way. They'd spend time with Katharina. She shouldn't go to Phys Ed classes for the next little while. Otherwise, they'd better all forget the whole thing. Helene sat in her car, waiting in the second row of mothers lining

[39]

up in front of the school. Everything would be resolved reasonably. Helene began to have doubts. Should she have sided with the teacher. The loss of the father. Wasn't that frightening enough for a child? Had she actually formed an alliance with the father against the child? To hear a kind word from him? Had she thereby harmed the child? Had she failed? First Gregor and now the children? Should she have defended Katharina differently? But she'd only wanted to protect Katharina. Helene was no longer sure of anything. During lunch, she asked Katharina why she didn't want to participate in Phys Ed class. "It's so stupid," the child said and continued to eat. She was cheerful and had a second helping. Helene was glad. She didn't ask any more questions. She had to leave right after the meal. For Weidlingbach. The sun screen company had its laboratory there, and Professor Sölders would provide her with information. Professor Siegfried Sölders. Helene washed her face and completely made herself up again. Foundation. Mascara. Eye shadow. Powder. Lipstick. She put on a skirt and a jacket. She would make the very best impression.

Helene had never been to Weidlingbach. Had only passed through. Next to herself on the passenger seat she put the paper with the directions on how to find the company. The woman on the phone had even given her the number of turns the road took up the hill to the laboratory. Helene found the intersection. The road went uphill. The sun was shining. The sky was dark blue. The buds on the bushes were ready to burst. The laboratory was in the middle of a forest in a Gründerzeit villa. Another section had been added in the 1950s. Plain, a bunker with windows. In the foyer of the main building a woman sat behind a desk. She wore a white coat, like a nurse or a lab technician. She looked up at Helene. Yes, the Herr Professor was still busy. But would

she please take a seat. W[...]
woman showed Helene to [...]
coffee table and chairs. The [...]
read. Helene sat down. She [...]
was quiet in the room. In fr[...]
and trees which made the r[...]
paper. She stopped again. [...]
feel insecure. Should she b[...]
she wait? What was her sta[...]
nally went into the foyer. The [...]
there. Nobody was. Helene [...] ...room.
After 40 minutes a different woman appeared. Older, with
dark hair. She, too, wore a white lab coat. And black patent
leather pumps with very high heels. The professor was sorry.
He'd been held up. But he'd be with her soon. Did she have
everything she needed. The woman spoke to Helene in an
unfriendly manner. With animosity almost. Helene nodded to the woman. Yes. Yes, everything was perfect. And it
was all right. After an hour, the professor arrived. He was
an old man. A well-groomed white mane fell in waves around
his head. He was the spitting image of Walter Rheyer, an
actor at the Vienna Burgtheater. He wore his white lab coat
unbuttoned over flannel pants and a pink tailor-made Ox-
ford shirt and looked as if he'd just had a particularly pleasant nap. The blonde woman from the foyer came in and
asked if the Herr Professor needed anything. The professor
declined with a smile. He had exactly 10 minutes to spare,
he said to Helene. But then they talked for more than an
hour. Helene filled her pad, page after page. She would need
to quote the professor verbatim. She was well prepared and
asked the right questions. With flying fingers she wrote
down the professor's sentences. The sun, the fountain of
life, was also the fountain of death. What was good in mod-
eration was harmful in excess. Benefit and harm were only

ar's breadth. Professor Sölders made these
Helene as if she were a good little girl in need
tion. Patiently he reeled off the lecture. The dark-
woman entered. Did the professor need anything?
th a smile, he declined and carried on. Helene filled 7
pages with his pronouncements. She thanked him for having gone to so much trouble. But it was nothing, said the
man. But now he had a question for her. How old was she,
by the way? Helene said, 30, and looked at him in surprise.
The professor kissed her hand. As a skin specialist, and at
his age. He was allowed to ask such questions. And he had
to tell her. She had the skin of a twenty-year-old. But she
should stay out of the sun, always. It's the best treatment
for beautiful skin. Helene said bravely, "Or else I'll use your
sun protection." "Yes!" Professor Sölders laughed. That was
another option, of course. He took her to her car. He put
his arm around her shoulders. The two beautiful women in
their white coats stood in the foyer. Professor Sölders called
out to them that he was just taking the young lady to her
car. After all, he was the host. The women watched in silence. At the door, Helene turned back to them. They didn't
return her smile. Looking back above the white sleeve of
the professor's arm, Helene saw the two women stand in
the door and gaze after them. Professor Sölders opened the
car door for Helene. The car was dirty and full of crumbs.
Paper bags. Rags. "My children," Helene said apologetically.
"Oh no. Children as well. How delightful. I hope they are
proud of their beautiful Mommy." He once more kissed
Helene's hand and shut the door of the car for her. The
motor died at the first attempt. Professor Sölders leaned
forward in commiseration. Helene hastened to start again.
And left. At the gate she glanced back. Professor Sölders
was strolling back toward the villa. His coat was flapping.
He had crossed his hands behind his back and walked with

a spring in his step. The two women in their white coats stood at the door and watched him coming.

Helene met the Swede in the Museum Café. Like the first time. She didn't know if he'd stayed in Vienna or had come back from Milan. He had phoned on Friday. Again he sat by the window immediately to the right. He jumped up, kissed her on the cheek, helped her out of her coat. He ordered a coffee for her before she could say anything. Was that all right, he asked. Helene nodded. Smiled. Didn't know what to talk about. Henryk sat at the window, she across from him. Outside in the Operngasse cars were backed up. Stopped at the lights. Started to move. Glided past the window. Picked up speed. Zoomed past. Stopped again. It was too noisy in the café. Helene couldn't hear the cars. "If we want to go for a walk, we'd better leave now," Helene said. They paid. Helene would have loved to take the children with them for the walk. But they'd gone with Gregor to see the Aichenheims. Johannes Aichenheim was a colleague of Gregor's. Gregor was also taking his Frau Gärtner there. Helene had forbidden that the children meet her. She wasn't sure if he was complying. And she didn't ask the children questions. They shouldn't have to lie. Susi Aichenheim would give her a call anyway. Helene no longer visited the Aichenheims.

Helene had left the car on the Schillerplatz. They went there, without talking. But then in the car. Passing the Vienna Provincial Courthouse, Helene asked Henryk if he really was in the mood for a walk. She always drove a fair way out of town. Some people thought it too much trouble. But countryside. You wouldn't find real countryside any closer. And she knew a path where you wouldn't see a single transmission tower. "Could be interesting," Henryk said. Helene crossed the North Bridge toward Stockerau. The Danube on the left. The forests along the river banks. Or what was left of them. The trees still gray, without foliage. Near Stockerau, Helene continued toward Prague. The hills opened out. Everything looked neat and clean. The edges of the fields formed a sharp line along the roads and banks. In Höbersdorf Helene took the secondary road. The railway gates in the village were down. Helene stopped and turned off the motor. They waited. Behind them, other cars lined up. Helene asked Henryk if he'd recovered. The Swede lifted his head in surprise. Then he said, "Yes, yes." Before Helene could ask any more questions, the train came into sight. It stopped at the station. Then continued. Even as the train had become visible, all the drivers behind Helene had restarted their engines. The running motors behind her urged her on. They honked at her while the train was still passing the gates. Helene turned on the engine and drove off. As soon as possible. She only remembered Henryk's astonished reaction when they had already reached Obermalebarn and were turning into Kellergasse. Helene parked the car in front of one of the old cellar doors. The door to this cellar hadn't been opened in years. Bushes had grown tall, almost hiding the door. They got out. Helene walked ahead. Right after the cellar doors and the trees in between, a path opened in front of them. It followed along a range of hills, halfway up. To the south, on the right, the slope rose higher up. Behind it the sky. To the north, on the left, fields stretched along the floor of a broad valley. Groves, hills, then again fields. "The children call it the Long Path," Helene said. The sun was still high. The range of hills rose into an azure sky. The furrows in the fields appeared to draw toward the sky. Helene and Henryk walked quickly. Helene had put her hands in the pockets of her jacket. She felt light. Farther away from the road all they could hear were the larks. The birds flung themselves high into the sky. Helene tried to follow the flight of one lark with her eyes. She didn't succeed. Again and again, one of the birds would let itself drop out of the sky. Drop like a stone. Stop its fall only at the last moment and hurl itself back up into the air. And the warbling continued. Without a break. Helene would have loved to run. She walked in silence. Lowered her head. The sun and the larks. Why hadn't she stayed home. She had ironing to do. Did she come here often? Henryk asked. Far too rarely, Helene answered. They walked faster. Talked. How much fresh air children needed. Why Henryk needed a particular hammer piano. Why Italian food was preferable to French. Or why it wasn't. They came to a crossroads. Helene always turned back at this spot. Henryk carried on. Helene hesitated. She wanted to tell him she never went beyond this point. Then she followed him. They talked. The larks tumbled high in the sky and filled the air with their trilling. They reached a village. Henryk slipped his arm through Helene's. Could they get some wine here, he asked. Wasn't this region called the Weinviertel? They couldn't find a wine tavern, a Heuriger. The place seemed deserted. They didn't meet anybody. In front of a house stood a car with a Viennese license plate. Another farm house had been remodeled as a Spanish villa. Plaster pillars had been added, whitewashed. With a whitewashed rock garden in the front, and a display of Spanish scenes. There was a bull, a tiny torero holding up a little ragged cloth, a small windmill. They turned around and went back along the path. Every so often they could see a car on the ridge of the hill. They still couldn't hear anything. Only the larks. In one spot, boxwood bushes rose into the now paler sky. Between the bushes, a tall wrought-iron cross. The wind was blowing in their faces. They walked very fast. It had gotten colder.

Henryk put his arm around Helene's shoulders. They laughed at their haste to escape the cold. The light lost its clarity. Mist rose from the valley bottom. They had to reach a Heuriger, they both agreed. Helene laughed. Did Henryk know what mulled wine was? No? Mulled wine was a sin. The wine is heated. Then you add cloves and cinnamon. Ghastly stuff. A wine compote. To a connoisseur, undrinkable. But in this cold, unavoidable. And you had to have a slice of bread and drippings with it. She shouldn't be wearing such a light jacket, Henryk said. Helene laughed again. No, she wasn't cold. Since she'd lost so much weight, she never got cold anymore. They ran the last steps to the car. In Hollabrunn they found a Heuriger. Helene ordered 2 red mulled wine. And 2 slices of bread and drippings. Without onion or garlic. The Swede looked at the bread. Doubtful. Can you really eat that? All Helene wanted was laughter. She began eating her bread. She showed Henryk how much salt he had to sprinkle on the drippings. Normally you eat it with onion. Henryk wanted to give it a try. In the end, each of them had drunk 3 quarter-liters of mulled wine and had eaten 3 slices of bread and drippings, 2 of them with onion. By now, they both couldn't stop laughing. It had gotten dark. They were giggling in the car as they went back to Vienna. They tried to find out how fast Helene's Renault 5 would go but couldn't get it up much beyond 170 kilometers per hour. They drove back to the Museum Café. Their old parking spot in front of the Academy on the Schillerplatz was empty. In the café they ordered two tall Braune. To sober up. Henryk wanted to go to the movies. It was only 7 o'clock, and they had eaten. Hadn't they? The Swede looked up the movies in the Kronen-Zeitung. Yes. There was something on, he said. "Il deserto rosso."

They walked across the Karlsplatz. At one place they could look down into the construction site for the Underground. Machines roared, vibrated in the light far below. They went through the Bruckner Strasse, past the French Embassy, onto the Schwarzenbergplatz. The fountain was still hidden beneath planks. The Russian War Memorial was brightly lit. Ilona Faber's body had been lying next to the third pillar from the left. Helene's grandmother had used Ilona Faber's fate to illustrate all her warnings and fears. All the things you weren't allowed to do, or you'd end up like her. Nobody had ever spelled out what had happened to her. Helene had become afraid of every bush in the dark, without knowing why. The shrubs around the Russian War Memorial were well lit. She couldn't walk or drive across the Schwarzenbergplatz without imagining the mangled body of the raped and murdered victim. She straightened up as she walked. She had checked it out. There'd been a rumor that Ilona Faber had been killed during an orgy at the French Embassy. Helene let her shoulders sag again. Henryk took her elbow. Helene felt like crying. But that could just as well have been caused by the wine. And Helene didn't want to have to admit she'd drunk too much. And too fast. In the movie theater they both had another short Braunen. Leaning against one of the high tables in the foyer of the City cinema, Helene told Henryk the story of Ilona Faber. Sipped at her coffee. And told how they'd found her. Naked. Strangled. And how the rumors wouldn't go away, because of the orgy. And how nothing was ever solved, because of the occupation. So much for justice after the war. Ilona Faber was among the war's losers. Indeed many girls had been abducted, after the war. Helene bought rum balls to have during the movie. They sat in the second to last row. There was hardly anyone in the theater. Henryk took a pair of glasses from the chest pocket of his jacket. He looked serious with his glasses, respectable and smart. Helene was drowsy. She snuggled into her seat. It was warm. She missed the beginning of the movie. The many shots of the industrial landscape became a blur of reds. She woke up when the woman in the movie drove her little car down a narrow quay that ran into the sea. Where she could stop, right at the water's edge, but not turn around. Later she appeared to be stranded on the quay. Way out. The man had to come and help. From then on, Helene hated the movie. When the woman went to see her husband's business friend and simply crawled into bed with him, Helene wanted to leave. She was hot. It was too hot in the theater. Her stomach hurt. And her neck. A headache began to move from her neck toward her forehead, lingered under her part, then seeped behind her eyes. Helene looked over to the Swede. He was watching the film. From the side Helene could see his eyes follow the action. Helene controlled herself. Sat up straight. Took deep and even breaths. She gave herself breathing exercises. She sat there. To the end. When the movie was over and they left, blinking, the Swede said, "Great, wasn't it? Fantastic!" Lies, lies, lies, Helene thought. She said nothing. How could she explain that everything was wrong? And was right. Therefore. She had no words for it. She only had a feeling. Powerlessness. She felt powerless. Henryk wanted to go for a drink. Helene said goodbye. They stood in front of the theater entrance. The light fell on him from behind. She couldn't see him clearly. Cars were turning from the Rennweg onto the Schwarzenbergplatz. They rumbled across the cobble stones. The Swede held on to Helene's elbows. He looked down at her. "I thought. We. I mean . . ." Helene began to feel miserable. She'd completely forgotten. This question was bound to come up. At some point. Without fail. "Yes," she said. She tried to joke. But her voice wasn't steady. "I think . . ." He held her shoulders. In a movie, it flashed through Helene's mind, people would kiss now. She looked up at the man. He looked at her. Quizzical. A little hurt. A little embarrassed. They weren't in any rush, were they, Helene managed to say. And she wasn't feeling so great. The bread and drippings. Maybe she really wasn't used to these things anymore. Henryk took a step back. He put his hands behind his back. Well! He'd call. Helene walked back to her car, alone. She crossed the square. Past the Russian War Memorial. She looked into the dark corners along her path, challenging them. She didn't care. She'd hit out at an attacker. She'd defend herself. Bite. Pull. Beat. Kick. She'd lost her fear. She'd defend herself. In the car, she felt tired again. She had trouble getting home. Then, in bed, she cried. Her man hadn't come to help her. Wouldn't have come. Was that because she wasn't as beautiful as Monica Vitti? Her man had turned away. Had climbed into his car and driven away.

Next morning. Helene sat in her bathrobe in bed and had coffee. She wanted to read. When she woke up, it had snowed. Heavy wet March snow that was melting fast. Helene leaned back into her pillows. She stared into space, a book on her knees. Basically, she thought, the movie was right. Everything was how men want it. As long as they want it. The difference was Monica Vitti. The woman in the movie, the woman she'd played, this woman had been desirable to everybody. According to the script, anyway. And no wonder. She was beautiful. Helene imagined how it would be to embrace Monica Vitti. To press her gentle curves against her own body. Her smooth skin against her own. Breast against breast. To look into her slanting eyes. She remembered. Ashamed, she pulled up her legs, very close. Her knees pressed against her breasts. She'd been waiting for Gregor. Toward the end, he wouldn't come home until 1 or 2 in the morning. Every night that late. And he had a different smell. Helene had pretended she'd fallen asleep in an armchair after her bath. She sat in one of the leather armchairs in the living room. Draped. Had let her bathrobe slide open. She could also have sat there naked. But she wouldn't have been able to explain that. She'd waited for hours. Motionless. She'd pretended to herself she was asleep. Then Gregor had come. Long after 2 o'clock. He entered the room, turned on the light and asked her what she was doing there. She'd catch a cold, sitting there like that. Helene acted as if she were just waking up. She'd practiced, before. She tried to embrace Gregor sleepily and lovingly. As if waking up she couldn't remember the scenes they made. Gregor pushed her back into the armchair and closed her bathrobe. What was going on, he wanted to know. Helene had imagined he'd stand there for a long time, gazing, and then sink down and take her into his arms. And then. Shortly after that, he had stopped coming home altogether. Couldn't even be reached by phone. Aichenheim would answer the phone in the department and tell her Gregor wasn't available at the moment. Was busy. Would phone her back. And how was she doing. Why didn't she come over anymore. Susi would love to see her again. Asshole, Helene thought. She drank her coffee. The children ran into the room. Flung themselves onto her bed. Helene had trouble not spilling her coffee. The warm small bodies pushed themselves against her under the blanket. Helene wondered if she should ask Katharina about the swinging in the rings. But it was too pleasant right now. Neither did she ask how things had been at the Aichenheims'. Who'd been there. They lay around for an hour, giggled, dozed. Then they decided to get dressed. They went to the Türkenschanz Park. To make angels in the snow before it melted.

At the office things were the same as usual. Helene wrote her report about sun protection in the tanning studio. She quoted Professor Sölders extensively. Herr Nadolny was pleased. Helene sat in her room. Again, she felt redundant. At lunch time she decided to have a serious talk with Gregor. She called and told him so. Gregor passed on Susi's and Johannes' regards. And it was good she was calling. He was just about to pick up the phone himself. He wouldn't be around for Easter. Yes. That's the way it'd worked out. And he needed a rest. She had to understand that. And . . . Helene hung up. She could have heaved over her desk. Tossed the books out the window. And screamed. Could have scratched out his eyes. Stabbed his eyes over and over with her fingers. And run screeching into the street. Everybody should know. She sat there. Quietly. She put her hands in front of her on the desk. She looked at the hands until the trembling inside could no longer be felt. Frau Sprecher came into the room. Spoke to her. Helene was startled. Began to tremble again. Went and got herself a coffee. Frau Sprecher's tomcat was doing better. His blood count wasn't that bad anymore. The vet no longer insisted on putting him down. Frau Sprecher was happy. The cat had liver cancer.

The children had their Easter break. Helene didn't get any time off. Her sister wanted to take Barbara with her to the Waldviertel. To friends, with children, on a farm. The Hietzing grandparents wanted Katharina to visit. Helene's sister picked up Barbara. The child had organized her backpack. Helene had prepared an overnight bag. Barbara didn't want any breakfast. She carried her pack around all morning. Her teddy bear in her arm. She skipped up and down and told Katharina everything she was going to do in the Waldviertel. With the other children and the animals. And that Katharina was only visiting the grandparents. How boring. Katharina sat there. Sucked her thumb, quietly. Helene said nothing. She sent Barbara to tidy up and took Katharina on her lap. She wrapped her arms around the child. Katharina sat quietly. Helene was furious with herself. She had to create a happy world for these children. That was her job. She asked Katharina if she'd rather stay with her. She could come to the office with her, too. Katharina sucked on her finger. The child leaned against Helene for a long time. Said nothing. Helene's sister rang the door bell. Barbara dashed outside. Down the stairs. "Aunt Mimi, Aunt Mimi," she shouted down the stairwell. She dashed out on the street. Ran and stood next to the car door. Helene kissed her. Told her to take care and come back safely. Barbara climbed into the car as quickly as possible. Let herself be buckled in. Sat there, full of anticipation, with her teddy bear pressed against her. Helene asked her sister if she should give Barbara some money. Mimi shrugged. Helene gave her 1000 schillings. In case they went out for a meal. They should treat their friends. Getting into the car, Mimi called out to Helene that the grandparents had the phone number where she could be reached. In the car Barbara demanded loudly why they weren't leaving yet. Helene watched the car disappear. Barbara was so small Helene could only see Mimi's head.

After work, Helene took Katharina to Hietzing. To her parents. Katharina had whispered she wanted to go to the grandparents. She had her pack ready when Helene got back from the office. Gregor's mother came over. She was whining how lonely she'd be, without the children. Helene suggested it would also do her some good to be without the children for a change. And on Sunday they'd all be back of course. Helene added that lately the old woman had been complaining quite a bit. About the strain of baby-sitting. Katharina sat quietly in the car. Helene took the Johnstrasse. She tried to chat with Katharina. The child gave only short replies. Or remained silent. In the rear-view mirror Helene saw her looking out the window. Now she could see Schönbrunn Castle, Helene said. Helene drove down the hill on the Hütteldorfer Strasse. "Dad won't be coming." Katharina continued to look out the window. "No," Helene was forced to say. "No, he won't. He can't. He won't be back in time. He can't. He's on a trip, you know. He needs a rest, he says. But. You'll stay with Grandma and Grandpa. The Easter bunny will go there too. On Saturday, Barbara and Aunt Mimi will join you. And I'll be there for the Easter egg hunt. And then we'll go back home. By the way, what would you like to get from the Easter bunny? You haven't told me yet what you want. You know, he's going to ask me. A new paint box? How about a really big paint box? Would you like that?" Helene talked and every so often looked in the rear-view mirror. Katharina looked out the window. Unblinking. "Can I watch TV? At Grandpa's?" "Yes, of course. Of course you can. Or. Would you rather stay with me. Tell me now. We don't have to go there." Katharina said no more after that: At the grandparents' she sat down in front of the TV. Helene stayed for supper. She wanted to help her mother set the table. She couldn't find things. Her parents had gotten their kitchen and dining room renovated, with all new furniture and furnishings. "Since it's just us, now," they said. Mimi was living with the parents. Continued to. Helene looked for the cutlery. She didn't want to ask her mother anything. She didn't want to be alone with her mother in the kitchen. Her mother might ask questions. What could she have answered. She knew the baby-sitting was organized to help save the marriage. A few days without the children. And the young couple would rediscover each other. A bit of a rest. And all would be well. And no disruptions from the children. Helene's parents knew nothing about Gregor's move. They only knew about disagreements. Helene would have to let Gregor get sick again for Easter. Or say nothing. Maybe no one would ask. What reasons were there, after all, to prevent a university math lecturer from spending Easter Sunday with his family? The correct answer would have been "his secretary."

After the meal, Helene drove back to the Lannerstrasse. She had put her arms around Katharina, had wanted to take her, keep her in her arms. The child had clung to her neck, her legs wrapped around Helene's waist. "My little spider-monkey," she had whispered into the child's ear. "Give me a call. If anything happens. I'll pick you up right away." Helene got home at half past 8. She locked the apartment door and left the key in the lock. So nobody would be able to get in. She should have gone over to visit Gregor's mother. But she didn't want to see the woman. Helene sat down in the living room. Stood up. She should make the most of her freedom. Go out. Be merry. She gave Püppi a call. There was no answer. Helene went to bed early. She couldn't sleep. The Swede hadn't called. Probably he'd expected it all to go faster. And easier, Helene thought. She took off her night-gown and sat naked in front of the TV. She got herself a Cointreau. She went and stood in front of the bookcase and saw herself reflected in the glass. She'd become skinny. The curve from her hips to her chest was more pronounced. Her breasts small again. As they'd been before the children. Only her nipples were flatter. Softer. Darker. She turned to the side. No belly. Looking down she saw the skin around her navel getting looser. Not wrinkled yet. The way Helene had seen it in older women in the sauna. You could tell where one day the wrinkles would run across. Helene sat down on the couch. The cover felt cool. There was a western on TV. She hated westerns. With their ever-lasting riding and shooting around and beating each other up. Helene tried to imagine one of the heroes naked. She touched herself between her legs. She twirled some pubic hair around her index finger. She led her middle finger slide further. It was warm, almost dry, hard. She could feel her pubic bone. Helene tried to stroke her nipples. She wanted to feel at least the tickling in her throat and under her navel. Her nipples only got hard when she pressed them tightly. Stroking didn't help. She had the taste of wood in her mouth. She squeezed her nipples till they hurt. Then she gave up. At least her period was back all right, sort of. Finally. Her period had been overdue for half a year. Helene went back to bed. She couldn't fantasize anything, either. She couldn't remember anything. Couldn't remember how it had been with Gregor. The men before him she had long forgotten. And Alex. If he'd phoned.

On Good Friday Helene did her spring cleaning. Washed the windows. Waxed and polished the floors. Cleaned out the cupboards. Washed down the children's bunk beds. Thoroughly tidied up their room. Put everything in its place. Changed the sheets. She dragged herself through these jobs. She worked late into the night. Listened to Los Paraguajos. She cranked up the stereo. Ached for faraway places because of the rhythms. Around midnight she fell into bed. She looked with satisfaction from her bed into the living room and into the kitchen beyond it. Without the children she was able to leave all the double doors open. The apartment sparkled. She had packed some of Gregor's clothes and books into boxes and locked them into a cupboard. You simply had to do your spring cleaning.

On Holy Saturday Helene had nothing left to do but to go shopping and bake the Easter cake. For lunch she ate a bun with lots of meat. She took a particularly avaricious bite. At that moment the phone rang. It was Henryk. Helene choked on the bun. Was she sick? She sounded odd. Henryk wanted to see her in the evening. Go for a meal. Not to a Heuriger. Decent wine, real wine, please. Helene accepted. But she'd have to be home early. The Easter cake had to be glazed. You could only do that in the evening. After the cake had cooled off completely. They agreed to meet in Café Sacher. This time he'd come for sure. He was looking forward to it.

Helene felt young. She had phoned and asked how the children were doing. She had talked with Katharina. The child had been cheerful. The empty apartment was a joy. No toys were lying around. Helene could wash her hair without being interrupted halfway through to settle an argument between the children. Again she put on the Balmain dress. She had everything ready for Easter. Except the cake. She'd given the grandparents the gifts for the children already on Wednesday. For hiding in the garden. Helene left the apartment. Locked the door carefully. She felt quite different, not as she usually did. Nobody asked when she'd be back. And if she could bring them a little something. The Swede was waiting in Café Sacher. From there they went to the Greek restaurant in the Mailberger Hof. They sat in a corner near the entrance. Helene had feared the people walking past them would be a disruption. But they soon forgot the world around them. In the end the waiter bothered them when topping up their glasses. Or asking if they needed anything. They only had eyes for each other. Helene was elated. They were both elated. Helene came to her senses in the bedroom of an apartment belonging to some friends of Henryk's. They had driven to the Hofmühlgasse. The apartment was on the 3rd floor. They had walked up the stairs, talking. They had talked nonstop all evening. Had spun out their ideas without a break. Had discovered perfect agreement. There wasn't a subject for which this wouldn't have been true. In the apartment Henryk walked straight through to his room. The furniture stood in their way. Big and dark. They kept having to avoid it as they walked through the rooms. Helene hit her shin on the protruding carvings of a sideboard. Henryk's room was behind a concealed door in the parlor. Bed, cupboard, small table, armchair. The room was a large bay window. From the 3 windows you could look in 3 directions. Distant street noise drifted up from below. The street lamps cast a silver-gray light into the room. There were no curtains. Henryk didn't turn on a light. He sat down on the bed, took off his shoes, lay down. His arms folded behind his head, he asked Helene if she wouldn't at least sit down next to him. Helene went to the windows. She looked at the road. Up the road. Moved to the left. Looked down the road. Looked at the houses across the way. People were walking. The traffic light ran through its colors. Cars stopped. Drove on. It wasn't late. Maybe half past 10. Helene couldn't speak. Her throat was constricted. Her head was far away from the body. The body was a heavy shapeless thing. She stood in the bay window and didn't know how to move or how to speak. She felt like slapping her face with her hands and starting to keen. She saw herself swaying backwards and forwards while uttering little wailing sounds. Beyond that, she couldn't picture herself. She couldn't get beyond that. The arms were hanging down. She couldn't feel her hands. The

[57]

head felt thin and drafty inside. On the edge of a fainting spell. Rooted to the spot. Legs immobile. She wanted to escape. Run. Hurry. Hasten down the stairs. And laugh at the front door. Laugh about her getaway. Some time later turn around and see that the enemy had been unable to follow her. "I have to go," Helene said. "Why?" he asked. "I must finish the Easter cake. The glaze." She walked toward the door. The Swede laughed softly. "You're just making excuses!" Then she suddenly sat on the bedside and fell into the Swede's arms. She saw herself bending toward him, pulled by him. Her lips on his. Lifting her legs onto the bed and lying next to him. Slowly. Slowed down. During the long sinking down she thought how she hadn't explained anything to him. She opened her mouth to speak. Lifted her head. Took a breath. Henryk pulled her head back down and kissed her.

Helene began glazing the Easter cake at around half past 1 in the morning. She'd cried a lot. Had cried afterwards. She had felt his body against hers. Hot. And racing. She had wept. Sobbing, she had pressed her chest against his belly. He had tried to soothe her. Helene's hips still hurt from the unfamiliar movements. On the inside her thighs were sore from his hip bones. She could no longer remember. Could no longer imagine anything. It was all a chaos of limbs to her. Surfaces of bodies. Skin against skin. Having it inside. She was exhausted and empty. She warmed the chocolate with the butter. A real chocolate glaze with feathered icing was now impossible. She poured the soft brownish-black mass over the cake. Let it run down the sides. She stuck little marzipan bunnies around the edge, marzipan chicks, and colored sugar Easter eggs. She put the cake on the kitchen window sill to get hard. Went to bed. In bed she wondered whether to try now. Would it perhaps work now.

She placed her middle finger between her still swollen lips. Giving it a try, she began to move it up and down the wet furrow. Then she realized. She had given no thought to the consequences. As if the question had been erased from her memory. Her period had been just about exactly 2 weeks ago. And what about AIDS. Really, what did she know about him. Helene rolled over. She put her arm around her 2nd pillow and fell asleep. He hadn't talked about it either.

Helene wasn't able to think of Henryk again until late in the evening on Easter Sunday. Nor of anything else. She had spent the whole day with the family. She had taken Gregor's mother with her. To her parents. She had delivered the cake. She had watched the children hunt for Easter eggs. The day had been cold and windy. The children were zooming around in the garden. She stood on the porch with her parents and sister while Gregor's mother was out there with the children. They stayed in Hietzing until after they'd had coffee and cake in the afternoon. Helene had said right at the outset that Gregor couldn't make it. Nobody had reacted. Because of Gregor's mother. Also, Helene's mother had tried to talk to her in private. But Helene had managed to escape. Later, back in the Lannerstrasse, the children attacked the apartment. The immaculate apartment reverted to chaos in no time. The children were noisy and happy. They strewed their presents all over the rooms. Ate sweets. Dropped wrappers everywhere. Got grumpy. Couldn't be put to bed. The grandmother wanted to have another talk with Helene. Helene was to come over, to her apartment. It turned out to be about money. The phone bill. Their floor used to have only one phone. Two had been installed after they had divided the floor into two apartments. You could switch from one to the other. The old woman had said that she didn't need a phone much anymore. It would work fine this way. And she had wanted to pay the bill. As her contribution. Now she suddenly wanted a share from Gregor. He should pay. But she couldn't get hold of him. That Aichenheim always said he'd pass on the message. But Gregor never phoned back. Could Helene understand that. "Well. He probably doesn't want to talk to you," Helene suggested. The mother-in-law said there had to be rules. Things weren't working out. And anyway. Gregor probably had his reasons for avoiding the house, didn't he. From her, his mother. He'd never walked away from her, he'd stayed. Until Helene had shown up. Helene replied that it hadn't been her who'd brought up this man. Spoiled him, rather. That was the core of the problem, wasn't it. His upbringing. Drilling him to become an egotist. Mothers simply projected too much. Onto their sons. Particularly if the mothers were widows. The son as substitute husband. It couldn't work. The mother-in-law showed Helene out of her apartment. Helene said that she'd never wanted to come into this apartment in the first place.

Helene was lying in bed. She stared at the window. A lighter square in the darkness. She was tired. Couldn't get any rest. She tossed from side to side. Turned her blanket around. Piled up pillows. Pushed them away. She tried to remember. What had it been. With Henryk. What had they talked about. How had he embraced her. Kissed her. When had she undressed? How had she gotten home? She was no longer sure of anything. Everything was in a tumble. And then. Where was she supposed to find the money for the phone bill. And why should she pay. If she were alone. Alone. Nothing would have been a problem. But how much more could she justify. Before the children. Gregor had consumed all the chaos. Used it up. For her, only order was left. She had to put everything in order, would put everything in order. As much as possible. The restlessness rose from her belly toward her heart. Pulsed, irregular. Spread in her rib cage. Formed a second cage. Which heavily pressed on her. The Swede hadn't phoned either. Later. Afterwards.

Helene woke up on Easter Monday with her face in pain. On the right side, her upper lip was puffy and taut. She fingered her face. The right side was swollen. Then she saw it in the mirror: a cold sore. She'd never had anything like it. Gregor had suffered from them all the time. Helene's blister was huge. Her cheek was so swollen the right eye looked small. Helene stared at herself. She looked as if somebody had slapped her hard on the mouth and cheek. She felt sick at the sight of herself. She went back to bed. She stared at the ceiling. Stayed in bed. She didn't go to the pharmacy. If it had to be this way, it had to be this way. She didn't even cry. She didn't talk with the children. She only told them to leave the key in the apartment door and eat cornflakes if they got hungry. Barbara came every so often to the bedroom door and wanted to get Helene to the phone. "I'm sick," Helene yelled before the child could say anything. "I'm sick. Damn it. Can't I even be sick. In peace." The child withdrew in a fright. Helene lay there. The whole day. She'd had it. If she also had to be disfigured, then she'd really had it.

In the evening, around 8 o'clock, Barbara burst into her room. There was a man outside, and Grandma was talking to him, but he wanted to see her. Helene couldn't imagine who it could be. She left her room. Why did her mother-in-law have to meddle again. Helene held a big white handkerchief against her mouth. There was Henryk. Her mother-in-law leaned against the door frame. She was just laughing about something the Swede had said. Helene stood in her doorway. The mother-in-law and the Swede turned to her. What was going on? Why wouldn't she come to the phone? Helene couldn't say anything. She would have started to cry with her first word. Henryk told the old woman he'd take care of everything. Not to worry. Helene wanted to send him away. She didn't need anybody. She was glad to be alone. And her mother-in-law should go away. Finally. How could anybody stand all this? She didn't want to see anybody. Henryk eased her back into her apartment. He closed the door behind him. He took the handkerchief from Helene, looked at her, and couldn't help grinning. Helene immediately had tears running down her cheeks. She turned and went back to her bed. Henryk followed. He asked for her car keys and some money. He had no Austrian money left. Where was the nearest pharmacy? He sent Helene to bed. Explained to the children that their mother was sick. They should be quiet. Helene buried herself under her blanket. Going through the apartment she had seen the mess the children, left to themselves, had created in a single day. She lay on her left side. The right one hurt. Throbbed. Helene wept about the apartment. Then she wept about weeping for such trifles. Henryk returned and brought ointments and pills. He sat down next to her. Then he went to the children. Helene heard them talk. Mostly Barbara's high voice. Then Katharina's too. Dishes rattled. Cutlery. Helene dozed. The children came to say good-night. Henryk had cooked spaghetti, and they had cleaned up the kitchen. They'd go to bed now and would be very quiet. Katharina looked at Helene in horror. No, Helene said, she wouldn't kiss them good night. Otherwise they'd look like her. It was very infectious. And maybe she should look for a new job. As a monster, in the movies. The children didn't laugh. They left. Henryk brought her an apple. He had peeled and cut it into small slices. He had dripped lemon juice over it. It tasted wonderful. He sat on her bedside. When Helene wanted to say something, he forbade her to speak. Talking was difficult for Helene. The right half of her face had swollen even more during the day. When she spoke, she sounded like a drunk. "I'll just calm your mother down," Henryk said. "Mother-in-law," Helene murmured. "Mother-in-law, okay," Henryk smiled. He came back afterwards. Everything was fine. Helene slept.

Helene got off the train. The other passengers pushed her toward the exit. The through coach from Vienna had been coupled to a local train in Mestre. Helene had to walk along the train to the front. With Gregor, Helene had always taken the car to Venice. And had walked from the autorimessa to the vaporetto. She had hardly slept. She'd sat at the window and stared into the darkness. She'd managed to give Henryk the arrival time of her train. Then the connection had become so bad that Helene couldn't tell if he'd been able to hear her. Henryk had shouted he'd be there. That was the last she'd heard before she lost the connection. And Henryk hadn't phoned again. What was she to do if he weren't there. The idea of having to spend even a single day in Venice and not to meet him. Knowing Henryk was in the city, somewhere, and no chance of reaching him. The idea was unbearable. Why hadn't she asked him for the hotel where he lived? Helene walked past the brown Italian coaches. At least she had no heavy luggage. A coffee, Helene thought. A cappuccino in the station snack bar. And wasn't there a train going back to Vienna this same morning. And why hadn't he given her his phone number. Why hadn't he phoned again. Henryk stood at the end of the platform, leaning against a cast-iron pillar, scanning the crowd of passengers for her. Helene saw him first. Walked toward him. Then he saw her. Pushed himself away from the pillar.

Walked toward her with big steps. Took her bag off her shoulder, put his arm around her, kissed her cheek. Helene put her arm around his waist. "You probably need a coffee." They went to the snack bar. Helene stood with her cappuccino. The coffee tasted wonderful. She felt that if she left her mouth slightly open, people would hear her gurgling with joy. She giggled. Then she made mean comments about her fellow passengers. And about the people around them. She didn't want to let on how happy she was. How triumphant. A success! They had found each other. To Venice for a day. A sensible person wouldn't do that. "You must be awfully tired," Henryk said. They drank their coffees. Then they went to the Pensione. Henryk had a room in a Pensione near the Ognissanti church. Helene walked behind Henryk through the narrow alleys. She wore new shoes. After a short while she felt the burning dampness at her left heel. A blister. She struggled not to limp. She tried to push her foot to the front of the shoe with each step. To avoid touching the heel. It didn't work. Helene concentrated on walking and soon lost her sense of direction. She only knew that Ognissanti was toward Zattere. The sun was scorching. The white walls of the houses gave her a headache. And Henryk always ahead of her. He walked fast. Long strides. In the beginning they had talked. But it was wearisome. The paths along the canals were too narrow to walk next to each other. Henryk had to turn around halfway when talking to her. Helene had to shout her answers at him. She limped along behind Henryk. At the hotel she breathed a sigh of relief. They climbed up to the 4th floor. A narrow staircase. On the stairs, Henryk saw Helene's heel. He had let her go first. Why hadn't she said something? That was just silly. In his room he told her to sit on the bed. Fetched a Band-Aid from the bathroom, made Helene take off her stockings, stuck the Band-Aid over the burst blister. The heel looked ugly. Disgusting. Helene was embarrassed. New shoes on a trip. She really was incompetent. Helene sat on the bed. She looked at her naked feet. White. On the burgundy wall-to-wall carpet that was old and worn and coarse against the soles of her feet. Helene suddenly didn't know why she was there. In this room, in this city. Wasn't it all exaggerated? She blushed. She felt her pulse like waves across her cheeks and eyes. She had wished so badly. To see him. To talk to him. And. In Venice. But. Women don't do such things. Wasn't it up to the man to carry the burden? Helene looked from her feet to her hands, which, clasping each other, lay on her thighs. Henryk leaned against her. Together, they fell back into the pillows.

Helene slept through lunch. They made it to the piazza San Marco at around 4 o'clock. Over tea in the Florian they told each other what had happened since their last meeting. Henryk was hoping to submit a project to the Fiat Foundation. That's why he was in Venice. And it really didn't matter why they were there, did it. Main thing, they were there. Henryk held Helene's hand. Or leaned against her. They couldn't keep their hands off each other.

The next day Helene woke up. The chamber maid was poking her key into the lock. Henryk called "No!" Half asleep. They turned toward each other. Rolled into each other's arms. Helene by now knew Henryk well. Knew where she had to stroke him. To trigger little quickened breaths. And where to trigger deep ones. She knew how his cock felt. How it felt to close her hand around it. How its hardness throbbed. And how to feel it slide into her. And how to stop knowing. And only exist there. Down there. Far away. But she. Henryk put his hand over her mouth. She couldn't remember having cried out. She was embarrassed and had to laugh. Hid her head on his shoulder, his chest. Helene gave herself to all that followed. Had to laugh every so often. Then they lay pressed against each other. Sunshine fell through the window. A spring wind made the curtains billow. And bells began to chime. From all directions, bells were chiming. It was Sunday. Helene felt buoyed by the pealing. And then felt sad. She didn't really know the man next to her. She would have liked to implore him not to leave her. Never to leave her. To hold her like this forever. Never to climb out of this bed, not again, not ever. She would have liked to throw herself before him, to lie at his feet and plead with him. Now, at this very moment, it was possible. To start another life. Only now. Helene lay next to him. The words were jostling in her throat. Around her navel some pain. Her breasts numb and heavy. And a feeling of pleasure. Helene smiled at how it all had happened. She turned over to Henryk. Looked at him. Henryk was crying. His eyes were wet. He whispered something. Helene had to lift her head first to understand. "I think this has been the most beautiful morning of my life," Henryk whispered. Again the maid put the key in the lock. She knocked. Loud. "It's past 11," Helene said. Again Henryk called "No!" Forceful. The maid hissed something behind the door. Angry. Henryk laughed. Yelled "No! Grazie!" and pulled Helene back into his arms. "Who needs their beds made?" he asked. They laughed.

Helene took the night train back. On Monday morning she staggered into the office. At home everything had been fine. Gregor hadn't done the dishes. The kitchen was full of dirty dishes. At the office everybody was in a bad mood. Frau Sprecher's cat hadn't eaten. Herr Nadolny didn't arrive until 11 o'clock. He went straight into his office. Locked the door behind him. Frau Sprecher put her head into

Helene's office and raised her eyebrows. Meaningfully. Helene wanted only peace and quiet. But she smiled. They both knew what Nadolny did behind his locked door. He would pick up the receiver. Push the button for an outside line. Then he'd go to the bookcase and take out Knaur's Encyclopedia, 1934 edition. From the bottle of Four Roses behind the encyclopedia he'd pour himself a few fingers of bourbon in a water glass. He'd put the bottle back and place the book in front of it. Standing at the window, he'd empty his glass. And make a lot of noise and mutter orders to himself. Once Helene and Frau Sprecher had stood outside Nadolny's door and listened. They laughed so much they had to race for the washroom. One had sat on the toilet while the other had skipped from one foot to the other in front of the mirror. Since then there was laughter at the office when Nadolny needed to start drinking in the morning. In the afternoon. Helene had picked up the children from school. Had given them buns with cold cuts for lunch. And cocoa. Had started washing the dishes. The dishwasher still hadn't been fixed. In the afternoon. Back at the office, Nadolny asked Helene to see him. There'd be a new job, a great job. Everything would change. Her first task was to talk to a Dr. Stadlmann. A Dr. Justus Stadlmann. A most difficult man. At least that's what he, Nadolny, had heard. A scientist. And much hope rested on her skill at being obliging. On her charm. "Your charm, Frau Gebhardt," Nadolny said, "is an asset. Don't underestimate it." He, Nadolny, he'd take care of Herr Nestler. Who was a businessman from Switzerland and wanted to launch Dr. Stadlmann's invention in a big way. Helene wanted to know what kind of invention this was. "Medical. Frau Gebhardt. Something medical. You'll see. Interesting." Helene arranged an appointment with Dr. Stadlmann. He wouldn't be free before the end of the week, Dr. Stadlmann's mother said.

No. Helene couldn't talk to her son. If she wanted to talk to him, she'd have to come on Friday at 12:30.

After work Helene drove to the market on the Sonnberg Platz. In the Obkirchergasse. She bought fruit and vegetables from the produce merchants, Herr and Frau Leonhard. Bought some meat from the butcher where the writer Thomas Bernhard had always bought his ham. As the butcher kept telling everybody. With her two bags full of fruit and vegetables Helene then went to the fish shop. She wanted to prepare a decent meal for the children. To make up for the buns with cold cuts they'd had for lunch. The fishman stood at the cash register. He only left the spot when he had to filet a fish. Then the heavy man would drag himself to the chopping block. The fishwoman stood by the deep fryer. Helene ordered 3 portions of fried plaice. The woman grabbed the breaded plaice filets from a table behind her. For a moment she looked up at Helene. The woman had swollen red eyes. "Yes," she said, "my uncle's died." "Oh. I'm sorry to hear that." Helene felt stupid. And superficial. The fishwoman had put the plaice filets into the deep fryer. She looked out the window. "And then nobody talks about you any longer," the fishwoman said. The fishman cleared his throat. He let the drawer of the cash register clang. No. It wasn't like that. You would think for a long time of the deceased. Forever. Wouldn't you? Helene tried to find something consoling to say. The wife came up to Helene. Clung to the display case. Bent over the case toward Helene. Helene had to force herself not to step back. The woman's face was very close. She felt the woman's breath. "In the beginning. Yes. They all talk. And cry. And then?" The woman turned away. She walked back to the deep fryer. Took out the plaice filets. They were still too pale. She dropped them back into the oil. "They'll forget you. Simply forget you. And what's it all about anyway?" Again the woman stared out the window. Again the fishman made the cash register clang. Nobody spoke. The oil sizzled quietly. Helene paid. The fishman took the money. Helene took her white plastic bag with the fried fish wrapped in foil. On her way to the car Helene was overcome with yearning for Henryk. What might he be doing just now? She longed to walk next to him. She remembered his legs, his handsome slim legs. Why did he have to be so handsome, on top of everything else, Helene thought. She got furious. Why was she kept away from him. She threw the fish into the back of the car. Flung the bag. They could eat crumbled fish for all she cared. And what nonsense she'd talked. Of course they'd forget you. She should have cried with the woman. Maybe she should cry a lot more. Even more than she did already. And go to Venice. And stay there. Helene took the Höhenstrasse home. Drove on in Grinzing, drove off in Neustift. The sun was shining. Forsythias and almond trees were in blossom. Green veils of young leaves hung around the willows. Otherwise everything was still bare. Helene drove underneath the naked beech trees. Between the branches, the sky was shining blue. Henryk was supposed to come to Vienna next week. He'd said so in Venice. When would he phone? So far, she hadn't heard from him. She had to get home. What if he called. Now. This moment. Helene drove home as fast as possible.

Helene was to meet Dr. Stadlmann at home. His place. In the Linke Wienzeile. Almost up at the Gürtel, near the Mollardgasse. Helene left the office. She had considered taking the tram because she'd found a parking spot right in front of the building. She took the car. She wanted nobody next to her. Enclosed in her car, she crawled with the traffic across the bridge by the Urania building with its domed planetarium. Across the Ring. Through the Operngasse. And into the Linke Wienzeile. On the bridge Helene's mind drifted off. She moved the car forward. Changed gears. Braked. She slid along with the flow. Automatically. Inside her, pain spread along the abdominal wall. Smarting, as if after a long incision. After Venice, Henryk hadn't phoned anymore. Helene had tried the number in Milan. Hesitant at first. She had cautiously dialed one digit after the other. On Tuesday for the first time. She'd wanted to know if he'd gotten back safely. Nobody answered. On Wednesday, she'd phoned 20 times. From the office too. Private calls abroad were, of course, forbidden. She had sat in her room. Frau Sprecher could be heard outside. Nadolny wasn't in. Helene had listened to the ringing of the phone in Milan. She had no idea what his phone looked like or where it was. She didn't even know what Milan looked like. Helene had never been to Milan. She'd had to force herself to hang up. With each ring, the memories had drifted further away. Away. Gone. Helene had looked at the table top and listened to the phone. She'd felt as though she herself were vanishing. Like her memories. Hanging up became an effort. She would have liked to keep listening. On and on. In the car, driving along the Ring, it was the same. The traffic carried her. Pushed her forward. Forced her once to drive a bit faster, then again to stop. Something behind her eyes prevented her from seeing clearly. The eyes stared. Didn't adapt well to anything. Helene reminded herself that they had promised each other nothing. That they were both grown-ups. And that it wasn't the first time for her. Hadn't she survived it each time? And hadn't it been right each time? The sentences remained in her head. High up there. The eyes rigid. In her belly, the pain. On Wienzeile Helene looked for the correct number. She slowed the traffic. Furiously other drivers passed her, honked, gesticulated. Helene yelled

in her car they should go to hell. It hadn't been her choice
to look for an address here, had it. She didn't want to stop
here. She bent over to the left to find the number.

Stadlmann's apartment was on the 3rd floor. Helene rang
the bell. She heard voices behind the door. Only after the
3rd ring did somebody come toward the door. A chain was
pushed back, 2 locks unlocked, the door opened. An elderly woman stood there. Looked at Helene. Indifferent, dis-
approving. "You want to see my son," she said. Helene
merely nodded. The woman pointed Helene toward an armchair in the long narrow hallway. Helene sat down. The
woman disappeared to the left. The hallway led deep into
the back. From there Helene could hear the voices more
distinctly. A man was explaining something. A woman asked
questions in between. Doors were on the right, windows
on the left side of the hallway. She could see into a yard.
Onto the top of a tree. Between the doors and the windows
were racks and boxes. Technical equipment was piled up.
Measuring instruments, computer parts, monitors, what
appeared to be medical instruments, electrocardiograph
machines. Everything was covered in dust. The windows
dotted with specks. It smelled of fried onions. The door at
the end of the hallway opened. A dark-haired girl stepped
out. Her long hair fell over her face. Hid it. She moved
slowly. Dragged one of her legs. A woman followed her.
Older, elegant. She was talking to somebody behind her.
"Thank you so much, Herr Doctor," she said. "Oh. You
have no idea how grateful we are. We've already been to so
many places!" Helene heard the man repeat over and over,
"Good-bye, Ma'am, good-bye." The two women walked past
Helene. The younger one didn't turn toward her, but the
older one gave Helene a nod. "Are you Frau Gebhardt?"
the man asked. He'd remained at the back of the hallway.

Calling out to the front. Helene got up and went to the back. The corridor was narrow. Helene had to squeeze herself past the racks. The man stood in the doorway of a room. The Stadlmann mother had appeared and unlocked the door for the two women. Locked the locks behind them. Noisy, rattling. Helene walked up to the man. It was dark that far down the hallway. "Dr. Stadlmann?" she asked and followed the man into the room. Dr. Stadlmann hurled himself 3 steps into the room. Then he dropped himself into a big upholstered office chair. He wore orthopedic boots reaching well above his ankles, almost to his knees. When he sat, the legs of his pants rode up high. Both boots were attached with braces. When he walked, he'd fling each leg forward and then put it down with a jerk. "Polio," Dr. Stadlmann said. Helene nodded "I see!" And "A girl in kindergarten got it too. She's become a doctor." "Well there you are," Dr. Stadlmann replied. He sat there waiting to catch his breath. Helene sat on a tiny white armchair. The room looked like a doctor's office, all glossy white paint. But everything was covered in dust. Helene knew from her files that Dr. Stadlmann was a physicist. Helene looked around. She didn't understand why he surrounded himself with the props of a doctor. Stadlmann caught her glance. "So what do you already know?" he asked. "Nothing whatsoever. Herr Nadolny thought I should hear it all from you." "I dare say you're right," Dr. Stadlmann said. He gave Helene a lecture. About magnetic Band-Aids. The healing power of magnetic fields. In Japan Dr. Stadlmann had developed a magnetized foil and had applied for patent protection for its medical use. Herr Nestler was funding it. Had Helene met Herr Nestler? Helene shook her head. Yes. Well. This is how these magnetic Band-Aids work. Soon Helene had pieces of thick, shiny golden foil stuck to her neck. To her wrists. She had to admit it was getting warmer underneath.

Whether she felt any better, she couldn't tell. The magnetic Band-Aid was for arthritis. Joint problems such as tennis elbow. And was generally soothing for soft tissue and joint inflammation. Creating harmony. Healing. You applied the Band-Aid in a certain direction. The direction had to do with the acupuncture meridians. All right. This is how you put it on. The door opened. Dr. Stadlmann's mother entered. She put a bowl of soup on the desk. Dr. Stadlmann rolled his chair behind his desk and started eating. Helene had to swallow. She was hungry, and the soup smelled good. Dr. Stadlmann pointed with his spoon at a poster on the wall. It showed a naked man, from the front and from behind. The acupuncture points and meridians were indicated. With a black felt pen Band-Aids had been drawn in. On the neck, on the back, along the spine, and on all the joints. You just had to wear the Band-Aids long enough. Then everything would be well. Dr. Stadlmann ate his soup. Beef with vegetables. Everything had been cut up. He ate with a spoon. Helene sat covered in Band-Aids in front of him. Lower down than he. Dr. Stadlmann was talking without a break. Helene could see the bolus in his mouth. How he moved it around and chewed as he continued his explanations. Helene should carefully study the material. He'd give her everything to take home. Then together they would produce a brochure. And a film. A video. So everything would become as understandable as possible. It was most important, wasn't it, to avoid any suspicion of impropriety. Of quackery. He was definitely aware of the potential dangers. Well! He. Now that he'd eaten he'd have to lie down. He had to lie down at regular intervals, unfortunately. It took a lot of time. But. After all, you can also think while lying down, can't you. Helene jumped up from her tiny chair. She peeled off the pieces of foil. Black edges remained on her skin. That was still a weakness, Dr. Stadlmann remarked. But a trifle. The Band-Aid on her neck had pulled hair out as it came off. Dr. Stadlmann gave Helene a stack of papers. He accompanied her to the door. Limped ahead of her down the hallway. Stopped in front of each piece of equipment and explained to Helene its benefits, its uses, its cost. All his money had gone into these instruments. And his mother's. And. The instruments were already obsolete. Could happen within months. Depending. And. The woman Helene had seen leaving with her daughter. Earlier, when she'd arrived. She was a countess. The daughter was suffering from arthrosis in the hips. The poor child. Would have liked to be a model. Would have been pretty enough all right. But with such a defect. The foil was helping. At least the pain wasn't so severe anymore. In any case, the child was able to walk again without a cane. Helene. Anyhow. Helene should consider herself lucky to be involved in such a project. She should call him. Monday. Or would she be free on Sunday. No. She had children. Yes. Well! Helene promised to phone on Monday. She went downstairs and into the street. At a little store around the corner she bought 2 buns with sausage and dill pickles. She got into her car and ate. Rushed. Stuffed herself. Munched the buns. "Magnetic foil," Helene talked to herself. "Magnetic foil?"

Early on Saturday morning the children climbed into Helene's bed. Helene hadn't been able to sleep. She'd sat by the phone. Late into the night. She hadn't phoned again. There. Milan. Later she'd put the phone next to her bed. She had lain down close to the edge of her bed and, lying on her side, had looked at the phone. It rang around 11. Helene let it ring 3 times. So it wouldn't seem as if she'd been waiting for the call. She was sure it would be Henryk. Gregor's voice immediately triggered the thought that now

Henryk couldn't reach her. Yes? she asked. Yes. Gregor should come. He always came Saturday mornings, didn't he? Yes. She'd been asleep. Yes. Sometimes she'd just go to bed early. Helene hung up. She had tried to keep the conversation as short as possible. But then it had taken a long time. Gregor had noticed she was trying to get rid of him. Helene was certain Henryk had tried just then. And now wouldn't phone again. She had stared into the darkness. Waiting to sleep. She tried to tell herself that other people had a much harder lot in life. They were always alone. Lonely. Didn't even have the bare necessities. It didn't help. In the morning she was tired. The children crept to her under the covers. They promised to be quiet. They laughed. Giggled. Then calmed down. Crawled around a bit more. Katharina got herself a book and sat at the foot of the bed. She put her feet under the blanket. She tickled the soles of Helene's feet. But then there was quiet. Katharina read. Barbara went back to sleep. Helene dozed. She didn't hear Gregor come into the apartment. Suddenly Gregor stood in the bedroom. He'd brought rolls. Was waving the little cloth bag with the rolls. He wouldn't mind some breakfast. Was hungry. Helene slowly sat up. Barbara disappeared under the blanket. Katharina sucked her thumb. Helene felt heavy and numb. Wouldn't it be better to drive to a coffee house. To Haag in the Währingerstrasse. They had baguette buns with egg salad there. What had he bought the rolls for, Gregor wanted to know. In that case. It was just about 10 o'clock. Perhaps people could make an effort to get up. Helene sat leaning against her pillows. Barbara was snuggling up to her. Helene said, "Why don't you make us breakfast? We'll get dressed. And you get started with the breakfast. In the meantime." Gregor stood in the middle of the room. That wasn't what he'd come for. If he wanted to make himself breakfast, he could do that anytime.

He was interested in having breakfast with them. Not in making breakfast. Helene was about to get out of bed. And go into the kitchen. At that moment Katharina came crawling to her. Climbed on her lap, slipped under the blanket, snuggled into her arms, fiercely sucked her thumb. "But, Gregor, don't you see how tired we are." Was she finally making breakfast or what, Gregor asked, bored. "No," Helene said. She'd like to stay in bed. And then go to a coffee house. He could join them. It'd be more fun. And the rolls would be eaten, too. Sometime. And anyway. His mother wanted to talk to him. He should go over and see her. Was she going to make breakfast after all. Gregor spoke to Helene as if she were her little children's sister. "No," Helene said. Gregor stood at the edge of the bed. Looked down at her. Barbara had crawled out. Sat there, sleepy, snuggled against Helene. Her hair tussled. Her cheeks rosy. Gregor asked again. He looked at Helene in anger. Stepped close to the bed. Helene pulled the children closer to herself, pressed them to her body. "This is the last time. Are you making breakfast now?" Gregor was leaning forward, over the bed. Helene unclasped her arms from the children's shoulders. Moved Katharina aside. Bent forward. She felt exposed in her nightgown. She said, "No," and waited for the first slap. Gregor stood hunched over her and the children. Unbudging, tense. His eyes narrow slits. "You asshole," he hissed. Helene looked at him. Gregor's face was red and swollen. He threw the rolls on the floor and stomped out of the room. The door's glass panels rattled as the apartment door slammed. Helene and the children sat quietly. Then they began to titter. Cautiously at first. Then loudly. They couldn't stop anymore. They lay in bed, flailing their arms about with laughter. They didn't calm down for ages. Again and again there'd be fits of laughter. Helene took the children to Café Landtmann. She ordered everything the children wanted. Cake. Juice. Chocolate. Then they drove to Schönbrunn and watched the butterflies in the butterfly house. They visited a newborn hippo. And a young elephant. They went to the Dommayer. Ate frankfurters and drank lemonade. They got home at 5 o'clock. Helene found a note from her mother-in-law. A Herr Heinrich had called. He'd phone again. And could Helene please switch over the phone before leaving the apartment. Helene wasn't interested in any of that. She unplugged the phone. She watched TV with the children. Put them to bed. Sat down in the living room. Turned up the TV. Loud. She no longer wanted to know anything. Or see anybody. Or speak to anybody. She wanted to be alone. The children hadn't mentioned it again. The incident in the morning. Helene forbade herself to say it. She'd start crying again. The words: Now you know this one too. Good. Now she knew what it was like when your husband wanted to beat you. Good. Many knew how it was. Many had to put up with it. She shouldn't get so upset. After all, he hadn't really beaten her. Her father had been less restrained in this regard. Though. He would never have called her an asshole.

On Sunday Helene had to have lunch with the children at Gregor's mother's. The children didn't want the Wiener Schnitzels. Gregor's mother was no longer a good cook. All of a sudden you could no longer eat what the old woman prepared. She didn't seem to notice how inedible her dishes were. The children sat in front of their Wiener Schnitzels, burnt on the outside and raw on the inside. The meat was too tough. It smelled unpleasant. In the end, Helene hid the meat in her napkin. The children snickered. The old woman ran back and forth between kitchen and dining room. Helene held the napkin with the meat under the table. She could feel how the napkin was getting soggier.

She wanted to smuggle the meat into her own apartment. And throw it out. For dessert, the grandmother had bought ice cream. So lunch ended peacefully. Helene took the children back to her apartment. She put the napkin in her kitchen and went back to the grandmother. But the old woman didn't want any help. Again Helene couldn't bring herself to say anything about the meal. The old woman was bustling about. And kept repeating how much trouble all this was for her. Too much. It was far too much for somebody her age. Helene would have liked to say in that case it might be better they didn't come over for meals anymore. And the old woman should finally admit to being old. And act accordingly. It suddenly sounded as if Helene and the children had forced themselves upon her for the lunch. Helene wondered if she should go back, get the meat, and hold it under the old woman's nose. But in the end she left and threw the meat out. She poured herself a whiskey and sat down in the living room. She needed her own place. It wasn't working out. The old woman was unbearable. Helene felt a rising anger. At the old woman's comment that she was doing everything anyway for Helene. And for the children. This comment. This accusation. Helene could have screamed. She sat in her living room. She had another whiskey. She understood how murder happens. It would only take a knife to fall into the hand, ready to strike. Done. Helene got herself a 3rd whiskey. Would it hit Gregor hard. If she . . . his mother. Gregor would say he'd known all along. Suspected. Foretold. And because he'd known all along, nothing surprised him. And nothing hurt him. Helene became light-headed. She had a 4th whiskey. Should she take the bottle to the sofa? She left the bottle where it was. Lay down on the sofa. She fantasized how it would be. Getting drunk. Going to Gregor's department. And telling everybody how Gregor really was. How he was cheating on her. With the departmental secretary. That he didn't give her any money. That she didn't know where he lived. That he beat her. Well, meant to beat her. And how he'd been talking about everybody in the department. Everybody should know what a swine Gregor was. Barbara woke Helene up. Grandma wanted to know what was going on with the phone. Helene got up. For a moment she was completely confused. Didn't even recognize her own living room. She plugged in the phone. All the grandmother had to do was switch over to her own phone. Helene couldn't see why she had to be constantly available. "Grandma says it's forbidden to unplug the phone," Barbara said. Reproachful. Imitating the grandmother. Helene yelled at the child. She wanted some peace. Peace! And to be by herself. Here. Just for once. And think. It might be news, but she had to do that sometimes too. The phone rang. Helene snatched it up. She said in a sharp voice, "Yes. Hello." "Helene. Is that you?" Henryk. He was about to leave. Where had she been? He could have phoned earlier, couldn't he, Helene said. Then they might have made some arrangement. In time. After all, he knew how things were for her. Helene's head hurt. Pounded. A migraine attack spread from her neck all over her head. Couldn't she at least come to the station, Henryk asked. His train would leave at 19:30. He wanted to see her. He loved her. Helene agreed. She wanted to finish the conversation. For now. And sit down. She was confused. Shaky. Miserable. She made coffee. Dissolved 3 Aspirin in the coffee. Poured lemon juice into the coffee. Drank the concoction. Trembling. Couldn't see clearly. The children were hiding in their room. Katharina had tried to snuggle up to her. Helene had pushed her away and said, "Go and thank your dad for all of this." She knew she shouldn't say things like that. Didn't mean to either. Wasn't allowed to. She said them with a deep satisfaction. The child

[79]

disappeared. Helene soaked little cottonballs in cold water and put them on her eyes. She called Katharina. Told her not to listen to her today. That today she was. Well. She didn't know. She was sorry. She had to leave for a little while. And then they'd do something together. Katharina should think of something. Helene lifted off the cottonballs. The child was gone. Helene went into the bathroom. Her eyes were swollen. Helene fought the redness with eye shadow and mascara. She couldn't remember having cried. But it looked as if she had. She remained for a long time in front of the mirror. Dawdled. She had to drive fast in order not to be far too late. She drove along the Gürtel. Drove fast. Sneaked into every gap. Passed whenever possible. Changed lanes. The driver of a dark Mercedes honked at her. His blonde wife sat in the front. 2 little children on the back seat. Helene gave him the finger. The two cars came to a stop next to each other in the lineup at a traffic light. The woman on the passenger seat glared at her with indignation. Then turned to the front. Indignant with Helene. The husband looked at Helene. Said something to his wife. Helene smiled at him. She licked her lips suggestively. The man shook his head and turned away. Helene laughed. She cut off the Mercedes. The man had to brake hard. Helene blew him a kiss.

Helene put on her sunglasses. In the rear-view mirror, her eyes had looked normal. But then in the car mirror you always look good. Henryk stood in the main concourse. Near the Venetian lion, as promised. Helene saw him first. She was coming from the parking lot, through the side entrance. He was watching the main entrance on the other side. He stood next to the brown leather travel bag Helene had seen in his closet. He had his hands in his pockets. His tweed jacket was bunched up. He stood there tall and slender, relaxed, confident. With the Burberry over his arm. Helene walked up close to him. Waited behind him. "Hello," she said in a low voice. Henryk spun around. He snatched her in his arms. The coat dropped to the ground and landed between them. Henryk took off her sunglasses. Stuck them in his breast pocket and kissed her. In the end they stood in a tight embrace on top of his coat. Helene out of breath. She hadn't meant to kiss him. Hadn't wanted to get close to him. She had only wanted to ask him why he hadn't phoned. Simply demand the reason. And then leave. She no longer wanted to wait. "I love you," Henryk whispered. Helene picked up his coat. Henryk took his bag. They went to the station snack bar. The air was full of smoke. The smell of knackwurst and meatloaf. Goulash. Tables without table-cloths. The waitress wiped a damp cloth across the table. They ordered. Helene asked for white wine with soda wa-ter. Henryk for a coffee, a Melange. "Don't rest your el-bows on the table," Helene said. "You'll get stuck." Henryk took her hand. Laid it on the table. His on top of hers. The waitress brought the drinks. Helene tried to pull her hand back. Henryk hung on to it. Squeezed the hand. "Helene. I didn't call because I must think about it all." Henryk's eyes were greenish brown. His tweed jacket was of the same color. Helene looked into his eyes. "Well?" she asked. "Why don't men do that first? Why do you go all the way? And then you think. Can't you do that first?" "Helene!" exclaimed Henryk. "Listen." He wasn't as free as it had appeared. And. He'd fallen in love. With her. And. He'd go back now. And sort everything out. And. He'd contact her after. Did she have any idea what it meant for him not to be able to reach her. These last 2 days. After all, it was because of her that he'd come to Vienna. Helene thought of the days she had been waiting for a call. The weeks. She said nothing. She pulled back her hand. He was under no obligation. He needed to be aware of that. As she was herself. And. There was no reason. "But Helene. I really want to. I promise. I promise you that," Henryk said. He knew exactly what needed to happen. And they would have to see each other again as soon as possible. Ideally, next weekend. Helene couldn't tell if she'd be free. She thought of Gregor. She could no longer let him have the children. He wouldn't take them anyway. She knew that. She could hear him say that now she'd finally destroyed it all. Whenever he no longer wanted something, he came up with this accusation. That she'd finally ruined it all. Perhaps she could leave the children with her sister. Helene asked Henryk if he wouldn't like to eat something before his trip. How long would the journey take. Henryk ordered goulash and another coffee. Helene watched him eat. She should write to him, he suggested. He'd call. And write as well. He simply had to hear from her. Regularly. Every day. Helene sipped at her wine. She would have loved to hold him back. He wouldn't call. And he wouldn't write. If he'd wanted to do any of this, he could have done so already. Why then did he say these things? Henryk had to go up to the platform. He had no seat reservation. He wanted to be up there as early as possible. And claim a seat. They went up the escalator. He'd seen her girlfriend yesterday evening. Last night, late. He'd asked her about Helene. But she hadn't known anything. And Püppi had said she believed Helene had gone away. Her husband. Helene's husband had told her that. Helene felt the blood rise in her face. And felt a stab in her heart. Why on earth did Henryk have to talk with Püppi. Why did Püppi have to talk with Gregor. What did Gregor have to do with all of this. Fury. Powerless rage rose in her. Fury. She hadn't been able to leave the children by themselves. After the scene yesterday morning. But Gregor had. He'd been perfectly comfortable strolling around town and gossiping with Püppi. Helene lowered her head. She was cold. She was carrying Henryk's coat. Henryk had put his arm around her shoulders. Her thigh was touching his. She could feel his muscles. While walking. They walked, pressed close together. Helene would have gone with him at the drop of a hat. To a bathroom. A seedy hotel. If he'd asked her. She watched their feet walking along. She longed for him, desperate and urgent. But she couldn't imagine anything beyond it. Her fantasies ended with his cock inside her. What afterwards. What then. And what generally. She could imagine none of it. Helene trudged next to Henryk. Felt her knees go soft. She shouldn't have had the wine. Henryk found a window seat. He put his bag on the rack, hung up his coat, took a paper from his coat pocket and put it on the seat next to his. Helene sat down across from him. She would have loved to stay there. Go with him. Away. Into another life. And to bed. With him. She kissed him farewell on the cheek. When she got into her car, she realized that Henryk still had her sunglasses. There would have been time enough to go back up to the platform. Helene drove off. She didn't ever want to see Henryk again.

On Monday Nadolny let Helene know that Herr Nestler was coming to Vienna on Wednesday. And to the office on Thursday. By then she should have a general overview of the whole affair. And she should take Herr Nestler for lunch. As he wasn't free himself. And she should look nice. Helene pored over Dr. Stadlmann's papers. It was all very medical. She could only read through the articles and papers but didn't know what to make of them. It sounded as if magnetic foil could save the world. Helene didn't know anybody she could ask for advice. The doctors she had known were all friends of Gregor's. And Gregor would have burst out laughing if he knew what she was up to. She sat in the office with the papers piled in front of her. She should phone Gregor. About next weekend. And about the money. And. Had Henryk arrived safely in Milan? She dialed his number. During the dialing she found out that she knew the number by heart. Milan was busy. She got the busy signal right after the country code. Helene began to make a list of all the diseases that magnetic foil was supposed to help cure. Dr. Stadlmann would have to complete the list himself. They would need photos showing how to apply the foil. And testimonials to the effects. Helene developed a concept. At the end she added to her draft: 1 apparition of the Blessed Virgin Mary daily at 11:30 with an early lunch. Club of the Cured to meet every Tuesday. Café Hawelka. Private Party. No Cripples. Helene didn't feel like reflecting any further on the kind of work she was pursuing. Choosers are losers, she thought. More than likely this business was bordering on the criminal. She should consult her father about the quackery law. The Herr President of the Senate would know all about it. He'd advise her not to get involved any further. And would wait for her to ask for money. He'd always thought her incompetent. Because he was so convinced of her incompetence, he obviously believed he'd already given her money. At least that's how he kept talking. Helene had never gotten a penny from him. She didn't even know if she would accept any. But he talked as if he'd been bankrolling her for the longest time. Helene thought that very clever. How could she ask for something he believed to have already given her. He was confirmed in his self-righteousness. He saved the money. And she got nothing. Which was the whole point anyway, Helene thought. She had stood there in her wedding gown. The whole wedding organized for the benefit of her parents and Gregor's mother. In the doorway, her father taking back her house key. "You know," he'd said. "You know when

you go through that door you can never come back." He'd
said. But. I know what it was all about, Herr President,
Helene told herself. I know what it's about. I should forget.
Should have forgotten. Forgotten everything. And should
be grateful. I should be grateful for having only been beaten
up. How easily does a girl get thrown on the bed during a
thrashing orgy. He is probably still proud of his self-con-
trol, Helene thought. She had no idea if her father had beaten
her sister. Her parents would have said that Helene just
needed to make more of an effort to fit in. That if this young
lady didn't make such a spectacle of herself, she'd be way
better off. Helene got herself a coffee. So much the better
then to have Visions of the Virgin. Helene asked Frau
Sprecher how the cat was doing. "Dying!" Frau Sprecher
said. Helene went back into her office. She tried the number
in Milan again. Still busy. The coffee tasted thin. Helene
wanted to escape. Office supplies. They urgently needed
office supplies. She went to Café Prückl. She ate a small
goulash and drank a beer. Was she becoming an alcoholic
now? The beer helped against that sick feeling in the throat.
Helene hid behind the Süddeutsche Zeitung. For a moment
she shut her eyes and simply kept breathing. Maybe she
really would feel better if she put on a bit of weight. She
had the goulash because people have to eat. And because
otherwise she couldn't have handled the beer. An alcoholic
all right. On her way back to the office she bought office
supplies. 3 extra large boxes of paper clips.

Herr Nestler flew in from Zürich. In preparation, Helene
had to buy little coffee spoons. The old ones were tacky,
Nadolny had said. Hadn't she noticed. That was, after all,
her job. Style. So Helene had bought coffee spoons at
Rasper's in the Graben. Herr Nadolny didn't much like
the bill. Did she have to choose the most expensive. "Beauty

has its price, Herr Nadolny," Helene had said and flashed him a radiant smile. Nestler arrived at the office on Thursday morning. He was medium tall. Very slim. Dressed very expensively. Three-piece suit. Perfectly matching tie. He wore fine Italian shoes. And designer socks with a bold pattern. He sat down, and his pants rode up. You could see black-haired, tanned calves. He was generally suntanned. Helene brought the coffee. The men put their heads together. Helene should come to the phone. Frau Sprecher stood in the doorway and gave her furtive signals. It was Henryk. It was impossible with the phone, he said. He'd never been able to get through to her. In the evening. Could she phone him in the evening. He loved her. He needed her. Helene was listening to him. She wasn't able to say much. Frau Sprecher was listening. Yes. She'd phone. She couldn't right now. And hung up. Again she had been waiting 4 days. She should break it off. She couldn't handle it. Waiting. She was incapable of merely waiting. Others didn't seem to mind. Püppi had never waited for anybody. Helene envied her for that. Helene felt hollowed out by all the waiting.

Helene had to take Herr Nestler to the Sacher for lunch. The man was staying there as well. Helene explained everything about the Tafelspitz and the battles over the authentic Sachertorte. Was a Sachertorte a proper Sachertorte if the jam was under the glaze or if it was in the middle of the cake? That was the question. In Austria, such questions were settled by the courts. There was no argument about the jam. Everybody agreed. It had to be Marillenmarmelade, apricot jam. Herr Nestler was German, not Swiss, as Helene had assumed. He lived in Switzerland because of the taxes, Herr Nestler explained. In Switzerland, money was still appreciated. He had made a fortune in Canada. Lumber and agriculture. And in South Africa. And now he was financing projects that had some promise. Such as the magnetic foil. What did Helene think about Herr Dr. Stadlmann. Dr. Stadlmann, as it happened, was totally taken by her. Stadlmann considered her, Frau Gebhardt, a good person. Was that right? He too was thinking that she. That Helene. Would she mind if he called her Helene? He'd picked that up in the States. Well then. He thought so too. It would work well with her. Herr Nadolny was right. She was good for this job. So he was going to rely on her. Dr. Stadlmann was, of course, an ingenious scholar. But geniuses. She surely knew what that meant. The practical aspects weren't their forte, the business side, all the money stuff. Tended to be overlooked by such people. So this was to be her role. Dr. Stadlmann had to be looked after. And he, Herr Nestler, wanted to be kept informed. At all times. Also about how Dr. Stadlmann was feeling. All of it was important. For success. Did she know Stadlmann's wife? Helene said no. She wasn't aware of any wife. Yes. Yes. Nestler nodded. A wife and 2 children. But this woman. She had little sympathy for the project. She was, so to speak, putting the brakes on the man. A scholar simply needs somebody who believes in him. Who supports him. Pushes him. In a manner of speaking. And magnetic foil was an important matter, wasn't it. Lucrative too. But then you can't go for a project if it isn't. It's the law of the market. If there is no prospect of a profit, you can't put your money into it. After all, he was a business man. While Nestler was eating, he looked around the marble room of the Sacher. Helene felt stupid. The man was lecturing her. She had nothing to say. Good. She was his employee. But. While he gave her instructions to spy on Dr. Stadlmann and spur him on, his eyes devoured a tarted-up blonde. She was sitting in a corner with an older man. Helene rejected Nestler's offer of dessert. Nestler insisted on cognac. "To our cooperation," he said.

In the evening Helene phoned Milan. A woman's voice said "Pronto." Helene hung up. Dialed once more. Spoke each digit aloud. Again she heard the woman say "Pronto." And again Helene hung up. When the children were asleep, Helene left. She drove to Laxenburg. She went for a long walk through the park. It was about midnight. It was all empty. No cars. The moon a reclining crescent pointing southwest. It was muggy. No stars were visible. A few bands of clouds reflected in pale orange-red the lights of Vienna. The path began immediately behind the castle. The trees enclosed it completely. Helene stepped into a black tunnel. She stopped briefly. Her eyes adapted to the dark. But she could only guess where the path went under the trees. She wore sneakers. Which made no sound when she walked. She moved through the darkness in total silence. Buildings and monuments were but pale shadows. The lake a dark, glittering surface. The trees creaking and groaning. A wind in the leaves. The even hum of the autobahn. Every so often a little owl. Helene sat down on the bridge parapet, right next to one of those gigantic helmets that might have fallen into the courtyard of Otranto. She probably would have to give notice, Helene thought. She dangled her legs. The darkness was behind her back. She hadn't worked long enough. She wouldn't get any unemployment money. And there were no other jobs. She certainly had tried. This one had been pure luck. She had to take Gregor to court, sue him for support. But Gregor had threatened to destroy her if she tried anything like that. She wouldn't get to keep the children, he had threatened. She would have to get through it. She didn't know how. And. Go to her father. Admit that it had been wrong to get married. Although, really, her father had insisted on the marriage. And yes. It had been wrong to get married to this man. To get married so young. And yes. People had advised her against him. From the beginning they had told her how Gregor's affairs had been known all over town. And yes. It had been wrong to have children so young. Helene swung her legs up on the parapet. She stood on the edge. Propped against the knight's helmet. She looked down at the pond and the Gothic castle. Then she jumped onto the path. She couldn't give notice. It hadn't been wrong. It hadn't been not right. It had been right. These children were right. And she had done the right thing. Helene walked beside a broad meadow. She sat down under a tree. Above the meadow, it was a tiny bit lighter. Under the trees, there was darkness. Helene stayed there. Nobody in the world knew where she was right now.

Henryk didn't call. Helene wouldn't have had anybody to look after the children anyway. The grandmother had gone away on a trip with the church. She hadn't heard from Gregor. She took the children to Kreuzenstein castle. They could see the castle from the autobahn. During the whole long stretch between Korneuburg and Stockerau the castle lay in front of them. The children were jumping up and down on their seats with anticipation. They told her everything they knew about knights. Out of Mickey Mouse and Asterix. Out of children's books. And from legends. They ran the last steps to the entrance of the castle. Branches in their fresh green danced in the warm April breeze. White blossoms on shrubbery. Primroses and violets in the grass. The children stood on the drawbridge. Barbara immediately wanted to climb onto the parapet. Helene had to take her by the hand. In the outer courtyard other parents were waiting with their children. A guided tour was about to begin. You couldn't go into the castle without the tour.

Helene paid. The guide. An elderly man. Overweight. Wearing knickerbockers and a red vest over a checkered red and white shirt. He looked at the children in a fatherly way. Said he was giving the tour for the children only. Only for the children. The parents could follow along behind. Now for once the children were the center of attention. All the children clung to their parents. The man led them into the inner courtyard. He explained the basic history. How the individual parts had been bought up by a collector in the last century. And had been pieced together to construct this impressive complex. Then he took the children to a wooden rack in the yard. Here was something that would really interest them, the man said. He told Barbara to lie on the rack. Then he explained to the other children how the witches had been tied to it. And how with the wheel over there. On the side. How with the wheel they'd been almost torn apart. The witches would then readily admit everything. The boys were interested in the mechanics. How the ropes were attached to the wheel. Barbara stood up. "There are no witches," she said and brushed the dust off her jeans. "Oh," the guide said. "What makes you so smart? Such a little girl." Barbara looked at him. "And what do you know? Did you learn that at university?" she asked him. "I live here," the man advised her and led the group across the yard. Mentioned dates. When which part of the castle was bought where. Then they went into the armory. A narrow corridor ran through the gallery which was long and wide. On the right and left side were spears and lances. The shining pikes were stuck on burgundy colored shafts. A dark red forest of murder tools lined their path. The guide explained how to use each kind of weapon. Then they got to the instruments of torture. To the choke collars and all the other devices intended to teach women silence. At this point the guide addressed himself mostly to the husbands. Gave them rather a lot of advice on how they could have dealt with the missus. In the past. Hearty agreeable laughter followed his explanations. Helene could barely swallow. In her belly, behind the navel, cramps with each instrument. The instruments were real and had been used. The same with the weapons. As the guide kept assuring them. "And now this, ladies and gentlemen. This is the last hangman's hood," he boomed. "Virgins who dare to touch the cloth will be married within a year. With child." Laughter. Helene reached for the thing. It was made of felt. Dusty. Katharina pressed against her. Helene picked her up and carried her for a while. Katharina snuggled up to her. Clung to her. Barbara came up to them. It was so boring. Helene agreed. A few children had started to feign little duels. In order to attract the guide's attention. The rest had taken refuge with their parents. In the kitchen things became more tolerable. How many chickens would be fried. How Cinderella would probably have had to work in such a kitchen. The children were edgy. All the children were whining. Medieval bathrooms. Boudoirs. Four-poster beds. Libraries. Furniture. They didn't want to see any more. Wanted to eat. Helene stopped for a moment. She wanted to have a closer look at a cupboard. The group had moved on. Helene lost her way. Katharina and Barbara held each other by the hand. Katharina was sucking her thumb. Barbara asked over and over when they would have something to eat. When they could go to a restaurant. She had to use the bathroom. Urgently. Helene took the wrong way. They reached the exit. The gate was locked. The others arrived 10 minutes later. She'd missed the guns, the guide said. He stood in the archway and held out his hand. To avoid him Helene had to turn to the right. She didn't give him a tip. The man looked at her, full of scorn.

Helene went to the restaurant right next to the castle. Through the large window one could look across the Tullner Feld. Barbara wanted a Wiener Schnitzel. What was a fried chicken, Katharina wanted to know. It's breaded like schnitzel and fried in oil. Katharina looked up from the menu she had gradually deciphered. "Do they kill chickens here," she asked. The question could be heard throughout the restaurant. Helene ordered soup for Katharina. And Kaiserschmarren pancake. Everybody looked at them. Smiling. Or otherwise. The children were talking very loudly. What it had been like for the witches. If they had really been torn apart in the middle. Helene regretted having gone on this trip. On their way back to Vienna she was still busy giving explanations. At the same time she was thinking to herself about what had really happened. When a woman was put into the pillory. What had happened during the night. To what extent were others permitted transgressions as part of her punishment? And how would little girls be taught what to expect? At home she told the children she thought she'd caught a cold in the freezing castle. She lay down. No interruptions, please. Helene crawled into bed. She was cold. The castle had stored all the winter's cold. Helene put on woolen socks. Weight pressed on her. Bore down on her. Heavy. Her chest would no longer expand or contract. Helene rolled onto her side. Rolled herself into her blankets. Henryk hadn't even canceled.

Monday night Püppi called. It was half past 11. Helene had gone to bed. Was dozing. Püppi asked if maybe she'd like to join them. They were all going to Café Old Vienna. Püppi sounded like her old self. When she still lived in the Veltlinergasse and hoped to bring up Sophie and to paint. Before the philosophy professor from Graz had shown up. Helene got up. Dressed. Made herself up. Got into her car

[92]

and drove into town. The downtown traffic was brisk. She found a parking spot in the Bäckerstrasse. By the Jesuit church. For a moment she stayed in the car. People wandered along the streets, strolling. Mostly in couples, with their arms around each other. The night was mild. People were sitting outside in front of the restaurants. A police car drove past her at a crawl. Helene got out. She didn't know why she was there. And even less, why she was going to the Old Vienna. Her fears were well founded. Püppi wasn't there. Helene walked all the way to the back of the restaurant. Should she check the bathroom? Cigarette smoke was thick. Made it hard to see. Helene squinted. She didn't see a familiar face. She went back to the entrance. Sized up the people at the tables and at the bar. Groups of people were crowding around each other in tight clusters. People looked at Helene. Helene felt herself stared at. Sized up. She wanted to leave. Simply turn around and go home. Without seeing anybody. And without being seen by anybody. At this moment a table was cleared. To the left of the entrance, at the window. Helene asked if the table was available. A young woman nodded. Smiled. Helene sat down. She ordered a hot chocolate and got herself a paper. Sat in the corner, read, sipped at her hot chocolate. The loud chattering and laughing. The cigarette smoke, a pleasant backdrop. As if she belonged. Helene felt content. Suddenly she liked everybody around her. When Püppi arrived forty-five minutes later, Helene felt interrupted. Not only that, Püppi was bringing people with her. 3 men and 1 woman. Helene knew the woman by sight. She was a teacher and told everybody how her husband was beating her. Helene had once seen her in the Wollzeile, crawling on all fours. At the end of a night. The woman was a drunk. That one, Püppi whispered to Helene, the one with the beard. He was the celebrity hairdresser with the movie career. Helene remembered having read about somebody like him. In Adabei's gossip column in the Kronen-Zeitung. They placed their orders. And were silent. Smoked. Said nothing. Helene sat there. She was the only sober person at the table. The silence was awkward. Helene would have rather read the paper. She made an effort and asked where everybody had been. Before. Püppi answered. They'd all run into each other at the Kalb. And. Yes. By the way. That Karl had asked about her. But had stayed at the Kalb. Helene might want to go there, likely she'd still find him there. Then Püppi fell back into silence. Sat there. Sipping at her white wine, sucking at her cigarette. Everybody stared into space. Helene asked Püppi how she was doing. What was going on. With the wedding. Püppi shrugged. Suddenly the hairdresser-movie director pulled himself up. He looked at Helene. Said in broad Viennese, "Listen. Some guy should take you. Give you a good hard night in the gutter. A taste of reality." He gave Helene a friendly smile. "Right? Daddy's always given you everything." Püppi laughed. The teacher had a coughing fit. The two other guys got up and went to the bar. The hairdresser winked at Helene. "Well. What do you say?" Püppi laughed. Then she turned to Helene. What was happening with the Swede. She had thought. But obviously not. Nothing doing. Helene was sure to miss the boat. If she continued to be such a coward and run away from men. She had seen him yesterday, as a matter of fact. Or was it Saturday? She'd run into him on one of those days. Helene felt petrified. She put her hands carefully on her thighs. Helene was suddenly afraid she mightn't be able to leave the restaurant. She took a deep breath. She had to go, she said. She put 50 schillings on the table for the hot chocolate. She tried to stand up. Her thighs lay like wooden blocks in her chair. Helene took deep breaths. She couldn't remember a single mantra from the Relaxation Through Self-Hypnosis pro-

gram. With a jolt she pulled herself up against the edge of
the little marble table. Standing was better. She tottered away
from the table. As if her thighs were terribly sore. She left.
She thought people would think her completely drunk. She
propped herself up in the door frame. It was better outside.
She wandered down the street, toward the Jesuitenplatz. She
was afraid Karl might come out of the Kalb. She didn't want
to see him. Him of all people. She heard steps behind her.
Püppi came running. What was going on. "You haven't seen
him. It must have been last weekend." Püppi looked at
Helene. "If it makes you feel any better. Then I haven't
seen him," Püppi said. Turned around and walked back.

Helene got a letter from the bank. She left it lying around.
Didn't open it. But didn't throw it out either. She put it on
top of the TV. She could imagine what the bank had to tell
her. She didn't want to know how bad it was. Imagining
herself explaining her situation to the bank clerk made her
feel hot with shame. Should she look at the man with a sad
face and tell him that he needed to know. Her husband was
away. Gone. Had left her. She was supporting herself and
the children. With a 20 hour job at a dubious PR agency.
And the clerk would immediately show sympathy for her.
For this sad forlorn being. How she was sitting there, beautiful and wounded. He'd immediately increase her line of
credit. Helene had to talk to Gregor. She'd phone him from
the office. From there she wouldn't sound quite as pathetic.
Johannes Aichenheim picked up Gregor's phone. Helene
hung up. He would chat with her for a long time. But Gregor
wouldn't be available. Unfortunately. He'd be in a meeting,
a practice, a lecture, a seminar. Not available, anyway. In
the departmental office, Frau Gärtner would answer the
phone. Ilse Gärtner. Helene thought it particularly irritat-
ing. Found it scandalous. That she had to imagine Gregor

rolling around in bed with a woman called Ilse. Helene wondered. Frau Sprecher was gone. Some errand. Nadolny wasn't in. She plucked up courage. The Gärtner woman answered. Helene gave her name. As clearly as possible. Could she talk to Professor Freier. He was unavailable was the reply. In that case, could she speak to her husband. She had to wait. Then Gregor came to the phone. Helene had known that Freier wouldn't be in the department. It was Wednesday. And Professor Arnim Freier always went bike-riding on Wednesdays. Creativity pedaling, he called it. All the academics in the States did it. Every so often Freier would still drop by Helene's in the Lannerstrasse, visit her, sit down with her. Without prior notice. Would want to take her to the sauna. Nobody else in the department was still talking to her. They would greet her quickly and carry on. At the most, they would ask briefly why they weren't seeing her anymore at departmental parties. Nobody would wait for an answer. Gregor continued to work in the department. And so did the Gärtner woman. And the woman knew everything about everybody. The next tenured job was supposed to be for Gregor. But so far, his application for tenure hadn't gone through. The decision was partly up to Freier. Helene got her husband on the phone because the Gärtner woman knew about Freier's weak spot for Helene. She wanted to keep it short, Helene said to Gregor. But. The financial questions had to be sorted out. First of all, she wanted to have the child allowance transferred. Because Gregor was collecting the money and not passing it on. That surely wasn't the intention. Gregor was listening. Helene got on a roll. Did Gregor know how deeply in debt he was? In debt with her and the children. Gregor interrupted Helene. Yes. Yes. She'd hear from his lawyer. Helene hung up. She stared at the desk in front of her. Her heart raced, the rage inside was welling up again. This furious powerlessness. Why didn't Gregor die? In a car crash. Then he'd be gone too. Wouldn't live anymore. Most importantly, wouldn't live happily. Surrounded by friends. With a mistress. And nobody could say it always takes 2 when it goes sour. It would be tragic, really tragic. And she could cry in public. But. Things hadn't changed. Nothing had changed, absolutely nothing. Often Helene hadn't been able to go swimming for weeks. Or participate in Phys Ed classes. Because of the bruises on her arms and thighs. When her father. Nobody was allowed to know about it. She always got an extra beating for that. She was only allowed to cry in secret. And now. Now everything was out of the question. Not only the pool. Or Phys Ed class. Now it was life itself. The whole of life. Helene sat quietly for a long time. Stared into space. Much later, Helene got herself a coffee. "Well. How's it going?" Frau Sprecher asked. Helene hadn't noticed her come back. No. No. Helene shook her head. It was nothing. Just her period. She'd know. Frau Sprecher recalled days of complete paralysis, cramps and migraine attacks. Helene went into the kitchen. Her legs seemed far away. Her blood pressure. She hurried to get back behind her desk. The hot coffee burnt the roof of her mouth. Dr. Stadlmann phoned. Right away he asked what was going on with her. Her voice sounded strange. Helene said she thought she was getting a cold. That must be it. Dr. Stadlmann didn't want to believe that. She was a strong healthy person, wasn't she. What would she want to get a cold for? He arranged an appointment with her. They had to discuss the brochure. He'd be glad if she could come to his place again. It'd be less trouble for him. Helene asked if he couldn't make it any earlier. One of Nestler's instructions had been to get useful information printed as soon as possible. Dr. Stadlmann wouldn't budge. He did not have any time before then.

Helene drove from the office to the Weinviertel. The conversation with Gregor had left behind a restlessness. Fear. Helene could not have stayed at her desk for one more second. She should have driven home. Tidied up the kitchen. Done some ironing. The thought of it caused the nervousness to pulse into her very fingertips. A dry nausea was scratching in her throat. The children were with a friend. They didn't need to be picked up until 7 o'clock. Helene followed the Danube canal and took the autobahn to Stockerau. Then on toward Prague. In Schönborn she left the highway. Took the underpass to get onto a dirt road. Left her car behind. Climbed up a steep slope and sat down at the edge of the forest. It was better under the sky. She could breathe more easily. The sky was light blue with little white round clouds. The fruit trees along the road black and surrounded by a pink veil of blossoms. The forest around Schönborn castle light green. All shades of green. The castle roof almost hidden. The poplars along the dirt road like feathers. Rising up translucent. The Tempietto visible. Not yet hidden by the rich summer green of the bushes. Helene stared at the building. The little temple stood there. As if for all eternity. The hills undulating like waves. At some point, they'd been the bottom of a sea. And then had disappeared under ice. And been abraded. Helene remembered the trip to Prague, with Gregor. She had driven through this landscape for the first time. The road straight uphill, downhill, between blooming cherry trees. They weren't yet married. How happy she'd been. How beside herself with happiness. How could such happiness have ended. And Gregor had been just as happy. She knew that. When at first he started not coming home anymore, she had hoped it would pass. Hoped he would remember. Remember this happiness. And would want it again. He couldn't have it with another woman, this happiness. She had thought. Helene hid her head in her arms. What had she really thought. That she'd be put to the test? Like good old Mrs. Psyche? And when she'd come through all her ordeals, he'd be there? Smiling at her? And embracing her? And all would be well? Forgotten. Perhaps. Helene looked at the countryside. She knew she had transferred all her excessive Catholic passions into this love. She had made Gregor her God, her father. And as the father had let her down, so Gregor had to let her down. More than likely there was some theory or other according to which she, as the victim, had willed the situation into being. Now Helene felt released from her illusions. Without gaining any insight. She laughed out loud. She knew it all. Everybody knew it. It didn't change the pain. Nor her feelings. And not the sense of having reached her limit. All she ever reached were limits. This one seemed to have brought about all the others. And. How could she stand it? Or endure it? Helene felt the chill from the earth creep into her back. She had to get home. Pick up the children. She hadn't gone shopping. There was no food in the house. She should have stopped somewhere along the way. At least to buy milk. Helene remained sitting. She wrapped her arms around her knees. Her chin propped on her knees. She sat like that for more than an hour. At half past 6 she finally got up. She could hardly move. She wobbled down the hill. Her back ached. Her arms and legs were cold and stiff. Must be like this when you're 80, she thought. She wouldn't be able to pick up the children in time. What would the friend say. She drove as fast as her car would let her. She was hoping for a speeding ticket. To be stopped by police, an officer on duty. "Herr Inspektor. I'm speeding because of my children. You know how it is. They always need to be picked up somewhere." And he would talk to her. Ask for her license and ownership papers, for her first aid kit, and the traffic warning reflector. He would have to talk to her. And the speeding ticket. Wouldn't that confirm it. On such and such a day, she'd been driving too fast at such and such a time at such and such a place. She'd been there. Had existed. Helene was 20 minutes late. Her children didn't want to leave yet. Nobody had noticed she was late. But the children were hungry. She took them to the Heuriger in the Agnesgasse, to Haslinger's. The landlady at the Heuriger was pleased. As always, was astonished how much the children had grown. She briefly sat down with them. Asked about the husband. "Dad called Mom an asshole," Barbara said. Helene sighed. The landlady looked concerned. And left. Other people weren't interested in such things, Helene tried to explain to Barbara. She would have liked to ask if Barbara had already told everybody. But she didn't. What could she have said anyway. Barbara was right, after all.

Henryk phoned on Thursday. At the office. Helene was by herself. Herr Nadolny was away on business, Frau Sprecher was out buying her lunch. Helene picked up the phone. Henryk asked for Frau Gebhardt. Helene recognized his voice right away. It was her, she said. Didn't he recognize her? Henryk said he had to see her. It was vital. It was all very difficult, and Helene had to understand. He had to talk to her. Could she come to Bozen. There they could talk it all over in peace and quiet. On Saturday. At 7 in the evening. He didn't have a car. He'd arrive by train and wait for her at the station. And it was really important. Helene didn't know what to say. She hesitated. She didn't have anybody for the children. And should she always jump when he wanted her to? She heard Frau Sprecher put her key in the door. Yes. She'd be there, she said quickly. Henryk hung up. Helene sat with the receiver in her hand. Frau Sprecher gave Helene the apple she had asked for. Frau Sprecher asked

Helene if she had fallen in love with the receiver. Because she was looking at it with such yearning. Helene quickly put it down. She paid for the apple. Frau Sprecher was chatting away. How nice the weather was. The people she had seen at the Greissler. How the woman in the store looked ill again. That she probably had a terrible disease. The way she looked. When she would go to see her mother next weekend in the old folks' home. How exhausting the trip to Lainz always was. Helene stared at the apple. Didn't know what to do. It was obvious what the reasonable path to choose was. Not go there! Helene imagined Saturday night. How he'd wait in front of the station. She could phone Milan. She wouldn't come. Didn't feel like it. Could Henryk please be given the message. Yes? Thank you. Helene dialed the number in Milan. She knew it by heart. The woman answered, "Pronto." Helene hung up. She phoned her sister. Could she sleep at Helene's place on Saturday night? She had to go away. Yes. It had to be. Yes. One night only. She wouldn't have to do anything. Just be there. No. She couldn't ask Gregor. They weren't talking. No! Not at all anymore. She'd organize everything. And prepare a meal in advance. The children would be happy. She'd have to leave at noon. Yes. That'd be nice. Thanks so much. Helene hung up. On her way home Helene cashed in Eurochecks in different bank branches. She couldn't go to the Credit Union anymore. The letter was lying on the TV. She had to put it into a drawer before her sister came. Helene had 7 checks left. So far, her name was not on the list the bank clerks checked before paying her 2500 schillings per check.

At half past 6 Helene reached the first autobahn exit for Bozen. She took it. She hadn't looked up how to get to Bozen. Or where the station was. She didn't even know how big Bozen was. She hadn't paid attention in Geography class. And once she was driving, she hadn't opened the road atlas again. She hoped the way to the station would be well signed. Although that seemed pointless. Why would anybody put up signs to the station for people who drive cars? Helene shook her head at the thought. Paranoia, she thought. The exit road became a narrow road. Curved in a wide arch, close to the rock. Followed the bend of the river, went across a bridge, carried on through vineyards and orchards. Pink blooming trees, yellow and white blooming bushes. The fresh green of spring. Still some light around the branches. The sun high above the mountain peaks. Then narrow lanes. There were signs to the station. In German as well as Italian. At 10 to 7 Helene pulled into the circle in front of the station. A huge circular space. Circle and station unmistakably from the days of the Austro-Hungarian Empire. The station was even the same yellow as Schönbrunn castle. Henryk was waiting on the steps to the station. With his bag at his feet he stood there. Watched the cars circling the roundabout. Helene drove up to the steps. Henryk smiled and picked up his bag. He walked toward her. Came slowly down the stairs. As if she picked him up there every day. As if it were a matter of course. Helene suddenly felt miserable. He might not have been there. And. Shouldn't she rather quickly put her foot on the gas. And be gone. Henryk pushed his bag onto the back seat. Then he sat next to her. He looked straight ahead. Serious. "You're not on time! You're too early!" Then he swept her in his arms. Laughed. Kissed her. Helene's foot slipped off the clutch. The motor died. The car jerked forward. Henryk covered Helene's face with urgent kisses. Bit her ears. Did she know how he'd been waiting. And if she hadn't come. He'd feared she mightn't come. And now get going. Fast. Fast. Helene started the car. He told her where to go. They went back the same way Helene had come. They took a left turn into the vineyards and drove uphill. Steep. Helene couldn't help looking to her right. Was Henryk really there. They looked at each other. Henryk leaned over to her. Kissed her neck. Helene talked the whole time. About her trip. How the weather had been. How long she'd waited at the border. What the Lira was worth. What they were going to do. She felt like laughing. A clear laughter. Happiness tightened her throat.

They came to a mountain plateau. Vineyards covered the gently sloping plains. Cliffs rose steeply behind. Toward the valley were houses. And a small hotel. An old villa, converted. Henryk seemed to know where he wanted to go. He told Helene to make a turn to get to the hotel. She wanted to ask how he knew the hotel. She didn't ask. She didn't want to hear any of Henryk's stories. The hotel had just opened for its first weekend after the winter. The lounge smelled damp and musty. They could have a room. Did they wish to have dinner in the hotel. Henryk looked at Helene. Helene nodded. She didn't want to drive that road again, at least not in the dark. She wanted to stay in. They went up to their room. It had a balcony. Which was above a sun deck, facing south. Right on the other side of the deck, the mountain dropped vertically. Caught itself on small ledges and gentler slopes. All the way down to Bozen. From the balcony one could see far into the distance. The evening sun made the haze over the valley glow rosy. Henryk joined Helene on the balcony. Embraced her. Pulled her into the room.

Dinner was served in the lounge. From there, French doors led out to the deck. One could see the lights gleaming in the valley. Only 3 other tables were taken. The menu was tomato soup, trout, and a cinnamon parfait. Or cheese. An older couple asked for chilled red wine. The hotel owner was called. They didn't have chilled red wine. You don't do that. Chill red wine. "Oh yes, you do," the man said. "We've learned that from two sisters on Lake Garda. They told us always to drink red wine nicely chilled." The wife nodded. The hotel owner was unable to suppress a smile. Yes. If the lady and gentleman wished it that way. She was looking at the other guests. That she had to comply with such a request. Then she shrugged. Disdainfully. Had a cooler brought with ice and put the bottle of red wine into it. The couple turned to their food. Satisfied. Everybody else in the room exchanged glances. Helene had meant to ask Henryk to explain the woman's voice in Milan. The scene with the red wine made her sit in silence. Then she asked Henryk what his plans were. He talked about a concert in Stresa. And another one planned for Milan. Perhaps. His problem simply was that he didn't own a hammer piano. He depended on the availability of such an instrument. He needed to have his own. Which he could then take with him. The meal was soon over. Helene wanted to go for a walk. The night was cool. They walked along the road. There was no alternative. They kept having to make way for cars. Their conversation was interrupted each time. They had to walk behind each other. They returned to the hotel. Helene suddenly didn't know what they should do. It was still early. Too early to sleep. She hadn't brought a book. There was no TV in their room. She didn't know what to talk about with Henryk. In their room, Helene sat down in the only comfortable armchair. Henryk sat on the bed. He looked at her. What's wrong, he asked. Helene didn't answer. She felt like crying, or screaming. Felt lost. Wondered what she was doing there. Hated Henryk. How he sat there and said she probably had overexerted herself. Should go to bed and sleep. Helene wanted to go to bed with him. But he didn't seem to be in the mood. Helene began to walk up and down. He had to understand she was nervous, she said. After all, it was all rather complicated. This whole thing with him too. Or did he not think it slightly odd that a woman would answer his phone. And she didn't know, really, why she had driven such a distance. It was all too much. Henryk sat there, mute. Watched her. Helene walked up and down. Talked herself into a crying fit. Suppressed the crying fit. Tried to insult Henryk. To make him angry. So that he would say something. But Henryk only said that he hadn't promised her anything, had he. He couldn't understand her. They were dealing with love, not bookkeeping. Weren't they? Helene went out on the balcony. She no longer understood anything. Not herself. Not him. Not what she had just said. The moon hung, almost full, in the sky. In the valley, the lights of the towns glittered. A cool wind rustled down the hill. Henryk came onto the balcony. Helene stood still. Behind her, Henryk said she should lie down. "No!" Helene called. Should he get himself another room. Helene froze. "No," she whispered. Was immediately angry with herself, dashed into the room and threw herself on the bed. She didn't cry. The feeling of having done it all wrong and of still doing it all wrong kept her silent. Henryk went to bed. He kissed her cheek. He hoped she'd wake up feeling more cheerful, he said. He left her alone. And fell asleep. Helene lay on the bed, fully clothed. She listened to his breathing. She would have resisted had he touched her. More than anything she wished to feel him on top of her. Some time later she got ready for bed. She stood on the balcony in her long, thin nightgown. She was hoping he'd wake up. And look for her. Because he desired her. She would give in, then. And all would be well. Henryk was sleeping, calm. Helene was lying awake. She wondered how the children were doing.

She had to put her life in order. Content herself. Be satisfied. Helene woke up because Henryk's hand lay on her belly. In the warmth of the bed Helene sank into his caress. She couldn't distinguish between sleeping and waking. Knew nothing. Knew it would continue once more. Then. But only later. She let herself be moved around by him. Rolled over. Did nothing. When it was over, she lay there as if this was her first moment of life. Henryk drew himself up. Laughed softly. Helene asked what he was laughing about. He didn't answer. Helene sat up. The sheet and covers were soaked with blood. Huge bright-red stains with darker edges, shining with moisture. Helene let herself fall back. She felt sick. Only now did she feel the dampness. And so much blood. And not at the right time. Too early. Henryk pushed Helene out of the bed. He arranged the sheets into a scarlet rosette.

Helene was to give Henryk a lift to Kufstein. From there, he wanted to take the train to Munich. Helene didn't have breakfast in the hotel. She was embarrassed about the blood-stained bed. Henryk laughed at her. And could she pay. He didn't have enough money on him. He'd explain in the car. Then they would need to talk anyway. Helene paid. While she was waiting for the bill, she calculated in her head. Did she have enough money? And what to do if it wasn't enough. And. Then it was all gone. But. Wasn't it a sign of trust, somehow? Outside it was a glorious Sunday morning. A warm breeze was blowing through the open door into the small foyer. The hotel owner had finished writing the bill. Helene put her money down. Was it okay this way. She hadn't exchanged any. Could she pay in schillings? The woman took the money. Did they really not want to have breakfast in the hotel, the woman asked. Again Helene felt herself blush. She assured the woman it was absolutely necessary that they leave right away. An appointment. Henryk turned aside. He was laughing. Helene hurried to get out of the hotel. Henryk carried their luggage to the car. Stopped. Admired the view. Wanted to go for a walk. At least have a coffee. Helene wanted to leave. Get away as fast as possible. She sat in the car. Henryk still fussed with the trunk. Helene saw the hotel owner come out of the door. She started the engine, and Henryk got in. Helene drove off. In the rearview mirror she saw the woman stand in the doorway. Gazing after them. Henryk shook his head and laughed. Helene took the curves too fast. The tires squealed. "Yes," Helene shouted on top of the squealing. "Yes. I know. They have that sort of thing happen every day. But that doesn't help me. And you are right. It somehow has to do with my mother. She is just as fat as the woman in the hotel. And I don't like her. I hate my mother. But that doesn't help. It doesn't help to know that. I should have taken off the sheets. I shouldn't have let you stop me. And now I'd like a coffee."

They had a cappuccino in a bar in a village. They didn't take the autobahn. Because it'd be nicer. Helene wanted to save the toll. They had the whole day. Stopped at every little church along the way. And went inside. They drove into the Grödner Valley. Ate spinach dumplings with parmesan and melted butter in St. Magdalen. One portion. They saw the 3 Jungfrauen peaks. Climbed slowly up to the Brenner pass. Driving through Brixen, Helene thought of Alexander. Helene would have liked to tell him how good things were for her. How happy she was. In Brixen she kept an eye open for a phone box. She wanted to call the children. But she didn't see one. And she didn't want to look for one. Before entering Austria, they had their last Italian coffee. In Austria, too, Helene took the old road across the pass. She wasn't sure if she'd have enough money for gas and toll. Helene and Henryk chatted the whole time. Without a break. Their conversation jumped from topic to topic. Henryk told her of his grandparents in England with whom he'd grown up. Helene told of her grandmother whom she'd visited often. They rolled through the countryside, a late spring day. A breeze cooled the sun's heat in the car. Helene felt as if by driving she took possession of the world. For the moment, the world was where she was. And he. They drove down the road from Brenner pass. The Europa Bridge high above them. Henryk didn't understand people who commit suicide. Helene was silent. "Misery is rather kitschy. Don't you think?" she asked later. Henryk didn't answer. Near Innsbruck Helene took the autobahn. They hardly spoke until Kufstein.

In Kufstein the station was easy to find. Helene parked in front of the entrance. Henryk would now get out of the car. And then be gone. Everything became blurry in front of Helene's eyes. She didn't have to cry. She wouldn't have been able to cry. The blur began in her head, far behind her eyes. She should come with him, Henryk said and got out. For a short moment, moving seemed impossible to Helene. With angular movements and dry burning eyes she went after Henryk. His train for Munich would leave in 45 minutes. Henryk went to the station snack bar. Inside it was smoky and smelled of onions and rancid oil. Helene walked out again. Sat down at one of the green garden tables in front of the snack bar. It was cool. Helene felt chilly. The sun was still high. Henryk ordered a beer. Helene too. She couldn't think of anything else. She'd had enough coffee. The waitress brought 2 big beers. Helene had a large sip. It tasted ghastly. She leaned her head against the wall behind. Looked at the mountainside opposite. Among the firs, the larch trees shone in a lighter green. Helene began to hum. "If I were a little bird." She was humming quietly to herself. Henryk had drunk half his beer and leaned over to her. Did she love him. Helene began to count the larch trees on the mountainside across from her. This was very important for him. He said. He had to put his life in order, and then he'd come to her. Did she want that. Really. Helene had found the 21st larch. She fixed her eyes on the tree, narrowed her eyes. Yes. She loved him too. She believed. But then. She no longer understood things. And now they had to separate again. And that's how it'd always be. Probably. Henryk took Helene's hand and propped his elbows on the table. Helene could no longer see the 21st larch. Would she wait for him. Helene said defiantly that at any rate she'd have to be where she always was, wouldn't she. And that's where she could be found. Helene got up. She looked down at him, filled with unbridled hatred. She took her purse and turned away. Henryk stood up. Embraced her. He wasn't as reliable as he'd like to be, but he loved her. She had to believe it. He whispered into her ear. And she should love him. He pressed himself against her. Helene could feel his cock. Desire for him flooded her. She ran away. Dashed through the hall. Pulled the doors that needed pushing, pushed the doors that needed pulling. She could barely get the car key into the lock. She didn't turn around. She hoped Henryk would come and embrace her and never again let her get away. Never ever. Helene rummaged through the glove compartment. Pretended she was looking for something. Henryk didn't come. Helene wondered for a moment whether to go back. Also he didn't have any money. And she should talk to him. She hadn't talked to him at all. Helene didn't go back. She sat there. Stared straight ahead. Then started her car. And left.

Helene drove along the autobahn. She automatically did what was required. Immediately forgot what she'd done. Couldn't remember how she'd gotten to where she was. And would forget this too right away. She hadn't called the children. Anything could have happened in the meantime. She could come home to find their corpses. And she wouldn't have contacted them. Wouldn't have called. Wouldn't have found out what had happened. Irresponsible. One of the children could have been taken to hospital. And could have wanted to see her mommy. But. She had to die. The mommy of the poor child couldn't be reached. Hadn't found it necessary to phone. Had found it more important to drive after her lover. To throw herself at him. If things were like this, it'd serve her right. And she'd have to do penance for the rest of her life.

Helene arrived in Vienna. Katharina had knocked out one of her teeth. She had fallen off a table. Helene's sister had needed to take her to the Children's Hospital. Katharina had swollen lips and was crying quietly to herself. Helene thanked Mimi. She'd drop off the money for the cab trips tomorrow. Right now, she didn't have a penny on her. And no, she still didn't have an ATM card. Helene put Katharina to bed. She could have hit Mimi. How could something like this have happened. And Mimi was her older sister. Had always known better, everything. Helene went to bed straight away too. She unplugged the phone. Barbara crawled into bed with her and Katharina. The children were sleeping snuggled up close against her. Helene woke up again and again. Dozed rather than slept. But she didn't want to disrupt the children's sleep. She lay there. The little bodies pressing against her. Too tired. All feelings far away. The day with Henryk like any other day and long ago. Helene thought she should start writing her diary again. Already she wasn't sure if she'd be able to remember this day. If she'd be able to remember what a happiness it had been. To drive up this hill. And see three trees with white blossoms on top and a bench in front of them. How it had been to see those trees. To drive past them with Henryk next to her. She did love him. Sure she did. Most likely.

On Monday Helene had her appointment with Dr. Stadlmann. She copied the papers. She put together small files. Gossiped with Frau Sprecher. The cat had eaten a bit of liver, again. Wasn't that a good sign. With his liver cancer? Then Helene drove to Dr. Stadlmann's apartment. To Dr. Stadlmann's mother's apartment. On her way to the Linke Wienzeile Helene quickly did her shopping. Lining up with her shopping cart at the cashier's in the supermarket, she felt cramps again in her abdomen. She wondered whether to get another box of sanitary napkins. Others had already lined up behind her. She'd have to line up all over. And she didn't know where to find feminine hygiene products in this supermarket. At Dr. Stadlmann's it was again the mother who opened the door. Dr. Stadlmann sat in his white doctor's office at the far end of the apartment. Helene handed him her proposals and sat down. They worked. Dr. Stadlmann explained to Helene in great detail how the various applications of magnetic foil worked. They discussed how the applications could be presented. Without raising exaggerated hopes. Dr. Stadlmann explained the effects to her. Helene didn't understand all the scientific jargon. As he explained it, she found everything crystal clear. It sounded credible. Convincing. Dr. Stadlmann leaned back satisfied. He called for his mother. He rolled to the door in his office chair and called. The mother didn't respond. He asked Helene to go to the front and ask his mother if they could get some coffee. She'd like one, too, wouldn't she. Helene went. She knocked on the kitchen door. The woman came to the door. Helene gave the woman her son's request. The woman merely nodded. Helene tried to be especially friendly, but the woman didn't return her smile. She closed the kitchen door. Helene went back. Entering Dr. Stadlmann's office she saw the stain on the chair. She saw the stain immediately. She'd been sitting on a chair uphol- stered with white Naugahyde. Helene quickly sat down again. To hide the brown-red stain. Helene was wearing a thin dark silk skirt. She cautiously touched the spot, with- out interrupting her conversation with Dr. Stadlmann. The cloth of her skirt was damp. Helene continued to speak. It was vital not to let the conversation end. Helene got hot. The cramps hadn't been all that bad. Or maybe they had. Helene desperately thought about what to do. Get up. And pretend she had to pick up something. And in the process wipe the chair with her skirt? The mother brought coffee and some cake. A marbled Gugelhupf from Anker. The coffee tasted particularly good. Dr. Stadlmann was explain- ing his plans to Helene. How they could expand the busi- ness with the magnetic foil. Helene wondered if coffee would increase the bleeding or not. The longer she stayed sitting, the worse it'd get. Helene felt the blood drain from her head. Seep away. She could only think as if her head were in thin air. Somehow high up there. She said she had to go. And didn't want to claim more of his time. She'd prepare the copy and arrange the dates with the photographer. And nothing would happen without Dr. Stadlmann. She prom- ised him. After all, she herself didn't really know how it all worked. Dr. Stadlmann sat in his executive chair. He hadn't gotten up. Helene prattled on. Stood up, rummaged through her purse, fished out her handkerchief. She went to the lit- tle sink on the wall behind Dr. Stadlmann. She wetted the cloth. Went to the chair. Started wiping. The blood was easily removed from the plastic. Helene had to rinse out the cloth and then wipe the chair a second time. Helene carried on talking. Without a break. If she hadn't talked, she would have started crying. Or dizziness would have overcome her. She felt she must be white as a sheet. Her forehead was cold and moist. Helene didn't dare to raise her eyes up to the mirror above the sink. Dr. Stadlmann watched her. At first he didn't understand what she was up to. Then he made a move to get up but sank back into his chair. He began searching his desk drawer. Helene was wiping. Chattering away to herself. What a blessing the development of magnetic foil was. How grateful to Dr. Stadlmann people were going to be. And how they'd get along with this Nestler person. Dr. Stadlmann held a box of pills in his hand. He opened the box, checked inside, closed it. Offered it to Helene. She should drive home, lie down, and take a Valium. After all, periods that heavy were generally caused by stress. Did she have problems. His wife used to go through this before exams. Helene stood there, silent. The wet handkerchief in one hand. Her purse and the papers in the other. Dr. Stadlmann rolled up to her in his chair, opened her purse. Dropped the box of Valium. Rolled back behind his desk. Helene glanced at the chair she'd sat on. She could no longer see anything. She began to leave. She looked at Dr. Stadlmann and nodded. She shrugged helplessly. She dared not say anything. The first syllable would have cost her all control. She turned away. Closed the door behind her as fast as possible. He should not see the back of her skirt. She had taken care all through wiping the chair not to turn her back to him. Helene took the Standard she had bought in the supermarket and put it on the seat of the car. When she got out, there were bright red stains across the report about an earthquake in Los Angeles.

Helene drove home. She hurried. Maybe she'd still be able to pick up the children from school. At home in her bathroom she saw how heavy the bleeding was. For a moment it seemed dangerous. Then she quickly changed her clothes. Stuffed a second napkin into her underpants and drove to school. Katharina looked sad with her swollen lip. She immediately ran up to Helene. Helene had to call out to Barbara. But Barbara continued chatting to the girl she'd come out of the gate with. Then she came, too, and they drove home to the Lannerstrasse. Helene was glad that she had picked up the children. The idea of the children crossing the Hasenauerstrasse always scared her. Nobody did less than 80 kilometers an hour on this road. And nobody stopped to let children cross. Helene herself would drive there that fast. She phoned the office from home. Frau Sprecher could be told of the disaster. Frau Sprecher had experienced a similar thing, she immediately told Helene. At job interviews and her first date. But then, in the past, things had been so much more difficult with sanitary napkins. This wasn't a problem anymore nowadays, was it. And Helene shouldn't worry. She'd mention something to Nadolny. Helene hung up and felt liberated. Really, it's always people like Frau Sprecher that help you out. And she got furious with her sister again. Couldn't she have paid attention. The stupid cow. For lunch Helene had bought jars of baby food. "We all have to play baby," Helene said. "Because Katharina can't eat anything else." She warmed chicken with noodles. She fed the children, taking turns. They talked baby talk. Their noises and arm waving created a tremendous racket. Soon they couldn't go on eating for laughing. "But now you're 3 already and want to eat all by yourself." Helene passed around the jars of peach, orange and banana. Obediently the children spooned up their goop. They spilled their food and intentionally stained the napkins they'd tied around their necks. "And now it's time for a nap. Little children your age must have a nap." "I'm big again," Barbara said. "I'm going to read." Katharina wanted to sleep with Helene. She stood there, blanket in her arm, sucking her thumb. Helene took her back to her own bed, lifted her and tucked her in. Moms, too, sometimes need to sleep by themselves. And she had a headache. Katharina continued to play the 3-year old. She got up and climbed into Helene's bed. "I'm not sweepy," she repeated over and over. Twice Helene went through the game with her. Then she asked for quiet. She'd leave the door to the bedroom open. Wasn't that enough? Katharina was tired of the game anyway and got herself a book. Helene lay down. Only when she was lying did she feel how the blood was running out of her. She lay very still.

The next morning Helene was telling Nadolny and Nestler about her discussion with Dr. Stadlmann. Nadolny and Nestler sat on the sofa in Nadolny's office. Helene sat opposite. On top of the glass coffee table lay thick files and catalogs. Helene was soon finished. The gentlemen were pleased. Herr Nestler wanted to hear one more time what Dr. Stadlmann's cooperation would be like. No piece of writing, photo or any other thing was to be released without Stadlmann's approval, right? Nestler turned to Nadolny. Nadolny shrugged. You have to go along with it, for the time being anyway. If Stadlmann wasn't fully behind everything, getting the foil approved could become a problem. Even in Austria, approval of pharmaceuticals was taken seriously. Frau Gebhardt was to reassure Stadlmann. They'd hit it off well, hadn't they. Frau Gebhardt and Herr Dr. Stadlmann. Obviously they were getting along just fine. Weren't they? Nadolny grinned at Helene. But that wasn't the problem. At the moment. There were others. The men chuckled. Lewd. Nadolny and Nestler sat in front of their pile of files and catalogs. They seemed to want to clap their hands with delight. With a flash Helene imagined how little Nadolny had stood under the Christmas tree. Helene wanted to leave. No. No. She should stay. Nadolny got a cognac for himself and Nestler. Then they began to look through the models' comp cards and photos and through the modeling agencies' catalogs. Nestler started with the individual photos that had the models' names and phone numbers stamped or written with pen on the back. Those were the ones without agencies. But they had phone numbers. Herr Nadolny gave Herr Nestler a blissful smile. Once the men had examined the photos, they passed them to Helene. They put on serious expressions. With each sip at their cognac the men got more garrulous. The question of the model's attire in the photos was discussed. Nadolny favored her naked. No, no lingerie, please. No distraction from the product. Nestler immediately gave in to Nadolny's logic. "We don't need a face either. Actually." Nadolny argued. Did they really need her, Helene wanted to know. Yes. Yes. She had to provide the female eye. After all, women would have to buy the product. Nestler and Nadolny bent over a catalog of nudes. How could you meet these girls? Nestler sighed. Was there really not one independent model in the stack he'd have liked? Nadolny poured more cognac. Not a problem. Since he knew the owner of an agency. They were hunting partners. Nestler should say which one. Nadolny would take care of the rest. It wouldn't be easy. But could be done. For Nestler. They could be introduced. After that. The men laughed. After that, it'd be up to Nestler. Helene gathered the flood of photos and papers, brochures, posters. She could no longer distinguish one face from another. Helene avoided looking at the two men. They were bouncing up and down on the sofa. They didn't even try to

hide their erections. In fact, they seemed to enjoy each other's arousal. Helene hated the men. She thought their bulging flies disgusting. And was angry for being treated as if
she were invisible. As a woman anyway. Had she cast her
female eye on the photos long enough now? She'd propose
these three models. Normal figures. Of which only neck,
hips, knees, and elbows would be visible anyway. In her
opinion, they should go with a male model. The healing of
a male body would be more convincing. Nadolny leaned
over the coffee table. She shouldn't be selfish, Nadolny
winked at her. What was the good of a naked man to him?
When they'd be taking the photographs. And she didn't
seem to be giving any thought to Herr Nestler. What?
Helene was called to the phone. It was her mother-in-law.
Was she to cook lunch for the children. She couldn't remember what they had agreed on. Helene said she was to
cook Tuesdays and Thursdays. Because she herself would
be at the office. During lunch. But if she didn't have any
time? No. No, the old woman hastened to respond. It was
only that everything was so difficult. And the worries about
Gregor. And again he hadn't phoned. Her. In fact, she didn't
even know if he was still alive. She was at the end of her
tether. Helene stood next to her desk. If she had to drive
home at noon on these two days as well and be back at the
office by 2 o'clock. She might as well forget about the job.
Of course nobody needed her during that time. But
Nadolny wanted to have her sitting there. In case something came up. And he was always angry about Monday
and Wednesday. As if she were deserting him personally.
Helene asked the old woman, please, to think of the children. And mashed potatoes would be enough. Or a sandwich bun. And a glass of milk. She didn't need to cook.
And everything was in her fridge. Katharina wasn't able
really to eat anything anyway. Because of her swollen lip.

"Yes," the old woman interrupted Helene. How had that all come about? Not that she didn't like Helene's sister. But why had Helene not asked her? With her, nothing like this had ever happened. Helene tried to cut the conversation short. In Nadolny's office Nadolny and Nestler were laughing. "This one! Yes. This one! No question." Nestler exclaimed. Nadolny congratulated Nestler on his choice and walked across the room toward the cognac bottle. Helene interrupted her mother-in-law. She had to go. She'd be home at 4. Frau Sprecher put her head through the door. Your mother-in-law is a really nice woman, Frau Sprecher said while signaling with her eyes toward Nadolny's office. Yes. Her mother-in-law was nice. Helene's mother-in-law always asked Frau Sprecher how her cat was doing. Immediately afterwards, she'd report on her own cat Murli. Who was doing amazingly well in spite of her old age. Nadolny and Nestler went to Frau Sprecher at the reception desk. Helene sat down and tried to think what needed to be done next. Nadolny had closed the door to Helene's office. She heard Nadolny give instructions to Frau Sprecher. Helene tried to come up with phrases describing the healing power of magnetic foil without making it sound too much like a miracle cure. The men were going off to lunch and wouldn't be back. They had hardly left when Frau Sprecher burst into Helene's office. Frau Sprecher was outraged. Nadolny had asked her to invite 5 models for interviews. To the lounge at the Sacher. At half-hour intervals. And she'd been given strict orders in which sequence. But the first 3 were completely booked anyway. What was she to do? And what did Helene think they were to come to the Sacher for? Helene shrugged. Just think about it. "Frau Sprecher. You've seen the two of them. What do you think they have in mind." Frau Sprecher looked put out and went to phone the remaining models. They too were unavailable. Answering machines. Frau Sprecher didn't know how to explain the situation to these machines. She hung up. Sat, helpless, behind her reception desk. Helene consoled her. She should leave a message at the Sacher. There was no more she could do. And probably nothing would come of it. Nobody here had expected Herr Nestler to show up. In the end, Helene and Frau Sprecher were quite pleased with the failed attempt to parade models in the lounge of the Hotel Sacher. They had some coffee. Helene poured a healthy shot of bourbon from Nadolny's bookcase into their coffees. "Isn't this called a Pharisee?" she asked. Both of them had to laugh.

On Friday afternoon Helene's doorbell rang. A young man stood outside. He was thin and tall. He asked Helene if her name was Helene Gebhardt. Helene said, "Yes. Maiden name Wolffen." The man was nervous. Anxious. Helene stood in the doorway. She asked him what he wanted. It seemed he couldn't find a way to begin. How had he gotten into the house? He'd rung the bell for Gebhardt. And then the door had been opened. Mom, Helene thought. Yes, the man said, he was there on behalf of the bank. Yes. Well. The Credit bank. The Credit Union Bank. And. He made a long pause. He looked at Helene. Meaningfully. Helene had a feeling she should grasp something. Should have grasped something. But she didn't know what. She looked to the man for an explanation. He kept looking at her, challenging. Helene got impatient. She hadn't turned off the iron. What was the matter. Yes. Well. He needed to confiscate her Eurocheck card. He said "confiscate" and was suddenly angry. He made a step toward Helene. Helene immediately shut the apartment door. She stood behind the door. The man called from the other side, "I really must have it. Or there'll be legal consequences." Helene took a deep breath. Barbara came out of the children's room. What was happening? Helene sent her back in. She took the Eurocheck card from her purse. The purse lay on a chest in the hallway. Above the chest was a mirror. Fake Empire style, with gold frame. On top, sheaves of wheat in bows. Helene saw herself rummage through her purse. The man knocked on the door. "Frau Gebhardt," he called. "I know you're there." The asshole's learned that from TV, Helene thought. She went back to the door. She opened it just a crack. "Aren't you ashamed of doing this? Earning your money this way?" she asked the man. Helene looked at the card. She broke the card, bent it over in the middle. It had just occurred to her that she could be dealing with a crook. Someone who collects cards. She should have asked for his ID. But now it was too late for that. The man towered in front of her door. A threat. Helene offered him the card. A wide white stripe ran across it. On one side a gaping tear. The card was a total wreck. Helene smiled at the man. Radiantly. She had no checks left anyway. She wouldn't have been able to get any more money with this card. The man took the ruined card. Offended. "That was not necessary," he said. "Though. In other cases you should. Right?" Helene suddenly thought the situation hilarious. She would have been delighted if her mother-in-law had put her head through the door and asked what was going on. Helene was sure the old woman was listening behind her apartment door. The man got nervous again. He was doing a little dance. Seemed to get ready to apologize. Helene didn't want to hear why or how anybody was doing this sort of work. She closed the door. The man remained standing there for some time. Helene heard the locks of his briefcase click shut. Then he left. Helene was relieved. She had to laugh. She had 8000 schillings. And then there'd be nothing. Her salary would vanish in the overdraft when her account was closed. She had to sort it out. Helene went into her living room. She kept ironing till late into the night. While she was ironing, "Derrick" was on TV. Jealousy and greed were raging throughout the fancy doctors of Munich. Their houses were perfectly presentable. And nobody had to iron.

Püppi called on Saturday. How about they all go to the park? Helene hesitated. But Püppi sounded normal. Friendly. The children were asking for ice cream anyway and should be going outside. She drove to the Belvedere. The streets were empty. The Viennese were all gone. To their weekend cottages. Helene found a parking spot far up in the Prinz Eugen Strasse, almost at the South Station. They went into the park from the upper side. Past the Upper Belvedere. They were looking for Püppi and Sophie. Barbara and Katharina ran down the stairs to the Lower Belvedere. And up. And down again. The fountain was running, the water was splashing and singing, the sun was shining. The trees were green. Still light green. Late tulips in bloom, withered lilac blossoms. Helene slowly walked down the path. Henryk had only given her one short call. She was to be patient. Still. Please. The sinking feeling in her stomach got worse after the call. She longed to see him. To have him next to her. In bed. During meals. At every step. Always. And to be able to rest in the assurance that he existed. And nothing else. No thoughts. No time. No more time. The sun. The glittering water. The laughing children. All of it she could bear if he were there. Alone, she couldn't bear the jubilant day. Helene walked slowly. Locked inside, she carried the pain. The pain that pushed and pulled: Longing. Helene walked down the stairs slowly. Püppi was usually down there with Sophie. Between the geometrically pruned hedges and rows of trees. For a moment Helene felt as if everybody was looking at her. Coming closer, with their eyes getting huge. Precise and searching. The next

[121]

moment she felt as if nobody took any notice of her. Yes. Turned away. On purpose, scornful. As if she didn't exist. Shouldn't exist. The desire to put an end to it all rose again in Helene. Not to herself. Helene would have never wanted to put an end to herself. She wanted to put an end to it. To all of it. The children had found Püppi. She heard Katharina call "Aunt Püppi, Aunt Püppi." Helene walked toward the calls. She couldn't see the children and Püppi and Sophie. They were behind the hedges in the maze. "Hello, hello," she shouted. "Where are you. I can't find you." The children giggled. She could imagine how the children stood pressed against the hedge, almost bursting with laughter. Helene shouted again. She stopped in front of the hedge behind which she could hear the muffled giggles. "Where are my children," she said to herself. Said it again and again. Mournful. The sentence she'd never heard from her parents. At first it remained quiet. Then single giggles, no longer held in check. She heard Püppi "shhh." Then Katharina called "Mommy!" and came running around the corner. "Mommy!" She ran into Helene's arms and let herself be swung high into the air. Helene carried the child around the corner, perched on her hip. Sophie and Barbara sat giggling on the bench. Püppi was kneeling in front of them, taking photos of Sophie. The children were laughing. Püppi took countless photos. Helene sat down on the opposite bench. Katharina stayed on her lap. She started to suck her thumb again. Helene carefully pulled the thumb out of her mouth. Was that really necessary, she whispered to Katharina. The child nodded and put her thumb back into her mouth. She gave Helene a grave look. Helene embraced her and pulled her head close to her chest. "All right. If you must," she said. Katharina snuggled up to her. Barbara and Sophie had climbed onto the bench and were making contortions for Püppi's photos. They giggled nonstop. Barbara, spurred on by the much younger girl, was being silly. Katharina whispered, "Mommy. Mommy. When are we going to have our ice cream?" Helene promised Katharina she'd buy some soon. As soon as they left the park. You couldn't get any in here. Oh yes, you could. Katharina had seen the kiosk at the entrance. You could get ice cream there. Katharina wanted a Cornetto. They had them there. "Yes. We'll get one. When we go back." But Katharina wanted it now. Couldn't she go. She could get one for herself. Couldn't she? By herself! Helene wondered what might happen. She should go with her. But she was tired. She didn't want to go. She wanted to sit. Helene hesitated. Katharina had already begun to take money out of Helene's purse. Barbara turned to Katharina. Wanted to know what was going on. And wanted to go with her. The children had left before Helene could even tell them which way to go. The children were dashing off. Sophie started to cry. Püppi consoled her. Helene sat on the opposite bench. Püppi calmed down Sophie. The big children had simply wanted to run away. She was too small. Way too much could happen. Helene wondered if she should leave. She couldn't bear an argument. Didn't want one. Then Sophie came up to her. Showed her pink pebbles that she had found on the way. Helene admired the tiny stones. With Sophie she started to arrange the pebbles in patterns on the bench. She made a star, a moon, a flower. And a big S for Sophie. Püppi took pictures of Sophie laying patterns. Then she sat down with Helene.

Sophie played with her pebbles on the bench between them. Helene asked Püppi how she was. What she'd been doing. Püppi smiled mysteriously. Helene would be pleased with her. She should come with her. To the Karolinengasse. She'd be surprised. She'd taken Helene's advice to heart. No, really! Helene wanted to know details. Püppi shook her head. She'd see. But otherwise. There was more good news. Jack had shown up again. And confessed everything. The emerald rings. And the hunting knife. Which was the only other keepsake from her father. And he'd given Püppi 30 000 schillings. From the sale of the rings. "But. They were worth a fortune!" Helene exclaimed. Püppi shook her head. Possibly. But Jack didn't have to show up again at all. Didn't have to give her anything. "You should have reported him to the police. After all, he has a reputation for doing this sort of thing. At least the marriage is now off." Püppi smiled. Jack was much maligned. And the police. Helene shouldn't expect the police to be interested in her rings. They hadn't been insured. And she didn't know anybody who would beat up Jack. That would be the only language Jack would understand. Could understand. Püppi sounded proud. And all in all. She was in love with him. No. Of course she didn't want to marry him anymore. But you had to understand him. He's had such a hard life. He's been working for this Hugo Korpsch. And those trips. It's hard. Weapons aren't sold to the lambs of this world, after all. Helene didn't have a clue, really. In the desert, somewhere, Jack had been drinking from a water bag. Which had looked odd. He'd asked. What sort of a bag was it. The other men had laughed terribly. So Hugo had told him not to shit himself. Of course this bag had been made from a nigger. They'd cut off his arms and legs and sewn up the holes. And the other holes too. Ha ha. And then Jack'd had to puke. He'd drunk out of a person's neck. A person who'd been turned into a water bag. "Is anybody forcing him to be involved with this Hugo?" Püppi pitied Helene. "Once you're on the inside," she explained to Helene, "you can't get out. They won't let you." Helene didn't know anything, did she. Helene had to admit that. She also had to admit that the whole town knew

of such stories. And of worse ones. And nobody did anything about them. Helene looked around. The children had
been gone for a long time. Sophie diligently put the pebbles in a long row. Helene said in English, Sophie shouldn't
hear this. Püppi didn't respond. She'd started to take photos of Sophie again. Helene watched Püppi. Püppi had something jittery about her. Some unsteadiness. Helene couldn't
see exactly in what way Püppi's head was trembling. But it
twitched imperceptibly. When Püppi talked, she was calm.
And when she took photos. In between, she seemed to be
shaking. As if something in her was tearing apart. Within
her. Somewhere. Helene got up. She wanted to look for the
children. She went to the main path on the far right. The
children were just coming down. They were licking their
ice-cream cones. They'd both bought chocolate Cornettos.
They had chocolate smeared all around their mouths.
Barbara pressed the change into Helene's hand. The coins
and bills were warm from being held. They'd had to wait
for so long. Other people had pushed in front of them all
the time. Helene went with the children to the Lower Belvedere. And from there across to the other side. They should
eat their ice creams so that Sophie wouldn't see them. And
then want one too. When they came back to Püppi and
Sophie, Püppi was about to leave. She'd put all of Sophie's
toys under the stroller seat. She was just putting Sophie
into the stroller. Katharina and Barbara danced around the
stroller. Sophie yelled, "Mine, mine." The two other children also yelled, "Mine, mine." And pretended they wanted
to settle in the stroller. The stroller had been Helene's, and
both her children had been pushed around in it. Whenever
they saw the stroller, they played this game. With much
yelling and laughing they left the park. At the gate Helene
hesitated. Püppi took her hand and pulled her along. "A
surprise," she said. They all went to the Karolinengasse.

They climbed up the stairs. Helene helped Püppi carry the stroller. By the third floor Helene felt so weak she thought she'd faint. Each step seemed insurmountable. Helene was panting. The children had arrived upstairs well before them. They were impatient. Sophie sat in the stroller and squealed with delight. At the top, Helene and Püppi were flushed from exertion. They both had to laugh. In the apartment they sent the children into Sophie's room. Püppi went to the living room with Helene. The dining table had been moved to the window. Drawing paper and pencils were lying around everywhere. Püppi picked up a sheet. She passed it to Helene. In the middle was a tangle of pencil lines. Püppi smiled at the drawing. "I think I'm getting there after all," she said. She lit a cigarette and began to pace up and down the room. She told Helene how she wanted to go on from here. How she'd finally figured it out. How she suddenly saw everything quite clearly. How she felt liberated. How representation had dragged her down. And wasn't it a big step. She'd been promised an exhibition. Nothing more specific yet. But nevertheless. And now she would have to work. Helene was looking at the sheet during all this. The pencil line started at the top and got itself wrapped into a tangle that seemed to be pushing into the background of the sheet. Then found its way to the right. Helene was moved. She told Püppi that she thought this sketch was truly special. She gave Püppi a hug. Keep the drawing, Püppi said. It was all thanks to Helene, really. The result of the long talks in the Veltlinergasse. Then Helene and Püppi prepared supper for the children. Soft-boiled eggs with soldiers. Everything went peacefully. The big children played baby. Pretended they couldn't eat. Spilled their food. Delighted, Sophie showed them how to eat properly. Helene went home after supper. In the car, she put the drawing on the passenger seat. Next to her. At home, she found a folder and put it away. Why wasn't she able to draw. The afternoon had almost been like the old days. When Püppi still lived in the Veltlinergasse. Still wanted to draw. And when the philosophy professor from Graz had yet to bring his chaos into Püppi's world.

During the night the phone rang repeatedly. There was silence at the other end. Sometimes a chirping sound. Helene didn't unplug the phone. The calls stopped at last around four in the morning.

On Sunday Helene lay down after lunch. The children were working on their Mother's Day gifts. At school, this day was taken very seriously. It had been necessary to buy colored paper, glue, cloth, lace, and embroidery thread. Helene wasn't allowed into the children's room. She lay on her bed. She had to talk to Gregor. No letter had arrived from a lawyer. She had 7100 schillings left. Henryk hadn't called again. She should forget him. Her period hadn't really stopped. The scarlet flow of blood in Bozen had changed to thin brown spotting. It smelled odd. Not bad, but different from any smell she'd ever had. A small sharp shooting pain exactly over the middle of her pubic bone made her stop from time to time and wait for it to pass. And how could she explain to the children that she didn't want to celebrate a holiday embraced by the fascists. After all, they were preparing for it with such eagerness. Helene's heart began to beat irregularly. She lay there and permitted herself to feel her heart. Tachycardia didn't frighten her. She waited for the skipping to pass and her heartbeat to return to its unnoticed normality. The waiting made her sleepy. She dozed. She slept. She must have slept. From a moment in which she'd been unable to remember anything the question suddenly came to her, "And. What if you now get breast cancer. What are you going to do then?" The question rose up her breastbone, burning, and gripped her around the throat. All the papers in this spring of 1989 were full of reports on breast cancer. Full of statistics on the chances of getting cured of breast cancer. And on the chances of becoming sick from it. Helene had read one article that proved the statistical calculation was a lie. The statistics gave a survival rate of five to seven years. The patients whose cancers had been detected early had spent those years in therapy. The doctors had treated them. And had made money. Those whose cancers hadn't been detected early had gotten sick. They had died. But they had lived a few years undisturbed. Both groups had died roughly at the same time. And breast cancer. Women like her got it. Women. Uncertain of their gender. Who couldn't cope with their sexuality. Who were overwhelmed by the practical necessities of life. Who hadn't breast fed their children long enough. Helene rolled over on her side and hid her face in her arms. It didn't make the fear go away. She turned over on her other side. Got up. Went to the bathroom. Locked the door. Unbuttoned her blouse. Examined her breasts. Her breasts cupped warm in her hands. Her nipples hardened and pushed gently against her palms. She began to play with her nipples. She looked at herself in the mirror. She heard a child go into the kitchen and get a glass of water. She would have found herself attractive had she been a man. Didn't she look like Isabella Huppert? She was leaning toward her reflection. There were no lumps in her breasts. Not yet, she thought. An immense hatred attacked her with this thought. Raged around her stomach. While from her neck the hopelessness of her situation was pushing her down again. Helene unbuttoned her jeans. Let them slide down below her knees. She put her right hand into her underpants. Stroked her breasts with her left hand. And, angry, beat herself with her right hand.

She was leaning forward even further. As she came, she watched her pupils. How the iris for a moment lost all strength and slackened into a small ring and how huge black holes opened through which she stared down into herself. Immediately afterwards she felt miserable. She washed her hands and dressed with trembling fingers. Lay down again. She left her bedroom door open. The children walked past from time to time. Busy. They smiled secretively and waved at her.

Helene was to find out which was the best hotel in Salzburg. For Herr Nestler. And companion. And not the Österreichische Hof. Something farther out in the country. That'd be better for such occasions. Herr Nadolny looked at Helene, pleading for understanding. Helene could have recommended the Gaisberg Hotel right away. She'd always stayed there with her father. For 2 concerts at the Salzburg Music Festival. Since she was 14. 5 days in Salzburg with her father. Because he wanted to hear the music. And because her mother always went to a spa at that time. To Abbano. Helene went into her office. She made calls. Then she told Frau Sprecher she had to go to the Tourist Information Office. So she could get the brochures right away and Herr Nestler would have something to look at. Helene took the tram to the Opera. At Tourist Information she wrested brochures and price lists from a bored woman with particularly red fingernails. Then she rode the tram back. She got off on the Schwarzenbergplatz. Walked past the Café Hübner into the City Park. She went to the Park Café and took a seat on the terrace. On the right, against the wall. They offered Schinkenfleckerln, a ham and noodle casserole, and green salad for lunch. Helene ordered a small beer with it. It would make her drowsy. She got a paper. She felt she'd escaped. The sunlight filtered through the orange umbrellas. Everybody looked healthy. Tanned. Helene was looking forward to the meal. Her beer was in front of her. She read her horoscope in the Kronen-Zeitung. Frau Helga's smiling face appeared above the horoscope. Helene was promised the joys of love and important meetings. The Schinkenfleckerln arrived. The noodles were overcooked. The smoked ham was falling apart. The dish reminded her of coming home after long days at school. The Schinkenfleckerln would have been kept warm in the oven. Sparrows arrived, landed on the edge of her table, pecked gradually toward her food. Helene drove the birds away. Up close, they looked disheveled and mangy. She felt like having a short coffee. She should go back to the office, she thought. She looked for the waiter. She saw Püppi first. Holding Sophie's hand, Püppi was coming around the building. They walked toward the balustrade. Helene was about to lift her arm and call out for Püppi. Püppi had stopped at a table in the sun. Gregor followed behind with Sophie's stroller. He maneuvered the stroller into a corner and sat down next to Püppi. Sophie was demanding something, loud and excited. Gregor got up and took a stuffed animal from the bag on the stroller. He gave Sophie the animal. He said something. Then the waiter blocked Helene's view of the 3. Helene got up and went into the building. She avoided glancing in the direction of the table by the balustrade. She stood in the restaurant. An old couple sat at one of the tables. Other than that, the rooms were empty. The waiter hurried past Helene. The bill, please, she called out to him. He didn't hear her, or didn't want to hear her. Helene was afraid Gregor or Püppi might come in. On their way to the washroom. And catch her. Helene picked up a menu and calculated how much she had to pay. She took the money out of her purse. Her fingers were flying. She put the money on a table. Called out to the waiter that the money was here. She had to go. And ran from the building. She walked toward the Museum of Applied Arts. She walked fast. She didn't take the tram. She was aware of her movements. At the same time, she was petrified. Paralyzed. Other than that, she felt nothing. All she wanted to do was go on running. Running. Walking. Forever. Or sleeping. Sleeping for a long time. Forever sleeping. Helene didn't want to think about the meaning of any of it. Her children. His children. Gregor had never bent down in this way to one of the girls. And given them a stuffed animal. Not this way. Not so lovingly.

Already on the Ring, Helene was no longer sure if she'd really seen the 3. In the office, Herr Nadolny wanted to know if it was possible to get rail ticket coupons. Nadolny was all a-twitter, in nervous high spirits. Helene phoned. It turned out to be the way she had thought. There weren't any coupons. You bought the ticket. It was valid for 3 months. And you could return it. But Nadolny needed of-ficial confirmation. He was secretive. But then couldn't help blurting it out anyway. Couldn't keep it to himself. In spite of everything, he had managed to get hold of a model. The owner of an agency owed him a favor and had leaned on the young lady. And Nestler liked her. He was wild about her. Now they had to arrange a weekend. The young woman hadn't agreed to anything. Not yet. What about the hotel. Helene phoned the Gaisberg Hotel. They had a suite and a double room available. No, not two suites. Yes. Good. In that case she'd take it. One suite and one double room. Yes. Friday till Monday. She left a note on Nadolny's desk. Nadolny stood at the window and looked outside. He asked Helene if she knew what was wrong with the whole thing. Helene looked at him. "The man is not a hunter. He doesn't hunt. If he were a hunter, things would be much easier. A hunt. I can always arrange that." Helene returned to her desk. She sat there. She pictured in her mind how she should have dealt with the situation in the park. She should have walked over to the three of them. And said Hi. Totally cool. Said something. And then left. Should have left them behind. Turned and left. Gone. Should have deserted them. And smiled at Sophie. The child couldn't help it. And should have walked away. Not fled. But Helene knew that she wouldn't have been able to. She would have started to cry. Helene decided to get drunk. To postpone that moment. The moment when she'd be alone and go over this scene, endlessly. And to postpone the pain. And not to talk. Not even being able to talk. Not being able to tell somebody, anybody. Frau Sprecher asked Helene if she didn't want to go home. Today. Helene asked Nadolny if there was anything left for her to do. Nadolny stood at the window, again, drinking Underberg. Helene had organized a jumbo pack of bottles. Nadolny hadn't protested this unauthorized action. His bottom drawer on the left was now filled with the little bottles. Helene had to leave the office. And go home.

Helene drank 2 bottles of Grüner Veltliner, Ried Klaus from the Jamek Vineyard. After that, bourbon. The bottle had been almost full. She was already drinking during the children's supper. Then she sat in front of the TV and forced herself to take a sip of bourbon every 20 minutes. She put her alarm clock on the TV. As if she had to take a homeopathic remedy on time, at regular intervals. The children fell asleep peacefully. At 10 o'clock, the phone rang. Helene didn't pick it up. She continued to drink. The bottle didn't get much emptier. But she had trouble walking to her bed. When she lay down, everything was spinning around. She piled up pillows. She had to focus all her attention on grabbing and pushing the pillows the right way. With the pillows, the spinning wasn't quite as bad. But then the crying happened anyway. Helene had to cry because it had been the same stroller her children had sat in. Which Gregor had bent down to so differently and, as a matter of course, so lovingly.

The next day when Helene arrived at the office, Dr. Stadlmann was already there. The first photos were to be shot. Helene felt terrible. She had tried at least to repair the worst of the damage with makeup. But then she'd washed it all off again. Her hands hadn't been able to. She had smeared mascara everywhere. The eyeliner had wobbled. The foundation was uneven, her skin pale and her pores enlarged, her eyes swollen. Helene had dozed until 2 o'clock. Then the vomiting had started. In the office, the light was too bright. People talked too loudly. Driving to the office, Helene had repeatedly been late stopping the car. Or late starting off. She felt slowed down. At the same time, all her sensory perceptions were overly acute. Dr. Stadlmann turned to Helene. Searching. He said nothing. Helene didn't even try to pretend that everything was normal. She wondered why she hadn't taken the Valium. Which Dr. Stadlmann had given her. The model arrived as arranged. She was slender. But not as young as in the photos. She was wearing a particularly short mini-skirt and a kind of bikini top under a leather jacket. She asked Frau Sprecher who she'd be dealing with. Frau Sprecher wordlessly pointed her to Nadolny's office. Nadolny gave the woman a loud and hearty welcome. Then he closed the door. The photographer was late. Helene was to take coffee into Nadolny's office. The whole pot at once. She asked Frau Sprecher to take care of it. Frau Sprecher complied. With reluctance. Then Nadolny came to get a bottle of sparkling wine from the fridge. Dr. Stadlmann sat down on the office chair behind Helene's desk. Helene had to sit on one of the Thonet chairs. That meant posture. Helene kept thinking she'd pass out. She felt herself ebbing away from herself. It seemed funny. The way she was sitting, trying to stay straight. If she were to lose all consciousness. Dr. Stadlmann wouldn't be able to pick her up. Helene remained conscious. Fainting would have created too many problems. They sat there in silence. Waiting. Dr. Stadlmann floated up to Helene in his chair. Was she sick. Helene smiled. "I got drunk yesterday," she said. "Not such a great idea. It seems." Dr. Stadlmann rolled his chair diagonally up to Helene. He reached around Helene and put his right hand on her back. Helene felt like laughing. Dr. Stadlmann whispered, "Shhh." They sat like that for a long time. Helene felt the man's breath. Deep and regular. Helene looked up briefly. He had his eyes shut. Helene felt awkward about the whole thing. For a moment she thought she should push him away. She felt crowded. Harassed. But then she realized that she was getting warmer. She smiled and whispered, "I think it's enough now." Stadlmann shushed again. Frau Sprecher came into the room and turned back alarmed. Dr. Stadlmann continued to press his hand against Helene's back. Helene began to feel embarrassed. While her embarrassment grew, her stomach no longer felt bloated. Her head had become lighter. The feeling of wanting to die right away had gone. Helene straightened up and pushed Dr. Stadlmann away. The man opened his eyes. They looked at each other. Helene wanted to say something. Thank you. Or. How good that had felt. She said nothing. She was sleepy. Too slow to say anything.

Herr Nestler arrived at the same time as the photographer. The photographer looked hounded. He was actually a press photographer. He was only doing this job as a favor for Nadolny. Nestler disappeared into Nadolny's office. It got noisy. There was a peal of high-pitched laughter from the woman. The photographer walked around and looked at the rooms. He decided to take the photos in the foyer. The light was best there. Dr. Stadlmann had brought his own camera equipment. His camera case was bigger than the photographer's. He asked the photographer technical details about exposure, focal length, the lens. The photographer didn't know the answers to most of his questions. He said he was simply taking photos. He didn't know how it worked. He was only interested in the results. Dr. Stadlmann was about to launch into explanations. By now, the photographer was getting thoroughly stressed. And angry. He pushed his 2 photo floods around and asked if they could start. Finally. He was willing to take photos. But not exams. Dr. Stadlmann was tight-lipped. Helene called the model. Nadolny and Nestler stood in the doorway, watching. The photographer asked if audience participation was a requirement here. In which case, he'd charge admission. He wanted to be left alone with the model. They should tell him what it was all for. And let him get on with his job. In peace and quiet. Please. Dr. Stadlmann insisted on staying and suggested that Nadolny and Nestler should go and have some more sparkling wine. And that Frau Gebhardt should stay. He needed to show her where the foils had to be applied. So that she could do it without him later. The model stood in the middle of the foyer and kept asking when she should take off her clothes. And would the lighting setup take much longer. And should she add a bit more powder to her face. Stadlmann told her that he didn't need her face anyway. Nadolny and Nestler inched closer. Dr. Stadlmann established that, as far as he was concerned, the young woman didn't have to get undressed at all. She could leave her top on. Nadolny and Nestler edged another step closer into the foyer. The woman went to Nestler. She looked up at him, looked up into his eyes. She was here for nudes.

Which was an extra fee. For normal shots she wouldn't have gotten up so early. Because of the lines from sleeping. Or from the underwear. Nestler grabbed the woman's shoulder. Turned her round. They stood next to each other. The woman in Nestler's arm. Of course they were shooting nudes. The last thing he wanted were bikini straps in the photos of his product. He said that to Stadlmann. Stadlmann turned away. The woman undressed. She stood there naked, and Stadlmann started to stick on the foils. He coasted close to her with his chair and heaved himself up. He stuck a foil across the model's neck. The photographer and Stadlmann took photos of the neck. Then the hip with foil. The arm. The knee. Nadolny and Nestler watched. They exchanged glances. Helene was relieved that at least they weren't nudging each other. After a while they went back into the office. You could hear them laughing. The model became obstinate. She wouldn't keep still. Started making comments. About the foil. The adhesive itched. She didn't want this sort of stuff on her skin. She asked the photographer if he would want this sort of stuff on his skin. And she wanted to know from Stadlmann how come he was taking photos of her. She didn't want to show up in some collection. Dr. Stadlmann replied calmly she needn't think he depended on photos like these. The woman sized up his enormous black orthopedic shoes and the braces that disappeared up his pant legs. She shrugged. Which ruined another one of the photographer's shots. Helene stood in a corner. Frau Sprecher had retired to the kitchen. She sat there smoking. Helene didn't dare to leave. Every so often Stadlmann would speak to her. About the effects. How to apply the foil. And how the effects changed depending on where you moved the foil. Helene nodded. Then the model ended the session. She simply put on her skirt. Stuffed her panties and pantyhose into her purse. Slipped on her shoes.

Pulled her top over her head and joined Nadolny and Nestler in the office. She was hungry. The photographer started packing up. Helene asked Stadlmann if he'd gotten all the shots he needed. Dr. Stadlmann nodded and also began to pack his equipment in its case. Nadolny and Nestler came out of the office with the woman. They were going for lunch. The photographer wanted to have a quick word with Nadolny. Nadolny took him into his office. Then they all left. Nobody had talked with Dr. Stadlmann. Nestler seemed to have avoided it on purpose. Helene watched helplessly. She asked Dr. Stadlmann if he'd like to go for lunch with her. He said no. It'd be too exhausting for him. He had his car outside and had to go back. Some people, as a matter of fact, had to work. Helene apologized for the behavior of the others. Could she get him something to eat? They could have a bite right here. Or had his mother prepared a meal so that he had to go home. Helene managed to talk Stadlmann into staying. She left him behind with Frau Sprecher. When Helene left, the two of them were already chatting about the effects of magnetic foil on animals. Helene went shopping at the Greissler. Sausage. Meatloaf. Rissoles. Salad. Caraway rolls. Mineral water. Apple juice. Helene wouldn't have minded a beer. But she didn't dare. When she got back, Frau Sprecher had organized everything on the conference table in Nadolny's office for an office picnic. Frau Sprecher was wearing a piece of foil on her neck. For the tensions. Helene hesitated for a moment because of the table. Frau Sprecher reassured her. They wouldn't come back in the afternoon, she said. Helene wondered if Nadolny was going to cover for the meal. She had spent 289 schillings. All together, she now had 6621 schillings left.

Helene was alone in the apartment. She had come home and found a note. The grandmother had taken the children to one of her girlfriends. They would have supper there and be back by 9 o'clock. On the note, the children had drawn little hearts for her and were sending her kisses. Helene sat down in her reading chair. She felt too heavy to stay upright any longer. She was too tired to go to bed. She was afraid of lying down. And of how everything would press her down into the mattress. And leave no room for air. Helene leaned back in her chair. Closed her eyes. The headache was gone. Her head felt spacious. Too spacious. Bright. There was ample space for the questions when Henryk would call, why he hadn't called, if he was ever to call again. Helene started to cry. A wave of misery rolled from her abdomen through her chest behind her eyes. Tears flowed. Pressed themselves out under her eyelids, and the sobbing followed. Shook her with violent thrusts. She wanted to have him. She wanted to have Henryk. She had wanted to have him. She wanted to have him kneel in front of her. Be aware of his presence. She wanted to have his skin against hers. She wanted to know him. And it had to be now. Right away. 3 hours of a crying jag and still no miracle. Henryk hadn't been conjured up. The phone rang. Helene didn't pick it up. It could have been Püppi. What was left to say. And Henryk. If it had been Henryk. She had loved him until just now. And now it was over. She would have to die for this love to be prolonged. Into eternity. Helene kept seeing Gregor come onto the terrace. So matter of course, so carefree. How he'd played happy family with her best friend. She herself non-existent. Not present. How he'd played his part without any memory of his own children. Played the father for Sophie. And how at the same time Henryk probably had stepped, in a similarly carefree manner, onto some other terrace. And how this way, at least, there was no point in dying. Helene was shaken by another crying fit when the thought hit her that her children would have to go through the same thing. Inevitably. The phone rang again. Helene cried. Feelings of guilt. Because, mind you, it was only a private tragedy. It only affected her. And was it important. So many terrible things could happen. A child could be sick, or die. What then. Outside the May sun was setting. The treetops in front of the window were bending in a wind. You could see the evening sky orange-pink behind the treetops. Helene sat in her chair. The same way she had let herself fall into it. She was exhausted. She figured she should be glad. Actually. She hadn't had the opportunity to say all of this to Henryk. She hadn't often spoken the words either. Mostly she had only looked at him when he was telling her that he loved her. She hadn't made a fool of herself. Not too much. Not the way she had with Alex. And not at all the way she had with Gregor. No way. At least she hadn't done that. Put up with it, she thought. Put up with something, once again. She remained sitting, immobile. Her body no longer responded. Then she got up. She put clean sheets on the children's beds. The children were excited when they got home. They'd watched dogs at their grandma's friend's place. Aunt Seuter could get one for them as well. They wanted a dog. And they would take care of everything. And be very kind to the dog. Helene didn't want to discuss it. We'd have to think about it really carefully. They should have a quick bath now. If they liked, she'd read to them afterwards. The children went, reluctant. Helene read from Don Quixote.

The phone rang at 10 o'clock. Helene unplugged the jack and went to bed.

The next day they all slept in. It was Saturday. Helene woke because the doorbell rang. She had left the key in the lock. She didn't want to be surprised by Gregor. She should have changed the lock. But that would cost too much money. Helene put on her bathrobe. Didn't even look in the mirror. Not for Gregor. She even took delight in looking haggard in front of Gregor. She'd send him home anyway. Helene left the chain attached and opened the door a crack. "We're all still in bed. Your mother was out with the children till late yesterday," she said through the crack. "In that case coffee is required. It's almost 11 o'clock," Henryk answered. Helene slammed the door. For a moment she stood there frozen. Then she pulled the chain off the catch. Opened the door. Left it open and ran to the bathroom. He should make himself comfortable in the living room. She'd be with him in a moment. She was shouting through the closed bathroom door. Helene washed her face. She soaked the face cloth in freezing cold water and put it on her eyes. The bones around her eyes hurt from the cold. Helene put on some foundation. Immediately washed it off again. There was nothing she could do. She looked miserable. She went into the kitchen and started to make coffee. She went to wake up the children. Katharina was sitting at her desk, drawing. Barbara was asleep. Helene sent Katharina to the bathroom. She went back to the kitchen. Henryk sat in the living room. Helene asked him into the kitchen. He was a stranger to her. She didn't know what to talk about with him. Henryk looked rested. Healthy. An early morning glow. He hadn't been able to reach her. So he'd simply come. Had he made a mistake. He could easily leave again and come back later. For a long time, Helene said nothing. She busied herself with kitchen utensils. Groceries. Crockery. First of all, let's have breakfast together, Henryk suggested. Then we'll talk.

They sat at the kitchen table, having breakfast. Katharina was dressed. Barbara was in her bathrobe. Sleepy. She mumbled again and again into her cocoa that she could have slept so much longer. Helene hadn't had any time yet to get dressed. She wanted to get herself ready while the others ate breakfast. The doorbell rang. Urgently. Several times, impatiently. Helene was just sugaring her coffee. "That's Dad," Barbara called and raced to the door. Helene wanted to call her back. But how could she. How could she call, "You mustn't open the door for your father." Barbara turned the key which was still in the lock. The door sprang open. Barbara threw herself into Gregor's arms. "Daddy!" She pulled Gregor into the kitchen. To the table. Got him a plate and a cup. Helene could see the scene through Gregor's eyes. Katharina shy and slumped over. Helene fresh out of bed, in her bathrobe. Doing domestic chores. Her hair pulled back with an elastic band. Pale. Deep lines running from the inner corners of her eyes down her cheeks. From crying. Helene also got these dark shadows under her eyes after nights of heavy love-making. Who would know better than Gregor. And then Henryk. A stranger at Gregor's place at the table. Having breakfast. Barbara had to get an extra chair for Gregor. Henryk immediately got up to welcome Gregor. Barbara said to Henryk, "This is my dad." Henryk shook Gregor's hand. Barbara pushed the chair toward Gregor. Next to Katharina, who was drinking her cocoa. Who said nothing and watched everything. Helene poured Gregor a cup of coffee and left to get dressed. In the bathroom it occurred to her how similar the two men were. Both slender. Henryk taller. Both had dark hair and light colored eyes. Henryk's hair was darker. And longer. But otherwise. The same way of dressing. Henryk was 10 years younger than Gregor. At least. Helene didn't know exactly how old Henryk was. She washed her face. Then she sat on the edge of the tub and wondered. Why had Henryk come. He hadn't phoned even once. Daily calls had been promised. Why had Gregor shown up. How was she supposed to talk to him. What was going on with Püppi. Was Frau Gärtner still in the picture. Most of all, Helene would have liked to ditch the whole lot of them. But, then again, she didn't feel strongly enough about doing that either. There were no feelings. She was toneless inside. And nothing surprised her. She would have preferred to climb into bed and pull the covers over her head. Helene turned on the shower. Watched the water and listened to the drumming. But then she pulled herself out of her trance. She washed herself with the face cloth. Getting wet, particularly on her back, was too much of an effort. Helene didn't put on any makeup. Anybody who wanted to deal with her would have to take her as she was. She dressed and went back to the breakfast table. Katharina had left. The two men were immersed in a conversation about Italian politics. Barbara sat next to them and listened. Helene started to clear the table. Henryk jumped up and helped. So Gregor was forced to help as well. The men continued talking to each other while they loaded the dishwasher. Helene took Gregor's paper and sat down in the living room. She had no food in the house. She should quickly run to the store. Yesterday, she hadn't done a thing. How could she leave the apartment while Gregor was there. Or should she send Gregor away. The men were standing in the kitchen, talking. Then Gregor started to leave. He said good-bye to the children. He didn't have time to take them anywhere or do anything with them. He had to work. "Say hi to Püppi," Helene called out to him from the living room. Gregor came to the door. He looked at her. "What do you mean by that?" he asked. Cool. Helene gave a little laugh. "Just spare me your little speeches," he hissed. For a moment his face was distorted with fury. Helene smiled back at him. Gregor turned immediately to the children. Responded to Barbara's complaints that he never had any time for them in an exaggerated gentle voice. Helene laughed. Gregor left, slamming the door. Henryk came from the kitchen and sat with Helene. Helene continued to laugh for a long time.

Helene sat in the living room. Henryk was talking with Katharina. The child was leaning against Helene, propping herself up against Helene's knees. Helene wanted to send her away. But Katharina pushed against her. Helene asked Henryk how long he'd been back in Vienna. Or if he'd come from the station. How did he manage to look so fresh after a night on the train. Henryk sat there. Smiled, answered her questions. He told Katharina how it is when you have a shower at the station. Henryk had crossed his legs. He jiggled his upper leg. It looked very elegant. And confident. Helene sent Katharina to check on Barbara. And Barbara was to get dressed. The child left, reluctantly. Stopped and waited at the door. Had to be downright shooed away. Helene got up and walked to the window. She looked out into the green foliage of the treetops. Henryk remained sitting. Watched her. She spun around to face him. Quickly, violently. To yell at him. Said nothing. Again turned her back on him and looked out the window. Henryk sat in the chair she'd been crying in the day before. Helene hadn't been able to say anything. Just when she was about to accuse him she'd forgotten what it was she should say. Anything she might say was ridiculous. All of a sudden it was ridiculous to say it. How was this man to understand. He knew nothing about her. At least no more than she knew about him. And now the little she did know she no longer really wanted to know. She no longer wanted to go to bed with him. Didn't even want to remember it. She didn't want him to sit on that chair. Where she had separated from him. Separated from her idea of him. And wasn't this all terrible enough? How would she get rid of him. Ask him to leave? Just be polite and ask him to leave. Like the man from the Credit Union. Helene walked back to the couch. Sat down again. She would tell him to leave. And she should make a quick run to the store. It was half past eleven. The shops closed at noon. Helene was impatient. Henryk bent forward and said, "I've come to you because I thought I could stay with you." Helene looked at him. She heard herself say, "No problem." And, "Where's your luggage then." He'd left it in a locker at the South Station. But. It was just the bag she knew. Helene watched herself and listened to her voice. How the words came out. How he embraced her. Cautiously and brotherly. How she let herself be embraced. How they drove to the Meinl in the Krottenbachstrasse. How the store had already been closed for the weekend. How they drove back. How she took a duvet out of the closet. Gregor's duvet, which at some point she had put away. How she prepared the bed. How she wondered what she should say to the children. Or might have to say to them. Except for Gregor, no other man had slept there ever. And Helene watched herself not wanting any of this. How she hated Henryk. Because of the many hours he'd kept her waiting for a phone call. The hours she'd been staring at the phone. How she would have liked to yell at him for that. Hit out at him. And how she'd immediately accept. Any explanation he'd give her. And how all of it was happening because of Gregor. How it all was the way it was because Gregor had handed a stuffed animal to somebody else's child. How she was afraid. Of being alone with Henryk in the evening. And how she felt nothing of herself.

The children were no problem. Helene had no food in the house. It was a beautiful day. She wanted to be outside. The children stuffed a bag with books and apples. Helene packed a blanket, and they drove to the Vienna Woods. From her trips with Alex, Helene could remember an inn. Though they'd never actually gone there. Alex of course couldn't be seen with her. So they used to meet at the entrance to the Döblinger Cemetery and drive to the Vienna Woods. In her car. Because no one would recognize it. They'd talked and laughed. At home, Helene had an envelope with photos of their dates. Gitta had sent a private investigator after them. There were only photos of them driving along in the car. And one photo with their cars parked next to each other. And one of them drinking coffee in the Salettl. Months later, Gitta had still been bitter about the cost of the photos. Eventually she'd given them to Helene as a present. As she wasn't in the photos, after all. Helene still felt sick when she thought about it. Somebody had been following them, taking photos. And they hadn't noticed. On these trips Helene had always noticed the sign, "Fine Dining at Bonka's." That's where she was headed now. Bonka's was a rambling Gasthaus with a gloomy pub. There was a narrow front yard where patrons could sit. And they had Wiener Schnitzel with French fries for the children. And ketchup. After the meal, they walked along one of the wide paths under the beeches of the Vienna Woods. In a clearing, they put the blanket on the grass and sat down. At first Katharina stayed close to Helene. Henryk seemed to be enjoying himself. He chatted away with the children. Made jokes. The children talked about school. About their grandmother. And about what Aunt Seuter's dogs had done. What they were called. How cute they'd been. And how they were getting a dog. If Mom let them. Henryk was talking about his dog. A setter called Lord Byron. Henryk had loved him a lot. But he traveled too much. You couldn't do that to a dog. But he thought having a dog was important, particularly at their age. The children were thrilled with Henryk. They'd found an ally. Helene was tired. Henryk had found the clearing where they were sitting. Helene had gone along with it all. She'd paid the bill. She'd stopped the car where Henryk and the children had said she should. She'd followed behind on the walk. She'd sat down on the grass. She wasn't able to think back on the morning. About what it all meant. What Gregor must have thought finding her in her bathrobe at breakfast with a complete stranger. What it meant for her situation. She told herself to see a lawyer. She just had to find one her father didn't know. It couldn't be all that difficult. Helene sat leaning against a tree. Barbara was walking around. Katharina was sitting on the blanket, drawing. Henryk had brought the newspaper and started reading. Helene thought the whole thing wasn't working. She needed to rouse herself to do something. To find a solution. Rouse herself. The word alone made her drown again in fatigue. Helene dozed. In the past, she wouldn't have been able to. In the past, she'd always needed to be busy with something. She wouldn't have been able to sit around. Just to sit there. And look. The light made little bright spots dance on the ground. The grass was long and thin. Light green. The beech trunks silver-gray. They looked smooth. Against her back, the beech felt coarse and cracked. A breeze bent the tufts of grass. Made the light spots flare up with a flash and then die away in the shade. It was warm. Helene had had some beer with lunch. The drowsiness from the beer made her thinking even fuzzier. As she fell asleep, Helene suddenly remembered her dream from last night. She had dreamed she was able to play each and every musical instrument. She could remember nothing else from the dream. But she could still connect with the pleasure of having mastered all the instruments. She had to smile. When she woke up, she was alone in the clearing. Helene didn't hear a sound. Only the wind in the trees. Fear for her children shot through her into her nipples. She knew nothing about this man. Memories of movies flashed through her head. Henryk could have. The children. Helene sat there leaning against the tree. An instant would be enough. The instant of the crime, and nothing would ever be the same again. Her panic was smothered by resignation. By her desire to have nothing to do with anything ever again. Helene thought about how much she loved these children. Why was she not satisfied with just bringing them up. Why was she not satisfied. Helene could hear the children. They were squealing. Coming closer. Playing tag. Helene closed her eyes. She pretended to have been asleep the whole time. "Sleepyhead," the children called and danced around her.

It was not until late in the evening that Helene was alone with Henryk. They'd been to a Heuriger. Coming home, the children had rung the bell at Grandma's. The old woman had to be invited over. She had two glasses of sherry. Got rosy cheeks and gave Helene a wet kiss on the cheek when she left. She understood completely, she'd whispered to Helene. Henryk was on the best of terms with everybody. Even with Gregor. Helene got some water for her bourbon. The children had finally fallen asleep. The kitchen was still a mess. Helene had only just put the breakfast milk and butter in the fridge. The men had stacked the crockery in the dishwasher. But they had left the cutlery on the table. The jams. The sugar pot. The box of cornflakes and the napkins. The table cloth was stained and covered with crumbs. The coffee pot sat in the sink. The coffee filter next to it. Rags were lying around. The apples they'd taken on their trip but never eaten. On the fridge. The blanket from the picnic was thrown over the back of a chair. In the hallway the children had left their dirty sneakers. Dirty laundry was piled up in the bathroom. Wet towels. Sponges and face cloths everywhere. Tomorrow, Helene thought. She went back to Henryk. She meant to tell him that perhaps he'd better find himself a room. Henryk smiled at her. Helene couldn't remember at all what it had been like when they were making love. And why she'd been longing so much. For him. Henryk smiled at her. "I'm in your hands now. Totally. There's nowhere else for me to go," he said. Helene stiffened. The phone rang. Helene mumbled an "Excuse me, please" and picked it up. It was Püppi. Helene hung up right away. The phone immediately rang again. Helene pulled the jack. "Why's that?" she wanted to know from Henryk. "What's going on?" Henryk told her how he'd been living in Milan with a German woman, a doctor's daughter from Munich. He had separated from her. But he'd had to leave. For the time being. Until she moved. Then he would have the room until the end of September. And right now. Right now he had nothing. And of course he wanted to move to Vienna. And he would look for work. If worst came to worst, he'd give private lessons. And wasn't she in the least bit happy. Now they were able to be together. Helene was unable to grasp any of what he was going on about. "Let's go. First we'll get your luggage," she suggested. It was around 11 at night. The South Station surely would still be open. They drove to the South Station.

Helene took the Gürtel to the South Station. Traffic was heavy. It stopped again and again in front of the striptease bars and brothels on the Gürtel. Jammed. Helene made way by taking the outside lane. Cars were parked in the 2nd lane. Drivers in the 3rd lane slowed down. Sizing up the hookers tottering on their high heels, smoking. People lined up in front of ice-cream parlors. Or licked their ice-cream cones. Helene didn't speak. Henryk sat next to her. He looked straight ahead. Not for a moment did he pay attention to the blinking lights or the screaming, laughing, ice-cream-eating people. Through the whole trip to the South Station he remained silent. Helene found a parking spot on the side of the station facing the Swiss Garden. When she wanted to get out, Henryk held her back. Helene let herself drop back into her seat. She said nothing. Henryk held her wrist. He would go in there alone now. Not to worry. Oh yes, he understood. Wordless, Helene stayed. She looked at the road. Few cars drove past here. The station behind them was lit brightly. The lights cast the whole area in an orange-colored shadowlessness. Helene asked Henryk why he hadn't phoned. Nor given her any idea that he was coming. After all, he knew her situation. "I thought it's enough that I love you," he said. "But. Henryk. If you don't show me, how am I supposed to know?" "I thought love is above such things. I wasn't aware that I should have. I thought you knew. Surely you know. Helene. You must know that I love you." Helene tore herself away from sitting there. And from staring into space. She got out of the car. She felt hollow and nauseated. She had to laugh. She walked to the entrance. Men were standing around under the portico. Bearded, dark-skinned men, motionless. A Kurier vendor walked between them, waving his papers. But he too was silent. Helene walked through the group. She would have liked to bump into them. Jostle them. Start an argument. Have a horrific screaming match. The men didn't even see her. Let her thread her way through. Didn't make way for her. The lockers were straight ahead. "So what's your number?" Helene asked. Henryk reached into his pants pocket. Started to rummage. Patted the outside pockets of his jacket. Put his hands back into his pants pocket. Then into the inner pockets of the jacket. He repeated his search. He looked at Helene in despair. Bewildered. He stood under the neon lights in the hallway leading to the lockers. And began his search a third time. Hastily. Helene took his hand. She pulled him into the seedy station bar. "What we need is some absinthe," she said. "You'll find it vile. But that's what we need now." Helene ordered two sweet absinthes. Asked if they had any. The woman behind the counter said they did and put two shot glasses in front of them. Carefully. The woman poured the absinthe from a bottle. The little glasses were filled to the brim. About to overflow. The woman laughed. Helene drank without lifting her glass. She bent over her glass and sucked up the green liqueur. She had to giggle and almost choked. She looked at the woman. Both laughed. Henryk took his brimming glass, lifted it up and drank. He didn't spill a drop. "You were pretty generous," Helene coughed. The waitress was young and plump. Under her blonde peroxide hair, darker offspring pushed their way up and out. "It's my birthday today," she said. She burst again into loud laughter. Henryk invited her to have a drink. She was no longer up to it, she sighed with a smile. She'd had too much already. You could tell from the way she filled their glasses, couldn't you. She wasn't really sober anymore. Helene and Henryk drank another absinthe to her health. Giggling, Helene bent over her glass. "Now you'll have to wear Gregor's pajamas. He left them all behind." They laughed. The pants would be too short. Yes. "D'you think I'll need them?" Henryk asked. He put his arm around Helene's waist and pulled her close. Helene let herself fall against him. Later in bed she put her hand over Henryk's mouth whenever he would moan even the slightest bit. The children didn't wake up.

Helene had to get up many times to check that the bedroom door was really locked.

Sunday was Mother's Day. The grandparents in Hietzing wanted to see the children. Helene went there. During the long drive through the Vienna Woods and past the Schottenhof Helene wondered what to do with Henryk. Taking him to her parents was out of the question. Leave him in the car? Helene drove past her parents' house and parked a bit further down. She told Henryk she'd be back soon and let the children climb out of the car on the driver's side. If Henryk had gotten out of the car, they could have seen him from the house. Henryk just smiled. She should take her time. If she were gone for very long, he'd go for a walk. Helene smiled back, grateful. The children had already dashed to the garden gate and were ringing the bell. When they saw their grandfather, they began bouncing up and down and shouting they had something for Grandma. A secret. Helene had found her Mother's Day gifts on the breakfast table. Barbara had crocheted a pot holder, and Katharina had embroidered a pincushion. Helene had had to use the pot holder right away and had to hide how badly she'd immediately burned herself. The pot holder had been crocheted very loosely. The pincushion had already been filled with pins and put into her sewing basket. The children had paid close attention to the way their gifts were received. For the grandmothers the children had drawn little cards. With hearts and kisses. And all the best to the Grandmas too. Helene's father was happy to see the girls. He laughed and entered into the spirit of the secret. Helene watched him. With his grandchildren he became a stranger to her. And the children didn't fear him. Helene went into the house with them. She had nothing for her mother. She wished her all the best. Her mother knew from many terrible scenes over the years that Helene didn't celebrate Mother's Day. Helene was disappointed. Her mother no longer cared. She no longer got upset, was no longer hurt. She turned to the grandchildren. Helene stood in the hallway. She asked in surprise, "You don't really need me, do you?" "No. Not at all. It's okay if you want to go. But don't pick them up before afternoon tea." Her father didn't even look at her. Helene kissed the children. Told them to behave. Left. The short path through the front yard. Slammed the garden door shut and ran to the car. Yanked the door open. Threw herself on the seat and started the engine. She drove off with squealing tires as if someone were chasing her. Henryk looked at her astonished. He'd pulled a small book from his pocket and had started to read. Only after they'd reached the Hietzinger Platz did Helene begin to drive normally. "Well? What do we do now?" she asked. Helene would have liked to drive back. Home to the Lannerstrasse. And go to bed with Henryk. Without worrying about the children. For as long as they wanted to. She had imagined this when she asked her father whether she was really needed. "We'll go on a trip," Henryk said. "A Sunday excursion!" "North, south, east, or west?" Helene asked. She was disappointed. But she wasn't able to say what she had wanted.

Helene drove to the Burgenland. At first toward Laxenburg. Then on to Eisenstadt. The day was mild. Changing from sunny to cloudy. A light breeze made the petals swirl off the apple trees. Helene took country roads. Tulips and laburnum were still in bloom in the gardens. Shrubs too. Past St. Margarethen, Helene turned onto a dirt road. She drove up a hill. From here they could see Lake Neusiedel. Reflecting the light. Long and narrow. They got out of the car and followed the path. Henryk grabbed Helene's shoulder. They looked out onto the lake and sat down under an apricot tree on the edge of a vineyard. Sitting, they couldn't see the lake. Helene stood up. Sat down again. Wanted to sit in the tree. Henryk laughed and stood up as well. He embraced her. Held her tight. Helene felt him. How he pressed hard against her. They kissed. Henryk wanted to leave. He let go of her. Helene pulled him back into the embrace. Above his shoulder, she looked around. There was nobody there. It was lunch time. Nobody was on the road. Everybody at their Sunday lunches. With all the Mother's Day mothers. Helene pulled Henryk to the ground and bent down over him. She opened the zipper of his flannel pants and took it in her mouth. She licked, lapped, sucked, and rubbed his cock. With her lips. Her tongue. Her palate. His semen filled her mouth. For a moment she couldn't breathe. She could have gone on much longer. She had forgotten everything else. Helene swallowed the semen. A bitter white taste. Henryk had not made a sound. Helene did not dare look at his face. Suddenly she was terribly embarrassed. She jumped up and walked back along the path. Climbed up the hill. Looked from there out onto the lake. She felt terrible. She should have controlled herself. She stood on the hill and didn't know how she would get back to the car. Henryk stood at the bottom and waved at her to come down. Helene sat down on the grass. Maybe he'd come up to her. Then everything would be all right again. But he didn't come. Climbing down the hill, Helene slipped. She scraped the palms of her hands. On her right hand she grazed those same spots where she'd burned herself in the morning. She came back to the car with tears in her eyes. Henryk looked at her hands. Asked for the first aid kit. Dabbed disinfectant on her wounds and applied Band-Aids. He asked if she'd had her tetanus shots and wanted the car key. "Oh, Helene!" he said and kissed her on her forehead. Helene couldn't speak. Henryk took her in his arms and held her. Helene thought about having to cry now, after all. She leaned against him. Buried her face in his shoulder. She couldn't think anything. Let herself be held. Helene was sad. Deeply sad. In the darkness, leaning against his shoulder, she remembered the man and the woman. The woman had worn something red. The man had been dark. A suit. Distinguished. The two had stood at the corner of Lannerstrasse and Cottagegasse. They were bent over the child. The child had been half lying under a bicycle. It did not move. Helene had passed in her car. The man and the woman had just straightened up again. Had looked around. Helene had never been able to find out what had happened. Now, leaning against Henryk's chest, she saw over and over the woman half bending over the child. How she'd turned her head. And the man, straightened again, standing up. Turning his upper body. Looking around in all directions. The child motionless. Helene tasted Henryk's semen. Dry. Dusty. Bitter. And warm. The child lay motionless. The child had been lying motionless. The child had been older than her children were now. 10 or 12 years old. Helene felt the cloth of Henryk's jacket against her right cheek. She opened her eyes. The hill lay behind Henryk's shoulder. The sky above it. Blue with clouds. The sun behind a cloud. Helene looked into the sky. This way, she didn't have to see the child. How it had lain there. And how the adults had bent over it. Helene felt weak. Later they had lunch in Rust. Helene picked up the children at 6 o'clock. They had eaten a lot of cake. They didn't want any supper. Helene wanted to go to sleep. Henryk felt like going out. Helene gave him the keys to the apartment and the front door. Lying in bed, she tried. Before falling asleep. Tried to remember. When it had been. The accident with the child.

Helene woke up at 2 a.m. Henryk was coming in. She heard
the apartment door. How he unlocked and locked it again.
He tried not to make any noise and tiptoed into the bedroom. He undressed by the light of the street lamps. Helene
watched him. Henryk was undressing. Calm and careful,
he took off one piece of clothing after the other. Then he
stood there naked. Searched under the pillow for the
pajamas. While he was standing there naked, Helene suddenly realized. Henryk was circumcised. That's why his
penis was always long and full. And Helene had thought it
had been desire. For her. The beginning of it, anyway.
Helene was ashamed of her ignorance and her lack of expe-
rience. She could have screamed with anger at herself. And
shame. She wished she didn't depend so much on discover-
ies.

Helene went to the Ögussa branch in the Kaiserstrasse.
Henryk had borrowed 2000 schillings. Helene had tried to
explain to him how little money she had. But he had needed
it. She had to understand that. He couldn't be walking
around without a penny in his pockets. And he'd be earning money as soon as possible. And he was owed money
from Italy. And his parents could send him some. But
Helene's money was gone. On Tuesday she had prepared
Kaiserschmarren pancakes for supper. She had used one egg
less than the recipe called for. She'd had everything else in
the house. For breakfast, she'd opened the last tetrapack of
UHT milk and poured it over the cornflakes. But that was
the end of the cornflakes now too. She needed to buy bread,
eggs, and ham. There was no toothpaste left. Helene had
squeezed the tube with the back of a knife to get some toothpaste onto the children's toothbrushes. She had brushed her
own teeth with salt. The toiletries Henryk had needed because he couldn't find the key to the locker had cost a lot.

Helene drove to Kaiserstrasse before work. She had phoned. The shop opened at half past 7. The shop was small. A door with a glass panel. Gold letters, "We buy silver and gold," were glued on. And the Ögussa logo on the door. The door was gray and dusty. The glass panel smeared. Inside, everything was old and worn. Having been neglected for a long time. A very old woman and a man of around 60 stood in the store. Behind the counter, a man in a gray dust coat. He wore reading glasses that had slid down to the tip of his nose. He turned to the old woman. He spoke in a low voice, indifferent. Helene knew right away it would be pointless to negotiate with this man. The man didn't really see the people in the store. He addressed a point high up on the wall when he talked to customers. He had two silver spoons on a pair of scales. Coffee spoons. He watched the indicator until it stood still. "127 schillings," he said. The old woman made a reluctant sound. The man took the money from a drawer and counted it on the table for her. He turned to the man in front of Helene. The old woman looked at the money for a long time. Then she took it. And left. Helene saw herself, selling her last silver spoons. 127 schillings. That would be 9 or 10 sandwich buns with ham, perhaps. Or 15 with sausage. For three. Or now, for four. Could you live off that for a day. And hopefully there was still a supply of coffee. Helene wondered what she owned and might be able to sell. The man in front of her put little nuggets on the counter. In a few spots the nuggets were shiny. Otherwise they were gray. The man in the gray coat put a jeweler's loupe in front of one of his eyes and examined the nuggets. He held them with tweezers. Then he weighed them. "4426 schillings," he said. The man shrugged. Helene watched the money being counted onto the table and taken away. Helene waited till the man had put the money into his wallet and left. She had the necklace in the pocket of her jacket. She handed it to the man. The necklace was warm from her hands. Helene blushed. The man studied the necklace with his loupe, examined the hallmarks, counted the gold ducats hanging from the links of the necklace. Helene had inherited the necklace from an old neighbor. One day she had come home, and her mother had handed her a little box. This was for her, she had said. And turned away. Helene had opened the box and found the necklace. The old neighbor had written best wishes for a good life on a paper and tucked it under the necklace. For My Dear Helene, she had written. The heirs had dropped it off that day. The old woman had wanted Helene to have it. Helene looked at the necklace as it dangled from the hand of the man with the gray coat. Had the neighbor intended this ending for her necklace. "I can give you 9600 schillings for it," the man said. Helene was glad to be alone in the store. She took the money and left. On her way to the car she tried to remember the name of the old neighbor. She couldn't. This had all happened 15 years ago, roughly. She should ask her mother. Gratitude toward the old woman welled up in Helene. She could hardly remember her. Had never had much to do with her. The old woman had sometimes looked from her patio into the garden of Helene's parents and waved. Helene stayed in her car. Thought that all this wasn't too difficult. Having your Eurocheck card confiscated. Selling jewelry. The bailiff hadn't come yet. But no doubt the bank would send him, too. Suddenly Helene felt she could do it. She'd be able to. She had more jewelry left. For the time being, nobody would starve. Helene drove to the office. The nuggets the fat man had put on the counter were gold fillings. From teeth. Helene was sure. How would you get those. She hadn't been able to see the fat man's teeth. But could you simply yank gold fillings

out of your own teeth. That seemed difficult to Helene.
Where would you get such nuggets?

At the office Helene found the photos. They were useless.
What they had overlooked or had refused to see with their
bare eyes could no longer be ignored in the black-and-white
photos. The model's skin was wrinkled. On her back the
skin was flabby, depending on how she held her arms and
shoulders. Even worse along the costal arches. Dark stretch
marks on her shoulders, close to the joints. The skin was
bunched in wide folds and hung down over the elbows. It
looked as if the woman had been fat and had lost weight
very quickly. Cellulitis scars showed on her buttocks. Helene
suddenly realized why women in nude shots always stick
their bums right out. Or bend forward. For the shots with
the foil on her hip the woman had been forced to stand
upright. Helene showed the pictures to Frau Sprecher. They
agreed these photos were no invitation to use magnetic foils.
Helene and Frau Sprecher made fun of the model. While
drinking coffee. The woman's name was Sabine Novotny.
The name was on the agency's bill which had also arrived
in the mail. At last Frau Sprecher understood why the
woman had suggested Nestler call her 'Bee' or 'Bini'. She'd
overheard it when bringing the coffee. What a performance! And without justification. As indeed the incorrupt-
ible eye of the camera now showed. Helene and Frau
Sprecher were very satisfied. They had known it all along.
Helene was astonished. How could anybody not have noticed. She could still see the woman's tanned body. And the
two men in the doorway to Nadolny's office. And how
they had left. The two men with the model in their midst.
Swinging her mini-skirt, provocatively. And how everybody
had been aware there were no panties under this tiny skirt.
Helene presented the photos to Nadolny. Were they good

enough, she asked him. With every picture Nadolny grew more furious. He started hurling insults. At the woman. Who was a cheat. Had tricked him. Had shown up as a nude model but looked a tattered granny in the photos. Helene asked how they were to get any photos now. Nadolny threw the photos on his desk in disgust. "Now. We'll have to do the whole damn thing over again," he sighed. And Helene wasn't to send a penny to the agency. He'd look into it. And now they were in a sorry pickle. Nestler had taken a fancy to Sabine. Right away. They'd hit it off well. Maybe Sabine was even with him, in Switzerland. So they would have to use the photos. Really. But of course he could never show them to Nestler. Should he, Nadolny, display to Nestler what his floozy looked like. In reality. Without 5 glasses of Champagne and vodka tonics? On the other hand. Nestler would ask. Would want the photos. Possibly even enlargements. Nadolny groaned. Helene thought it perfect. Hadn't the men let themselves get totally carried away? It served them right. Nadolny bent over his desk. Would she stop grinning, please. He said to Helene. It was all her fault. In the end, it all came down to being her fault. What had been the point of having her there. After all, guys can't think straight with a naked woman in the room. She should have seen it right away. She should have noticed. Indeed. Nadolny glared at Helene. For a moment, Helene didn't know what to say. She was indignant. She immediately had to fight back tears. The injustice of the accusations. Then she got furious. Helene felt her eyes narrow and her cheeks blush. She took a deep breath. Would there have been any point, she asked. Or would it even have been possible. To say anything in front of Nestler. Well? Since both, Nestler and Nadolny, had been so convinced of the young lady's virtues. She herself couldn't care less. Because she simply didn't care about anything. If it was anybody's job to notice anything, it was the photographer's. Nestler and he, after all, had been like rutting stags. And he had picked the model. She had assumed he had some expertise in such affairs. That he was an expert. Why would she question that. Helene got up and went back to her desk. She had trouble closing the door to Nadolny's office quietly. She tossed the thick envelope with the photos on her desk and dropped into her chair. Frau Sprecher poked her head around the corner. Winked at her. Nadolny could be heard in his room. He was shouting at somebody on the phone. Brusque. Frau Sprecher withdrew. Helene stayed in her chair. Fatigue flooded her again. She should have left. But at least she had said something. She knew she should leave right away. This very instant. Now she should be at the door. Then down the hallway. Call the elevator. Get in and float down. Drive home. Henryk would be there. Henryk stayed in bed till 11 o'clock. She should lie down next to him. And make love. But Henryk never felt like it anymore. He had to think about his situation. And Helene didn't dare throw herself at him like in the beginning. She had to leave it up to Henryk. And Henryk didn't think of it very often. Not as often as Helene would have liked. So driving home was out. Instead she'd drive up the Kahlenberg. Sit on a bench and look around. Then Nadolny came out of his office. Helene still sat in her chair as she had dropped into it. Nadolny walked by. He was getting himself some coffee. He would always get his own coffee when he wanted to refine it with cognac. Otherwise Frau Sprecher had to bring him a cup. Or Helene. She should solve the problem, he said, on his way back to his office. You couldn't expect him to take care of everything. He had his limits, too. Helene booked a new model. A Phys Ed student. Yes. That was probably okay. The photographer was booked once more. He should talk to Nadolny about the fee. Yes. She'd put him through. Dr. Stadlmann was surprised. He had pointed out at the time, hadn't he, that the man should have used a different f-stop. And another lens. No wonder his pictures hadn't turned out. He couldn't come. Helene had to take care of things herself. But she knew what to do. The date for the shoot was set for the coming Friday. Helene informed Nadolny of it. And he should tell Nestler that the photographer had messed up the photos. She had re-arranged everything. Herr Nestler surely wouldn't insist on Sabine. He'd have long forgotten about her. Nadolny nodded and said he wouldn't be in on Friday. She should take care of everything. He didn't want to hear anymore. About this whole affair. Helene quickly went shopping and drove home. Henryk wasn't there. Helene had bought ready-to-eat schnitzels. And a salad. At the Greissler. She put Henryk's schnitzel into the fridge. In the afternoon she was alone in the office. Nadolny had left and wouldn't be coming back. Frau Sprecher had a doctor's appointment. At 4 o'clock Helene dialed the number in Milan. For no particular reason. Only boredom. And curiosity. A man was on the other end. Helene hesitated. He had said, "Ja. Bitte." Helene asked if she could speak to Henryk. The man said that Henryk wasn't there, at the moment. Could he take a message. He'd be back soon. He was expected back for the weekend at the latest. But. Who was she anyway. Helene hung up. Henryk had said his German girlfriend had a new boyfriend. And he would never go back there. Helene left the office half an hour early. She had stomach cramps. Sharp ones. She was glad not to have eaten a lot for lunch.

The phone rang at 2 in the morning. Helene was almost awake. Henryk usually came home around that time. He would get undressed. Try to be quiet. Climb into bed and pull her close to him. Helene would snuggle up. He would hold her in an embrace from behind. And they would sleep. Henryk smelling of cigarette smoke and red wine. He'd be gentle and not want to have sex with her. Helene was longing for it. Longing terribly. But. When he was tipsy, she felt odd about it. She was afraid he wouldn't know who she was. Might call her by a different name. And she would have to react to that. Cuddling was safer. And being sleepy helped. Helene thought it was Henryk. Calling to let her know he'd be coming home later. Helene picked up the phone. At first, she couldn't hear anything. Then. When Helene was about to hang up. A voice rasped, "Helene. Come. Please." Helene could hardly recognize the voice. "Please come," Püppi whispered. Helene heard the receiver at the other end drop and hit something. Then she heard sounds. Distant. Vague. Humming. Splashing. "Püppi! Püppi! What is it. Püppi," Helene shouted into the phone. She heard noises coming from her children's room. She hung up, climbed out of bed, got dressed. She had to look for the key to Püppi's house. After the discovery in the City Park, Helene had wanted to throw the key away. Then she had hurled it into a drawer where she kept everything that didn't belong anywhere else. String. Flower wire. Screw drivers. Old napkin rings. Aluminum foil. Birthday candles. Clothes pegs. Tea lights. Rubber bands. Light bulbs. Soap bars. Dowels. Nails. Keys. Helene ransacked the drawer. Took every key she could find. Was it once again a false alarm. A pill too many. A high turned into a bad trip. A glass of gin after which life no longer made sense. Helene was furious. Why didn't she phone Gregor. What a bitch. Helene put the keys in the pocket of her cardigan. She drove to the Karolinengasse. She had to wait behind a milk truck unloading in the Gusshausstrasse. She was impatient. She would deal with the situation. And make it clear that in future Püppi would be on her own. Maybe Püppi had a

number for Gregor. Püppi sure wasn't one to be put off
easily. The way she. Then she'd get Gregor and let him do
the worrying. Helene found a parking spot almost in front
of Püppi's house. She didn't see any lights in the apartment.
Helene searched for the right key. The last one unlocked
the door. She climbed up to the sixth floor. She gasped with
exertion. And rage. At the same time, fatigue again rolled
over her. An unwillingness to climb these stairs. To deal
with Püppi's problems. Or any other problems. With diffi-
culty, Helene reached the apartment door. Still breathing
heavily, she rang the bell. Cautiously. Touched the bell only
lightly. Helene heard Sophie. The child came toddling into
the hallway. Helene began to talk to the child. It was her.
Lene. Auntelene. Was there a key? In the lock? No? Could
she push the handle down. Just for her. The aunt. Sophie
ran away. Came back. Helene could hear the child lean
against the door. Trying to reach the handle. Sophie reached
the handle a few times. But the handle slipped and snapped
back. Finally she succeeded. Helene pushed the door open.
Carefully. So as not to push Sophie over. The door gave
way easily. Sophie stood there in her nightie. Looking up at
Helene. She beamed. Was proud because she had opened
the door. "Where is your mommy," Helene asked. "Good
evening," Sophie said. It was one of Püppi's games. Nobody was allowed to speak or eat unless they had greeted
each other with courtesy or had said "please" and "thank
you." "Hello, Sophie. Tell me. Where is your mommy."
"Good evening," Sophie said and looked up to Helene with
a serious face. Helene bent down. She held out her hand to
her. "Good evening, Sophie." The child took her hand and
shook it. Then threw herself into Helene's arms. Helene
picked her up and went looking for Püppi, with the child
clinging to her. Püppi lay in the bathtub. Vomit was floating on the water. And bubbles. Püppi's arms hung over the

sides. Her forehead was on the edge of the tub. The water moved slightly, and her face every so often slipped under water. The receiver lay the way it must have fallen from Püppi's hand. The busy signal was sounding. Thin, endless. Helene took Sophie to the bedroom. Put her on the bed. Sophie began to sob. She didn't cry. She sobbed with every breath. Helene talked to the child in a firm voice. Everything will be fine. She just had to get Mommy out of the water. Sophie. Yes? Everything will be fine. Not to cry. No point in crying. Everything will be fine. Not to cry. No point in crying. She'll see. Everything will be fine. It's a promise. Hadn't she always kept her promises. Her Aunt Helene. Helene put the receiver back on the phone first. Pushed the phone aside with her foot. Began to pull Püppi out of the tub. Püppi was very skinny. Her shoulder blades were sharply delineated under the freckled skin on her back. Helene tried to pull Püppi up so that she could put her arms around her and drag her from the tub. Püppi kept slipping away from her. Looking at the vomit, Helene could have started to cry. To scream. With disgust. She could hardly fight down her nausea. Helene finally got hold of Püppi under her armpits. Püppi's big breasts were in the way. Again she slid down. Helene drained the water. She was drenched. In the end, Püppi lay against her chest, and Helene pulled her out of the tub. She almost fell over when Püppi's legs snapped free of the edge of the tub and hit the floor. Helene dragged Püppi through the bathroom to the bedroom. Staggered. Groaned. Cried. Sophie was wheezing. She sat on the bed, her eyes opened wide. With each breath, her little chest convulsed in a spasm. Towels had caught under Püppi's feet. The bathroom mat. And toys. Helene dragged them all along and maneuvered Püppi onto the bed. Püppi's buttocks were coated, brown. Helene could barely breathe. For a moment all she could hear was her own heart beat. Was afraid she'd pass out. The smell of shit was spreading everywhere. Why did Püppi sit in the tub if she couldn't manage to wash it all off, Helene thought. She tucked Püppi in. She couldn't fight down her nausea. She picked Sophie up. The child didn't want to touch her wet clothes and started to scream. Helene put her under the covers and left to phone emergency. No. She didn't know if the person was still breathing. She had pulled her out of the tub, unconscious. Konstanze Storntberg. Yes. Helene spelled the name. She. Her name was Gebhardt. Helene Gebhardt. Helene talked with the man at emergency as if they were at a cocktail party. Was this important right now? Helene asked. Polite. And calm. Helene was squatting in the bathroom. The floor was wet. The trail to the bedroom very obvious. She believed it was very urgent, she said. They always did the best they could, the man said. Equally casual and polite. She was sure they did, Helene replied. A scream stopped in her throat. A screaming. Helene felt caged. Caged within herself and too small. Open the front door, the man said. Helene heard a siren. Could that be them? she asked. Yes. It was possible. The nearest emergency services were in the Nottendorfergasse. At night, that wasn't far. That could well be his colleagues. Helene said good-bye. Thanked him. Didn't want to hang up. Wanted to continue this civilized conversation into all eternity. She went into the bedroom. Sobbed again. Had snot running from her nose. Wiped it away with her sleeve. She grabbed a sweater from Püppi's closet. Yanked it over her head. Picked Sophie up and ran downstairs. Again she didn't know which key to use and cursed Gregor and Püppi and the City Park. Until then, the key had been in her desk drawer and no mix-up possible. Helene fumbled with the lock. In the transom she could see the emergency light, turning. The paramedics talked to her to calm her down . The keys fell from her hand. Sophie wheezed. Helene managed to open the door. Three men in white uniforms stood outside. "On the 6th floor," Helene said. "She's on the 6th floor." "Is she able to walk?" one of the men asked. "No." "Mommy! Mommy!" Sophie started again. The men got the stretcher from the ambulance and began to go upstairs. Helene ran up the stairs with the child in her arms. The men with their steady step passed her. They reached Püppi long before she did.

The ambulance drove to Franz Joseph's Hospital. Helene did as she was told. She spelled Püppi's name. Gave her date of birth. Her address. She didn't know any next of kin. Gave her own personal data. She asked to have Sophie examined. Could the wheezing be a false croup? The child was taken away. Shouldn't she stay with the child? She got no answer. Helene sat on a plastic chair in a corridor. Frosted glass with the words "No Entry" on the door to her right. And bright lights behind it. Shadows of people walking on the other side of the door. On her left, down the corridor, a long row of identical plastic chairs. Disappearing in the dark. Tall windows overlooking the gloomy park. "What does she usually take?" a woman in a white coat asked. She suddenly stood in front of Helene. Helene hadn't seen her coming. "I'm Dr. Stadlmann," the woman said. "She's stabilized now. But of course it'd be better to know what she took." "I'm just the one who gets called when there is another catastrophe." "Would you like some coffee?" the doctor asked. "Oh yes, please," Helene sighed. She was no longer too sure where she was and why. And didn't care either. At the moment. She probably looked ghastly. The doctor came back with coffee in a plastic cup. "We don't have any milk or sugar," she said. "Why are you so wet?" she asked. She fished a pack of cigarettes from her coat pocket. With a lighter, she lit a cigarette. Offered the pack to Helene. "No, thank you. She was in the bathtub," said Helene. "Yes, they like to do that." The doctor sat down next to Helene. Helene sipped at her coffee. With the woman next to her she was suddenly no longer afraid. She got sleepy. "And what about the child?" she asked much later. "Should I take her home?" "I don't know. It won't be too bad. For now." "Yes. For now." Helene stared at the floor in front of her. She leaned forward, elbows propped on her knees. The doctor sat leaning back, her head against the wall. Helene had finished her coffee. The doctor had stubbed out her cigarette in one of the ashtray stands. With her foot, she had pulled the metal stand close. Then the woman put her hand briefly on Helene's arm. "Take care," she said. "Don't get a chill." They smiled at each other. The doctor went back through the door into the room to which entry was prohibited. Helene kept waiting for a long time. Around 5 o'clock she was told Frau Storntberg was in stable condition. The nurse said it, accusingly, as if it was all Helene's fault. The child had been tranquilized and was asleep now. Helene should phone at 8 o'clock to find out what would happen next. The child could be picked up. Then. Most likely. Police and Child Protection Services would be informed. Helene probably realized that. Did they really need to do that? Helene asked. The nurse gave no answer and walked away. Helene stood up and walked off in the opposite direction. She would have liked to thank the doctor again. Helene had to wait a long time for a cab. She took the cab to the Karolinengasse, to her car. From there back to the Lannerstrasse. At 6 a.m., she was back home. The bed was empty. Henryk hadn't come home. Helene flung herself on her bed and cried. She'd been so sure she would be able to tell Henryk of all the terrible things that had happened. While everything had been so terrible, she had thought how she would tell him. And how then everything would be all right again.

Helene woke up at half past 8. She'd overslept. The children hadn't woken up either. Helene called the hospital. She should phone again at noon. By that time, they'd know more. At noon, Helene learned Frau Storntberg had signed out and gone home. She had taken the child with her. No sign out had been needed for the child. Helene didn't phone Püppi.

Helene came home from the office. On her way, she had bought fruit and vegetables at the Sonnberg market. She was carrying the plastic bags straight to the kitchen. From the living room she heard voices. "No. It's not your phone. You mustn't make calls." Henryk was talking to the child insistently. He was friendly. Tried to explain to Barbara why he had to make a call. They seemed to have been going at it for a while. His patience had grown paper thin. Barbara kept yelling at him. Henryk's answers got more testy. It wouldn't take much longer for him to lose his patience. Would he use force with the child? Helene dashed into the living room. Barbara ran up to her and started to cry. Henryk stood at the window with his arms folded. What was going on? Barbara sobbed that Henryk had been on the phone the whole time. And that Grandma would tell them off. Because it was so expensive. Henryk remained standing at the window. He pressed his lips together. Said nothing. Helene took Barbara's hand and went with her to the children's room. Katharina sat at her little desk and wrote into an exercise book. Helene sat down on one of the small chairs. She wanted to start a conversation. About who had what rights. Who was allowed to do what. And if she allowed somebody to use the phone, or the bathroom, or whatever.

How the children had to respect that. In the end, all Helene said was, "Can't you be a bit nicer." Looking up from her work, Katharina said, "Barbara just wanted to call Anita. And she couldn't do it. Because he was on the phone." Helene sighed. "Was he really on the phone all afternoon?" The children nodded and looked at the floor. Helene remained sitting. Just when she wanted to get up and go to Henryk, she heard the apartment door shut. Helene went to check. Henryk had gone. Helene stood at the window for a long time. There. Where Henryk had been standing just then. She was tired. She was worried about Püppi and particularly about Sophie. She was sad. She didn't know how things were with Henryk. For all she knew, it was over. What had he been up to last night. When she thought about it, her stomach contracted in pain. Pushed bile up her throat. Helene unpacked her shopping. Put everything in its place. She would have liked to sleep. But she was afraid she might lie awake all night as a result. She got the phone book and looked for G. G as in Gärtner. There were two entries under Gärtner, Ilse. Helene hesitated for a long time. It was half past 5. Gregor might still be at the department. And so might Frau Gärtner. Helene dialed the number of the Ilse Gärtner who lived in the 7th district. Helene thought she remembered Frau Gärtner had an apartment in the 7th district. She could be wrong. After the 5th ring, the phone was picked up. Frau Gärtner answered by saying her number. Helene recognized her voice right away. Helene gave her name and asked for Gregor. She had to talk to him. Urgently. Was he there. Frau Gärtner said he wasn't. Cool. Helene apologized for the interruption. But. Could Frau Gärtner be so kind and take a message for Gregor. It was about Frau Storntberg. She'd had to be taken to hospital last night. And was in very bad shape. Gregor should look after her. It was his duty. Also because of the child. Frau

Gärtner said nothing. She was sorry, Helene said. But this was an emergency. Frau Gärtner said, in a tight voice, she would pass it on. And hung up. Before Helene could thank her. Then she dialed Gregor's number in the department. Gregor picked up the phone immediately. As if he'd been waiting for a call. Helene said it was only her, unfortunately. Helene hated herself as she said it. Did he know what had happened with Püppi. Püppi had almost died last night. And he should look after her. She was in very bad shape. Why was she telling him this, Gregor asked. He said it provocatively. It really was none of his business. The child did have a father. Helene sat there. She almost crushed the receiver. Again she had the compulsion to plunge a knife into the man's belly. To stab him again and again. "I think the time has come for you to meet your obligations," she said. "What obligations?" Gregor was making fun of her. "Just listen," Helene said. "You're having an affair with the woman. Maybe she even did it because of you." "Did she say that?" Gregor asked. Sharp. Helene bent over and put the receiver down. She put it down very gently. Carefully. The phone rang. Each time it started ringing, Helene lifted the receiver and let it slide down again gently. Everything appeared to her infinitely far away and unreachable. Later she called the children. They went to the Türkenschanz Park. The children hung out in the playground. All the little children had already left. For home. Supper. All the equipment was free, and there were no dogs in sight pissing on the roundabouts and chasing the children. Katharina and Barbara were swinging and sliding and climbing and playing hide and seek and chasing each other. Squealing breathlessly. Helene sat on a bench at the side. Her stomach was a stone ball under her chest, pressing up against her heart. She smiled at the children. Waved. Blew them kisses when one of them waved to her from the climbing tower and yelled, "Mommy! Mommy! Look at me." At the same time she would again smell the water in the bathtub. The water had been cold, greasy. Somewhere beside her, or actually, behind her. Helene was thinking how it could all be over. And what a release. Then the pressure in her throat and the restlessness became too strong. Helene wanted to leave. Go on. Get moving. The children wanted to stay. Helene raised her voice. She heard her voice get higher and higher. Sullen, the children trotted behind her. I can't even leave when I want to, Helene thought. She had to take a deep breath. To relieve the pressure in her throat. Sophie's wheezing came back to her. She took the children's hands and asked what was happening at school. They arrived home talking about all sorts of things. Henryk was in the kitchen, wearing an apron. He'd cooked spaghetti. He grinned at all of them. Helene walked up to him. He opened his arms. While she took the three steps toward him, Helene thought she ought to talk to him. About last night, about the money, about making phone calls. Henryk closed his arms around her. She leaned her forehead against his shoulder. She realized that with each man in her life she had to talk about the same topics. Helene was tired.

Helene drove to Dr. Stadlmann's. The new photos had turned out well. The new model was also called Sabine. Sabine Pototschnigg. She'd been cheerful. Uncomplicated. She'd only asked for the window blinds to be pulled. Frau Sprecher had immediately complied with her wish. And then had made fresh coffee. Helene had been uncertain how to stick on the pieces of magnetic foil. She had done it exactly how Dr. Stadlmann had shown her. But Sabine Novotny's neck had looked different from Sabine Pototschnigg's. Helene hadn't known exactly where the neck ended. Or began. Sabine Pototschnigg was 20. During the shoot, Helene had understood what youthful freshness meant. Without Nadolny and Nestler, the job had been done quickly. Then they had all stayed for coffee. Sabine Pototschnigg and the photographer were cat owners. They'd chatted for a long time about the effects of spaying and neutering. And if you should let them once, before. Or if you should get it done right away. Helene had spoken up for free sex for cats. She didn't know what she was talking about, she was told. Dr. Stadlmann's mother opened the door. Helene smiled at her in a particularly friendly way. The woman showed her in. She didn't smile back. Helene went into the room at the end of the hallway. She felt the woman's distrustful eyes until she had closed the door behind her. Dr. Stadlmann sat behind his desk. He greeted her with a reproach. What was the holdup? They had to get on with it. Somehow. Finally. He'd expected more of Helene. Helene had looked forward to their appointment. She'd thought she'd done everything right. Helene put the photos in front of Dr. Stadlmann on his desk. She said nothing. She sat down on the Naugahyde chair. There were no traces. Or was it a new chair? Helene suddenly remembered how long her period had again been overdue. She should see a gynecologist. Was this why Dr. Stadlmann's mother had looked so reproachful? Just as well, Helene thought. She was waiting for Dr. Stadlmann's comments. Suddenly she lost all interest in them. She no longer was interested. Why should she let herself be bossed around by everyone? Did she have to? "You have to!" she said to herself in her mind. But she didn't have to like it. Dr. Stadlmann looked through the photos. "Well? What's the next step?" Yes. Well. If he thought the photos all right, she'd talk to the designer the next day. They already had the text, of course. And then the first brochure about the application of magnetic foil could go into print. Herr Nestler had requested proposals for the packaging designs. They would have to discuss those too. "I want a female figure. Like the Venus de Milo. Her arms raised. But in gold. She would have to be all in gold. As a symbol of healing power." Helene noted the request. Another nude, she thought. "You're certainly not particularly friendly today," Dr. Stadlmann said to her. Helene pressed her lips together even more tightly. She said nothing. Dr. Stadlmann gave her the number of a certain Professor Chrobath. Who had an institute for acupuncture at the hospital's outpatient service. Surely she knew. There. Where the writer Schnitzler had worked. Professor Chrobath was willing to test the magnetic foil at his institute. Nestler would discuss with him what further support could be given to the trial. Helene got up and gathered up the photos. She took the files and her purse. "I'll give you a call," she said. Offered her hand to Dr. Stadlmann. Said good-bye and left. She would have liked to have said something friendly. She left.

Henryk was leaving. Henryk said he had to go to Milan. To sort out some stuff. Helene took him to the station. The night train to Milan left South Station at 9 p.m. Helene had prepared sandwiches. There was no dining car. And no other opportunity to get something to eat or drink. If you were lucky, you might get something in Udine or Travis. On the platform. They bought a bottle of mineral water at the station snack bar in the main concourse. Diagonally across from the Venetian lion. They went up the escalator. It was still light. The sun low in the west. On the platform, they walked beside the train. Henryk wanted to find a seat close to the front. The sun was shining into Helene's eyes. She carried the plastic bag with the food, Henryk his little travel bag. Helene couldn't say anything. Her throat was compressed. She swallowed repeatedly. She still had to ask

Henryk everything. In all those days, she'd never gotten around to talking with him. During the days, he'd been looking for an apartment. He'd even had a good possibility of getting one in the Schwarzspanierstrasse. In the evenings, he'd gone out after supper. Helene had never joined him. She'd had to sleep. After all, she had to go to work. The children couldn't be left alone that often. And Helene was afraid she might run into Püppi. Henryk had never asked if she'd like to go out, either. He'd said he was meeting people he'd like to do something with. Something musical. Henryk had told Helene he'd stay with friends in Milan. Not with the woman from Munich. Who had a new boyfriend, of course. But even if he did stay with her, it wouldn't matter. He'd be faithful to Helene. She had to know that. Under all circumstances. Walking along the train, Helene asked, "And there's really no way for me to reach you?" Henryk put his arm around her shoulder. He'd call her. Regularly. It's a promise. Really. Helene shouldn't worry so much. Wasn't life quite easy? Actually? Henryk got on the train. He walked along the corridor through the coach and looked into the compartments. Helene walked along on the platform. Then Henryk disappeared. Helene could see him vaguely. Behind the window and compartment door. Vanished into a shadow. He hoisted up his bag, put it on the luggage rack, hung up his raincoat. Left the compartment and walked to the door, stepped down on the platform. Helene couldn't feel a thing. She'd be able to sleep without being bothered, she'd thought, as he was storing his luggage. And she wouldn't always have to keep an eye on how the children got along with him. Helene offered the bag with the food to Henryk. "Don't forget this." "You shouldn't wait. I'll walk you to the front and buy some papers. And you go home. There is no point in waiting here." Henryk took the food to his seat. Returned. They walked back. They cast long shadows which danced with each other as they walked along. Henryk had his arm around Helene's shoulders. They bought a Neue Züricher Zeitung and a Corriere. Then Henryk stood there. Helene gave him a kiss. She left. She didn't turn around. Or she would have had to run. Cling to him. Not let go of him, again. Not turning around was taxing. She bent forward as she walked. To tilt her face downward. And the ache under her breastbone. To reduce this dry burning. Helene was sure she'd never see Henryk again. When she got to her car, she wondered once more if she shouldn't go back. Had to. Wanted to. She could hardly breathe. She should run back. Follow the train. Helene got into her car and drove home, tears running down her cheeks. Over and over, she could see Anna Magnani. How she was running behind the truck. And how the bullets stopped her. And how she wanted to be her. But only in the movie. And Henryk ought to see it, should have to see it. And then cry and be haunted by the image for the rest of his life. Never again happy. Never again able to love. Never another woman. Each change of gears. Each acceleration. Each step on the clutch. Each hand movement and each breath were taking her further away from this moment. Helene bitterly watched herself functioning. The same as everybody else. Forever. People were forever taking leave. Orderly and calmly. Nobody screamed. Nobody wept. Clung to the other. Tore open their chests. Lamented. You could not see the tragedies in any station or airport. Helene suddenly thought it obscene. Nauseating. How they were all, calm and collected, gliding past each other. A perpetual funeral. At which nobody would look at anybody else. She could taste her nausea. She found herself confirmed in her opinion of herself. She was a coward. A follower. She would have liked a sip of bourbon. Against the metallic taste. "Well," Helene thought. "So that's what we've come to." And then she asked herself how Henryk's travel bag had turned up. Where had it been, all that time. Certainly not in the Lannerstrasse.

Gert Storntberg called Helene at the office. Could he speak to her. He wanted to thank her. And ask her advice. From Püppi's stories he had learned what she had done. Helene arranged a meeting. She couldn't think of any other place but Café Sacher. It'd be the easiest for him to find. He asked her to meet him that same evening. Because he had to leave again. Yes. If it had to be this way, Helene said. She didn't want to. Didn't see the point. At lunch time, Helene was to meet with a Herr Rocek. In the lounge of the Hilton. Nadolny had informed her as he was leaving. 1 p.m. Helene had never been in the hotel. She entered it from the City Park. How was she to find somebody she didn't know in this huge lounge. Why wouldn't Nadolny have asked the man to come to the office. Helene felt lost and abandoned. She went to the first table to the left of the bar. Sat down. Ordered a glass of sparkling wine. She held the stem of the glass in her hand and looked around. There wasn't a man, all by himself, in one of the sitting areas or at one of the small tables. At least I'm here, she thought. She decided to wait for 20 minutes. And then to leave. By now, all she looked at was her glass. Hoped this Rocek would be late and she wouldn't have to meet him. Helene drank her spar- kling wine in one gulp. It tasted tart. She paid. As she was getting up, a man from one of the tables nearby leaned to- ward her. Was her name Gebhardt. "Yes," Helene said. "Wonderful," the man said in English. He was small, stocky. His T-shirt was stretched over his biceps. His face tanned and full of pock marks. Next to him was a pale, oldish man in pin stripes. The man with the pock marks grabbed hold of Helene's elbow and swung her onto one of the chairs at his table. He didn't get up for it. "I'm Klaus Rocek. This is

Mr. Goldenberg." Helene nodded. Mr. Goldenberg didn't seem to want to shake hands with her. "Leo has recommended you highly." Helene looked at Klaus Rocek without comprehension. Then it struck her. Nadolny, of course, was called Leopold. "He has?" she smiled at the men. Rocek smiled back. Mr. Goldenberg looked at the table in front of him. Rocek ordered another glass of sparkling wine for Helene. He told Helene that he'd met Leo on a hunting trip to Hungary. And that he was a real good guy, that Leo. And Leo had offered to help solve their problem. They needed somebody with organizational talent and discretion. Rocek added "you know" to each of his sentences. And immediately explained why. He lived in New York. Worked there. And that's where you pick it up. You know. Helene liked Rocek. Mr. Goldenberg only stared at the table. Or leaned back, looking at the people walking up or down the staircase in the middle of the lounge. Much later. Helene had learned where Rocek was born. In the Burgenland. Where he had attended school. In Eisenstadt. And how he'd been sent to relatives in America at age 17. And had stayed. Suddenly Goldenberg leaned forward. "I want to state my business. If you don't mind," he said in English. "Okay Harry. Yes. By all means. Do!" Goldenberg was talking down at the table. "My friends. A group of friends. We are doing a tour of Europe. Come fall. And we like to do things in each place according to history. Roman baths in Rome. Corrida in Madrid. That sort of thing. You see. In Vienna we like to have a ball. In grand style. Baroque. You understand. The venue should be very private. And we think we should have shoes, silk stockings and crowns. Particular details you get from Klaus. I've got to lie down. I have to do business in the afternoon. Good bye." He'd looked at the table all the while he was speaking. He got up and left. Helene turned to Rocek. Rocek was following Goldenberg with his eyes. He seemed guilty and nervous. "He is pissed. I can see that. You know." But. She hoped it wasn't her fault, Helene said. "No. No. It's the business. It's always the business. Money is an unparalleled rival. You know." Rocek ordered another coffee for himself and another glass of sparkling wine for Helene. Helene should send him a draft budget. He gave her his card. They sat and drank. Rocek dictated the dates for Helene, the number of participants and where they would stay. Helene felt light in her head. Because of the sparkling wine. Rocek became more and more absent. Helene had to ask him repeatedly what they thought about an orchestra. Then Rocek said goodbye. He was confident she'd solve their problems. He charged the drinks to his room bill, signed the bill and disappeared into the back. Toward the elevators.

Helene hadn't changed for her meeting with Storntberg. She was sitting in Café Sacher. Again beneath the portrait of Empress Sisi. And was annoyed. Her gray linen suit was creased. The skirt was particularly crumpled. When she stood straight, the horizontal wrinkles made it shorter. Since her pregnancy with Katharina, Helene had a varicose vein on the inner side of her leg under her right knee. She was afraid it would be visible when her skirt rode up. Helene recognized Storntberg immediately. She had seen photos at Püppi's. And he resembled Sophie. Helene waved to him. Storntberg walked up to her. He was tall, broad, dark, immaculate in his khaki summer suit. He stood in front of her. From the start, Helene disliked him. She wished she hadn't come. She looked at his expensive shoes. This man would always get whatever he wanted. Helene was angry about herself. And about the way she looked. Storntberg sat down and ordered mineral water. Helene drank coffee. Storntberg thanked her for coming. Did he owe her money.

Did she have expenses, that night. Helene said no. She'd had to pay for the cab. Tips for the paramedics. But from Storntberg she didn't want to accept anything. What did the man know about money anyway. As a banker. No. Everything was all right, she said. How was Püppi. And Sophie. Storntberg shrugged. Helene watched as he sized her up. Who did he expect, Helene thought. "Yes," she said. "I am the respectable friend." Storntberg nodded. What was going to happen next? Well. He'd have to take Sophie with him. That was obvious, of course. Helene froze. She hadn't thought of that. It had never occurred to her. She'd thought Püppi could get money from Storntberg. Or move back in with him. To London. And away from everything in Vienna. Start again. Helene looked at the man. "I have a new wife. She's expecting. At first, Sophie will go to my mother in Hamburg. And then we'll see from there. What am I to do. I can't leave the child where she is. You must agree with that." Helene thought about Sophie. How she had stood there, saying "Good evening." "But. It'll be the end of Püppi." "Believe me. I've tried everything." Storntberg looked at his glass. "Do you see any other solution?" Helene looked at her hands. They lay in her lap, on the creased gray linen. With the index finger of her right hand Helene traced the thick blue veins on the back of her left hand. No. She didn't see a solution. She didn't know what was best for Sophie either. She didn't know anything that could be done for Püppi. She didn't know anything at all. In her mind, she told herself, "But I know very well that you carry some of the blame too. Storntberg. You bastard. I know that very well." She could have cried. She also thought how easy everything would be if she herself had a proper husband. Then she could have taken Sophie in. At least for the time being. But this way. When was all this supposed to happen? Sometime this week, Storntberg said. And could she take care of Püppi afterwards. He had to wait for his mother to come. Püppi, by the way, had agreed to it all. She'd signed everything. At a lawyer's office. Everything was settled. But he had to admit he wasn't sure Püppi really understood what was going on. She was on pills. "She's going to kill herself," Helene said. Storntberg ran both hands through his hair. He'd happily pay for anything. A spa. Detox. Therapy. Anything. But Püppi just sat there and smiled. He couldn't bear it any longer. Could Helene perhaps talk to her. Helene wondered if she could tell this man that, no, she couldn't. No, I'm not talking to her. Your divorced wife, Mister, is having an affair with my husband. I'm only her best friend. But Helene said yes. She'd talk to her. Take care of her. Use her influence. "This is all very sad," she said. Her throat was swollen and tight. She'd try. He should phone her. He had all the phone numbers, hadn't he. "I've tried endlessly to get her back," Storntberg said. Helene knew about it. She had overheard phone calls during which Püppi would yell she wouldn't have any of it. He should take one of his bimbos instead. "I know," she said. "I know." Helene finished her coffee. She was tired. Couldn't move her limbs. She had to leave. She had two children, didn't she, Storntberg asked. He had stood up with her. Helene glanced up at him. He had brown eyes. She left. She paid a waiter at the door for her coffee. She didn't want Storntberg to pay for any coffee she had. "You are a remarkable woman," he had said. You mean dull, Helene had thought. She hadn't shaken hands with him. What could this guy know, she thought. Later, in her car, Helene thought Püppi could have had the good life. Normal, anyway. The idea made her even more tired. During the conversation Helene had wondered what it would mean if Barbara or Katharina were to be taken from her. The idea was monstrous. Horrifying. Just how could Püppi agree to it? Helene thought she wouldn't be able to live without her children. She drove home. She pressed her lips together, tight, until her face hurt. She felt helpless. Storntberg had made it clear to her, once again, how the system works. And who wins. In this world. Helene was afraid. She imagined Sophie and how she'd walk off holding Storntberg's hand.

Helene lay on her bed. The sun sent oblique rays through an opening in the curtains. It was completely quiet in the apartment. Not even the fridge hummed. The children had gone to the park with their grandmother. No sounds came up to her from the street. Saturday afternoon peace. Helene was lying on her right side, with her head on her right arm and her left arm in front of her on the cover. She had fixed her eyes on the second hand of her watch. With each passing second the probability increased. At some point he simply would have to phone. He'd said, after all. Promised. Helene lay there and watched the hands move. She felt light. She didn't have the shortness of breath. Which she usually had when she thought of Henryk. Or the stone in her chest. Or the sharp pain in her stomach. Or the numbness in her arms and legs. Or the vice around her neck. It was as if she had this body only in order to look at her watch. To concentrate on how time passed. And she had loved him, in this time now passing. There was nothing she could do about that now, Helene thought. She woke up. Cars were parked in the street. Doors slammed. Men's voices shouted something about "winning" and "getting even" with each other. Probably the sons from across the road. Helene always saw them with their tennis bags, coming and going. She had slept for 15 minutes. Her composure was gone. Helene watched the sunlight. How the motes of dust were rising and falling. Calm and steady. Henryk wouldn't phone. Ever. Probably. She was alone. As always. And none of them found it necessary to tell her. Inform her. They let her know by not phoning. Let her find it out. Gregor hadn't told her either what was going on. He'd only gotten more and more furious. Angry with her. Enraged. Didn't she notice anything, he had yelled at her. Did she need it in writing? Helene would have been satisfied to know where Henryk stayed these days. Where he was. Existed. All of a sudden she felt everything. The stone in her chest. The sharp pain in her stomach. The numbness in her arms and legs. The vice around her neck. Shortness of breath. Headache. Helene was lying on her bed. Her watch in front of her eyes. The sun's rays became more oblique.

Helene walked from Bräuner Hof toward Neuer Markt. All day it looked as if there would be rain, thunder and lightning. Just as she was crossing the Dorotheergasse, a terrific downpour began. Rain was pelting down. Immediately the streets became deserted. Helene had parked her car at the Albertina Stairs behind the Opera. She dashed from store entrance to store entrance. She wore her gray pumps. The ones that matched her gray linen suit. They would get water-stained. Helene ran down the Plankengasse. A red Porsche stopped at the bus stop. A man leaned across the passenger's seat and opened the door. Helene dropped herself into the seat. Her face was wet, and her hair dripped. She laughed. The man drove off immediately. He grinned. Asked where she wanted to go. Helene continued to laugh. She didn't know the man. Getting into the car she had thought, for a moment, that she did. She thought it funny simply to climb into a stranger's car. And the man had addressed her as if they met each other regularly. "Werner Czerny," he said. In such a downpour you couldn't wait for your Auntie Prim to do the introductions. No you couldn't, Helene agreed. Still laughing. Indeed that wouldn't work.

Helene said her name. They talked about the weather. Only once in a blue moon would you get a deluge like this. Why was a blue moon so rare, Helene asked. The man sized her up from the corner of his eyes. He had to go to the Spittelauer Platz. Near the Franz Joseph's Station. He lived there. That would be great for her. Could he let her get out at the taxi stand. Shouldn't he take her home, Czerny asked. No. No. Helene didn't want to be seen in this car. And he shouldn't know her address. Wouldn't she have to invite him into her apartment for a drink? Because he'd saved her? They talked about the weather. The downpour continued. Water was rushing over everything. Streams were swelling in ditches. The rain formed a wall of water around the car. No other car moved. Czerny drove slowly and cautiously. The wipers raced across the windscreen. They could only see anything for fractions of a second. The next moment the windscreen was flooded again. They drove down the Boltzmanngasse. Past the American Embassy. The police had disappeared from the street. Czerny turned right into the Alserbachstrasse. Drove past the station, swung around to the left, and then past the station to the right. To the right of the station, tall apartment buildings formed a square. Old plane trees grew in the center. Czerny said they'd arrived. And she'd better come with him. A glass of something wouldn't hurt her. And he hadn't seen a cab. It was true. Helene hadn't seen one either. They both hurried to the door. Immediately Helene got drenched again. She didn't want to know what her shoes looked like. They were history. Czerny unlocked the front door. They walked into a splendid 1870's foyer. Colorful stained-glass windows. Glimmering golden lights. Marble. In the apartment, Czerny brought towels right away. And he asked Helene to take off her shoes. She slipped off her pumps and left them in the hallway. She wrapped a towel around her head. She followed

Czerny into a room. The room was big. Huge windows opened onto the square. You could look into the treetops. "Same as at my place," Helene said. "What can I get you to drink?" Czerny asked. Helene sat down on the sofa. "A sherry? If you have any." Helene looked at her toes. Why had she just used the informal address and said "du" to the man? As he had. She didn't want to look up again, ever. She was angry with herself. How could she have ended up in this place. Despair welled up in her. Every glance at the room increased her despair. Donald Duck ruled the room. Donald Duck lamps balanced light bulbs at the tips of their beaks. Donald Duck vases. Donald Duck heads held silk flowers. Pink and apricot. Donald Duck was painted on ashtrays. Sewn on cushions. Embroidered. Donald ran in narrow stripes across the curtains. Donald supported the glass top of the coffee table. At all 4 corners. Donald stood to either side of the double door, holding trays. There was a big Persian carpet on the floor. Helene put her sherry down in front of Donald's beak. Czerny was pacing, with a glass in his hand. He didn't look at her. They didn't talk. Helene went to the window. It was raining. The cloudburst had changed to a steady rain. One side window was open. It smelled fresh. The rain rustled through the leaves. "Why don't you sit down again?" Czerny stood, close, behind Helene. She could feel his breath. Her neck was unprotected. She had put her hair up with the towel. Czerny was the same height as Helene. In her shoes, she'd been taller. "Well, no," Helene said. Her voice was hoarse. Helene was upset about it. Cleared her throat. Gave a slight cough. She could hear herself breathing. Loudly. Puffing and panting. She felt as if something were pressing her down. She could imagine simply sinking into the floor. She had to get out of this apartment. Her apprehension grew. "You're nervous too. Why don't you admit it. Nothing wrong in admitting that sort of thing." Helene hesitated. For a moment. Do it with the man now? And then never see him again? Afterwards? Helene looked around. She had to go, she said. Now. Immediately. Yes. This very moment. Czerny turned her so she faced him. Tried to kiss her. He must have brushed his teeth when he got the sherry. He smelled of toothpaste. Helene pushed him back. She bent over and unwrapped the towel from her hair. She handed the towel to Czerny. Thanks a lot, she mumbled. He took the towel, folded it. He didn't understand a thing anymore. After all, she'd come with him. Hadn't she? He hadn't forced her. To do so. Or had he? "I'm sorry," Helene said. Left. Stepped into her wet shoes and walked to the apartment door. She went down the stairs. Czerny called after her, "Stupid bitch." Yelled other things after her as well. Helene no longer heard him. In the street, in the rain, she had to run. She couldn't help laughing again. She ran to the taxi stand at the station. After a long time, a cab arrived. She let herself be driven home. At home, she took a hot bath. She got her car the next morning.

Helene attended a lecture. While she was shopping, she had run into a woman with whom she had taken classes at university. They'd had a quick cup of coffee at the Meinl. Helene had asked the woman what was happening. In intellectual Vienna. She was no longer able to go anywhere. Helene hadn't remembered the woman. The woman had greeted her. Helene hadn't been able to remember her name either. That's why she had a particularly long chat with her. In the course of which she found out about the lecture. The one everybody went to. Given by a certain Fabian Andinger. And what he said about Thomas Bernhard was quite simply. De rigueur. Helene had never much enjoyed reading Thomas Bernhard. And 2 years ago she'd given up reading altogether. In the past 2 years, she hadn't held a book in her hands. The mere idea of opening one had been inconceivable. Helene told Frau Sprecher she had to get office supplies and drove to the university. The lecture was in lecture theater 41. In the main building. Helene followed the signs. She felt out of place. The lecture began at eleven. Helene had counted on academic time, the standard quarter-hour delay. But she was late. She walked through the door. The lecturer was already speaking. She had to walk past him. All the aisle seats were taken. She had to ask a man to let her pass. The student got up reluctantly. Helene found a seat near the middle of the second row. The speaker stood in front of her. He was forty. Dark hair with gray streaks. Slender. He had put his jacket on the lectern. He stood there in shirt and tie. His tie dangled and danced whenever he tried to describe something with special emphasis. He seemed to prefer subdued colors. The shirt, grayish pink. The pants, grayish green. A brown belt. The tie a mix of all these hues. He wore black Birkenstock sandals and black socks. He talked about the artist's failure to realize the Apollonian ideal. About the position of judge assumed by the different first-person narrators. About how these first-person narrators judged themselves at the beginning of the work. Until, in the end, they sentenced the others to death. Because of their failure vis-à-vis the ideal. That Auersberger should kill himself because he was a lousy artist. How the first-person narrator felt abused. How he had enjoyed the abuse. At first. And only later recognized it for what it was. Too late. And then had already been abused. How, in these texts, sexuality figured merely in the background, was encoded in adolescent idiom. How all texts were texts of madness. And how in the novel Cutting Timber the guilty ones survived. Got fat. How the victims miscalculated. And had therefore become victims. How women were feared. Rejected. Hated. How they played the part of the phallic, punishing mother. Or of the depressed, suffering one. But how they always were to be seen in relation to the man. How woman was desired and cursed. Helene was listening. All around her, people were taking notes. The student in the row in front of her was writing with a red felt pen on unlined paper. Helene read what she was writing. Auersberger = Lampersberger. She read. And "fat." And "musician in the Webern succession." "Homosexuality" was underlined. The student wrote in large letters, twisting her wrist. When the speaker turned to the side. Or read from a book. She took a small mirror from her purse and tugged at her hair. She took off her jacket. Then her sweater. She sat there in a top with spaghetti straps. Helene watched her. The student probably took this seat at the speaker's feet right after the previous lecture. Would already be waiting at the door. 2 older women sat next to the student. One of them had a tape deck in front of her. She checked every so often to see if the equipment was indeed recording. The women were writing into small exercise books with colorful covers. When the speaker said that Bernhard took revenge on the female principle by letting women get old and ugly. Fat and bloated they'd be left for younger ones. More beautiful ones. At that moment the two women turned to each other. They were both delicate. Elegant. Then women were no longer dangerous, the speaker continued. Only beauty. It was the female beauty that represented the danger. The lecturer was fluent and emphatic. Inspired by his subject. Helene had feared it. Somehow she'd even known it. None of this held her interest anymore. She was no longer interested in figuring out the artists' tricks. Helene followed the lecture, astonished at the extravagant amount of thought. Reflections. She became sad. She had dedicated herself to this for so long. Given herself to it. To figuring out what others had meant. And. Perhaps the lecturer, in his attempt to decode the biography via the oeuvre, had been taken in by the writer. Helene had always felt that with Bernhard's writings she was being punished in advance for something she had yet to carry out. A task. Commissioned in these writings. She had always understood his books as an assault. A personal one. Not an assault on a system. On her. As a woman, she hadn't been able to identify anyway. Nor would she have wanted to. You were invited to observe, with glee, the failure of men. Who then would pull women into the abyss along with them. Women who just as easily might have lived. She suspected something decidedly fascist at work, deeply buried. A secret envy of those who could be openly fascist. And a deep contempt for humanity. But perhaps this too was a way of being taken in. Because members of the master race could, after all, no longer be depicted. The opposite had to be illustrated. The losers. And women were to blame. For everything. And that was all they were good for. Nobody had any children. This way, the characters were spared growing up. Eternally reproachful children. Looking back at their evil fascist parents. Which parents they had allowed to take everything away from them. Everybody terminal. Not to be continued. Straitjacketed into the past. Helene sat there. Listened. Looked at everything. Let her thoughts run free. And hoped there would be no discussion. She wanted to get out of the lecture theater. But then there was discussion. One of the two older women, the one on the left. The one with the tape deck. Thought nobody had the right to make such demands of a person. The very highest demands. It was unfair. Helene looked at her bag on the desk in front of her. Somebody wanted an exemption, as usual. The woman was indignant. It was unfair, she repeated. Ha, Helene thought, taken in again. And congratulated Herr Bernhard. The woman was infuriated with the author. Ergo: Successfully seduced. By a writer. A man. Of course. But she did not want the rigor of his principle. Not to apply it. Surely it was too cruel! Although it had always been this way. And because she wanted to adore the man, she gave herself a moral dispensation. Released herself from the principle. Unfairness, she called it. Inhumanity. But if she'd seen through it. And through her own role. Then she would have had to take the signet ring off her little finger and throw it away. Her diamond ring as well. And hang herself with her Hermés scarf. Better she didn't get it, Helene thought. And how hard must it actually be, for a man, to have been abused? To have been possessed. Taken. Women got the hang of it. And for a woman? You got to keep the children. In the relentlessness of an all-pervading reality that, too, was freedom. The woman continued to talk with the speaker. She looked up at him. He said, "Let's not reproach the author for his characters, please." The student sat there twirling her hair. She smiled up at the speaker. Helene wondered if she too at some point had worshipped somebody in this way. She hoped not. She forced the student next to her to get up and let her pass. She was the first one to leave. The last will be the first, Helene thought.

Helene bought hamburgers at McDonald's on the Schwarzenbergplatz. And Coke at the snack bar at the tram stop. The children were ecstatic. She should go to lectures more often. They tore into the little Styrofoam boxes. They squeezed ketchup on their fries. Pulled the Coke cans open. Helene had a coffee. She wasn't hungry. In the mail was a note to pick up a registered letter. Another letter from the bank. Probably. And a letter from a lawyer had arrived. From Dr. Ronald Kopriva. He'd gone to school with Gregor. Helene had never liked him. He was one of those small fat men who forever had to allude. To their true greatness. And the like. Helene had found his much younger wife pleasant. Gregor had gone to him. Of course. She held the letter in her hand. She was unable to open it. But she would have to. There was nobody who could have done it for her. Helene sat with the children. They should do their homework. Afterwards. Yes. Barbara could go and see Nina. But only once everything was done. And Katharina? She'd stay home? Yes? Yes. She could get herself new paints. But she shouldn't dawdle too long. In the Döblinger Hauptstrasse. Helene left her some money. Should something come up, Grandma would be there. And she'd call them. See you later. Helene hugged the children and left.

Helene was driving toward the Höhenstrasse. She had put the lawyer's letter next to her on the passenger's seat. She drove down the Krottenbachstrasse. Along the Agnesgasse. Through Sievering up into the woods. She took the corners carefully. She didn't drive fast. On the Höhenstrasse, she took a right turn. Beneath the Cobenzl she stopped. She parked the car to the side. Got out. Vienna was below her. The Danube on the left. On the right, toward the downtown, the maze got denser. The General Hospital, two dark cubes. Helene looked into the distance. The sun was burning. She was afraid. She could hardly swallow. She knew what the letter would say. Said. What she would read. She had hoped. She had to admit she had hoped. Until the moment she found the letter on the pile in her hallway she had hoped. There had been no reason why. On the contrary. Now. Standing above Vienna, it seemed stupid. Pathetic. Miserable. If it hadn't been for the children, she could have dropped the letter in the garbage bin by the roadside. And walked away. Never be in touch again. Vanish. As if she'd never existed. She could have continued to love Gregor.

Who would have wanted to stop her. He wouldn't have known. She could have done what she liked. But as things were. Standing in the sun. Looking towards Hungary, Helene had a burning desire for Gregor to be dead. An end. And no arguments. Finished. Helene went to her car. She got the letter. For a moment, she held it in her hand. She thought she had to tear it up. Out of rage. Helene got back into her car, into the heat. She tore the letter open. It was what she expected. She was to get nothing. For the children, the minimum payments prescribed by law. Custody for her. Gregor wasn't even interested in maintaining his responsibility for the children. She was to be permitted to stay in the apartment. Until the children turned 18. From then on, she would have to pay Gregor rent. Any individuals residing in the apartment with them before that point in time would have to begin paying rent immediately. To the apartment owner. That is, to Gregor. Helene could just imagine how Gregor must have talked with Kopriva. About this. Helene could have knocked the man down. Or run him over. With her car. And backed over him. In reverse. She imagined how the tires would wobble across Kopriva's paunchy belly. Although it made you laugh. Gregor wanted to become her pimp. Cash in on her lovers. Gregor and Kopriva had set the rent at 15 000 schillings. Reasonable, given the neighborhood. That made. Helene calculated. That made 500 schillings a night. So that's how the situation had been assessed. Helene felt like throwing up. She bent over the steering wheel. Now she knew the worst. Maybe she should drive into a tree, after all. She wished dying took care of itself. She took a deep breath. Against the pressure in her throat. She started to drive. She had both windows open. Her hair was blowing in her face. She had to hurry. She should have been at the office quite some time ago.

Helene drove downhill, toward Grinzing. On her right and left, trees were gliding past. The car rumbled across cobblestones. She cranked the sunroof open. The sky was blue and cloudless. She wondered if it was harder to be unhappy in fine weather. Or better in bad weather. Helene longed for Henryk. She wanted to have him on top of her, a body between her and the world. And no longer to see anything. Sitting in the car, Helene felt she was crawling. She drove into the shady tunnel created by chestnut trees. She slid away beneath the treetops. Drove through Grinzing. Straight on to the Heiligenstädter Strasse and then to the Lände. She was sure. The endless phone calls when nobody spoke at the other end. Only the line buzzing. Henryk was trying to reach her. And the lines from Italy weren't working.

All afternoon at work Helene was busy finding out where to rent crowns. Crowns were the only item missing in her draft budget for the ball. Helene found crowns of normal width at Binder's Theater Supplies. You could order a sample. At Lambert Hofer Costume Rentals you could rent individual crowns for each ball guest. But it was expensive, and some damage was to be expected. So you had to pay insurance as well. But they had replicas of real crowns. The crown of the Holy Roman Empire. The crown of the Austrian emperor. The crown of the British king. Gilded laurel wreaths for those favoring Napoleon. The crown of the czars. There were a few tiaras. A brocade and fur cap for Genghis Khan. And the crowns that the Shah had commissioned for himself and his wife. They would have to borrow shoes and stockings. But the crowns. Helene wanted to find out the price for the little crowns worn by debutantes to the Opera Ball. Helene phoned the Austrian Federal Theater Association. There she was told that the office for the Opera Ball was not staffed. At the moment. She could leave orders for tickets. If intending to use a credit card, she should leave the number of her card. That wasn't the issue, Helene said. She'd like to know where the little crowns worn by the debutantes were produced. "Just a moment, please," the woman on the phone said. Helene listened to the recording "bitte warten—please hold the line" for a long time. Nobody answered. Helene phoned the Chamber of Commerce. She thought somebody there had a registry about where to get what products. Everyone had gone home from the Chamber of Commerce. Helene phoned the Max Reinhardt School of Dramatic Art. The woman at the other end of the line was sympathetic. She'd like to know too. But she couldn't help. There was nobody around. It was summer, after all. Helene thanked her. She would have liked to talk with somebody. But Nadolny wasn't at the office. He hardly ever came to the office these days. Nestler was in Vienna. They had discussions with professors of medicine. With the Health Department. Medical insurance companies. There were discussions with the Board of Pharmacists and pharmaceutical companies. Medicare should cover magnetic foil. There were even discussions about launching magnetic foil in Britain. The approval processes for pharmaceuticals being about as generous in Britain as they were in Austria, Nestler thought. And from there, they'd move into the United States. And on to the big money. Nestler wanted to be in on the market before the European Union standardized things. The discussions meant lengthy meals with stimulating drinks. In between, Nadolny had to recover. But he was in a good mood. When he was at the office, he'd stand by the window. With a little drink of cognac in his hand. He hadn't been seen drinking Underberg for a long time. He'd stand by the window, glass in hand. Gently swirling the cognac in his glass. Humming. By chance Helene had come across a Personals ad in the Kurier,

"New. Chocolate baby with big bosoms, supergirl with huge breasts, natural massages, long-term service, 1020 Ferdinandstrasse 2A." Helene had shown the ad to Frau Sprecher. Together they had speculated if Nadolny was spending his afternoons there. It was almost next door. Helene decided to wait another day. She wanted to find out the price for the little crowns for the Opera Ball. She didn't want to fax an incomplete estimate to Rocek.

Helene had to get up at 6 a.m. She had to wash and dry her hair and iron a blouse. Before making breakfast for the children. She leaned over the bathtub and let the water run through her hair. She was sick. She had to look good. At 8, she was to pick up Dr. Stadlmann. She had to take him to the Outpatients' Clinic. There would be a lecture at 10 a.m. about the effects and interactions of magnetic fields and acupuncture meridians. Professor Günther Chrobath would give the lecture. Dr. Stadlmann was to introduce the physical qualities and effects of magnetic foil. Before that, a TV interview was scheduled. Helene could not muster up the energy to hurry. She wanted to sleep. She had to wash off her mascara twice. She had slipped and smudged the black paint under her eyes. At first, under her right eye. Then under her left. Her eyes were red from rubbing off the paint. She started all over. She brushed rouge on her cheekbones so nobody would ask her if she was sick. Helene got to Stadlmann's apartment at 10 past 8. She had driven to his mother's apartment first. The mother had explained to her, reproachfully, that her Justus merely had his office there. He lived with his wife in the Arnsteingasse. It wasn't that far away. But with rush hour traffic and her detour to the Linke Wienzeile Helene arrived late. Dr. Stadlmann stood in front of his entrance. Helene honked and stopped. Immediately others behind her honked. Nobody could pass her in the narrow street. Stadlmann yelled at her that he'd already called a cab. She should go on, thank you very much. Helene shouted he should get in. Please! There was plenty of time. The cab couldn't get through anyway. Behind Stadlmann, a woman stepped into the street. She said something to him. Helene couldn't hear it. There was honking. Helene sat in the car. She had talked with Stadlmann through the passenger's side window. Helene tore her seat belt off and got out. Across the roof of the car she gestured to the woman and to Stadlmann that he should get in. The woman was not the doctor from Franz Joseph's Hospital. Helene had thought that she must be Dr. Stadlmann's wife. Helene was disappointed. The woman helped Stadlmann off the sidewalk. The cars behind Helene were honking. Stadlmann lifted his crutch and threatened the drivers. The woman urged him on. She maneuvered him into the car and immediately went back. She disappeared into the house without turning. Helene drove off as fast as possible. She wanted to apologize. Stadlmann was looking straight ahead. Was pressing his lips together. Was not open to a conversation. Helene felt guilty. She could have hurried. She should have considered what a hassle all of this was for Stadlmann. She couldn't get out a word. In silence, they drove to the Outpatients' Clinic. It had been agreed that a parking space be reserved for Stadlmann. In the yard. There was no space left. Helene pulled up in front of the building. She helped Stadlmann out of the car and into the building. Then she went to park the car. She found short-term parking in the Gilgegasse. She walked back to the clinic. Who would pay for the ticket she was bound to get.

The staircase in the clinic was crowded with people in white coats. As if there were only doctors in the building. It smelled like a hospital. Helene asked for the lecture theater. The security man showed her the way. Helene first walked to the Institute for Acupuncture. She carried a big box with brochures on magnetic foil, name tags and attendance sheets. In the institute, a TV crew was busy setting up lights and sound. Dr. Stadlmann was talking to a tall man with a full beard. Nadolny was standing next to the TV crew. He had his hands thrust in his pockets and grinned at the reporter. Her name was Sommer. Karin Sommer. She belonged to the science editorial staff. Helene knew her from the phone. Helene also knew the price of the bracelet that Frau Sommer was to get following the report on magnetic foil. Nadolny had asked Helene which of the bracelets she would choose. Had put two bracelets in front of her. Helene had pointed at the golden bracelet made from simple, heavy links. "In that case I'll take the other one," Nadolny had said and picked the thinner bracelet with little hearts with little glittering stones. Helene's taste was boring, besides which, the one she had selected was also more expensive, Nadolny had said. And had thanked her. For her help. Helene wore her gray linen suit again. The shoes didn't match. Her gray shoes had been ruined for good by the rain on her way from Czerny's house to the taxi stand. Helene's cash supply had shrunk to 3600 schillings. She wondered what to sell next. She walked over to Nadolny. Was everything okay. Nadolny welcomed her effusively. He introduced her to Frau Sommer. Without her, he said to Frau Sommer, without his Frau Gebhardt he was nothing. Helene smiled. Frau Sommer smiled. Nadolny took brochures and distributed them. Nestler entered the room. He stopped next to Helene. She should tell him who was who. The one over there was Professor Chrobath. He knew that, Nestler said. Dr. Stadlmann had insisted on negotiating with him alone. He shrugged. "Dr. Stadlmann still doesn't believe in the power of money," he said. He walked over to Frau Sommer. They greeted each other with kisses on the cheeks. "Karin," Nestler said loudly. "Did you have a good time last night?" Frau Sommer rolled her eyes suggestively. Helene left. She looked for the lecture theater. She found it still locked. She sat down on a bench in the hallway.

The lecture theater was almost full. Doctors in white coats. Business men. Male journalists. Female journalists. Dr. Stadlmann was sitting next to Nestler and Professor Chrobath at a table below the stage. In the front. At 20 past 10, Stadlmann got up. Heaved himself up. Grabbed the crutches leaning next to him against the table and started to haul himself to the lectern. It got quiet. Everybody was watching the man as he dragged his misshapen feet in the heavy black shoes behind him. And thrust them forward. Rebalanced his weight. Leaned on his crutches. Started the next step. Stadlmann arrived at the lectern. Leaned his crutches next to himself against the lectern. He pulled a piece of paper from his jacket pocket. Placed it carefully in front of him. And began his introduction. Helene knew the story by heart. How the development of magnetic foil had come about. She understood the physics while Stadlmann explained it. Immediately after the explanation, she got it all muddled up. She looked around. Beyond the dusty windows of the lecture theater you could look at adjacent buildings. Into other windows. Helene was seated on the side, hidden, below the stage. In the past, the beadle would have sat on the small bench. Would carry in the specimens. And carry them out again. Or the patients would have waited there. Those who were able to walk by themselves to be put on display in front of the students. Helene leaned against the wall. She could see Dr. Stadlmann from where she sat offstage to his left. As he stood facing the audience in the lecture theater. Helene wondered what Dr.

Stadlmann's cock looked like. When it was limp. And when erect. She pushed the thought aside. What did she care. But the idea of what it might look like kept pushing itself to the fore. She fished for a peppermint candy in her purse. She wanted to distract herself. She rustled. Irritated, Dr. Stadlmann looked in her direction. Helene paused. Feeling guilty, she sat there motionless. In her head, the thoughts were racing. How Dr. Stadlmann could do it. Could he kneel. Not likely. Probably his wife had to, on top. Helene remembered the wife. She would have liked the doctor from Franz Joseph's Hospital to be his wife. The woman who had helped Stadlmann into the car in the morning had looked haggard. Helene couldn't imagine the two together. Helene sat there. Calm. Composed. He'd be helpless. Rather helpless. At her mercy. The images were rising in front of her eyes. Could not be pushed away. Could not be forbidden. And not be enjoyed either. Seriously and in an orderly manner, little films unreeled. Only the chaos of the discussion released Helene.

Helene woke up during the night. She grabbed the phone. On the floor. Next to her bed. But it had rung only once. She heard a loud buzz. Nobody responded. Helene waited for another call. She thought it might be Püppi. Püppi had disappeared. To a spa. Storntberg had said. Helene was lying in bed. Who could it have been. She was waiting. Expecting another ring, she held her breath. She had to start breathing again. She swallowed the wrong way. Her throat was dry. She had to cough. Gasped for air. For a moment Helene felt she was suffocating. She sat up. Pulled up her knees. Wrapped her arms around her legs and rested her forehead on her knees. She sat in the dark. The desire to see Henryk. Or to speak with him. Or at least to know where he was. If he still existed. The desire pried her chest open. Helene thought she couldn't survive the pain.

Helene sat in Café Prückl. She had been to 3 print shops. The manufacture of packaging was complicated. Helene had to learn everything about embossing, folding and color selection. She felt she deserved a break. It was half past 2 in the afternoon. The café was almost empty. Helene had ordered an Einspänner. Had watched how an older woman at one of the neighboring tables had been served an Einspänner. Helene wanted such a glass, too, with its tempting black and white combination of coffee and whipped cream. Helene let the sugar slide down the side into the coffee and stirred carefully. She didn't want to stir the cream into the coffee. Helene started to read the Neue Züricher Zeitung. The photo was on page two. The photo was from South Africa. A black man cowered inside a tire. A big tire. From a truck or from building equipment. The man was shackled. His arms were twisted back. His feet couldn't be seen. Another black man was bending over the one in shackles. He held a burning torch in his hand. He held it above the tire, which was filled with gasoline. It said so in the caption. The two men were very close to each other. The one setting the fire held his torch, tight and secure. Competent. As if concerned about his plan. Tenderly concerned. The shackled man had dropped his head. His shoulders hunched. As much as his fettered arms would allow. The one setting the fire could have come to help him. Perform first aid. Untie him. Refresh him. Or wash him. If there hadn't been the flame of the torch. And the idea. The caption confirmed the idea. Of how the fire would leap up in a circle around the shackled man. How the gas would ignite. And the screaming. And the rolling around. And the smell. It would take long. Then it did take long. As the caption confirmed, the man with the torch ignited the gas right after the photo had been taken. Helene could imagine the screaming. She had a clear recollection of the various self-immolations from TV news. The one setting the fire probably had to jump aside. To escape the fire himself. Helene sat there. The whipped cream was sinking in streaks into the coffee. Through the glass Helene could watch the white creamy streaks floating up and down. How the coffee gradually turned from black to brown to light brown. She couldn't drink the Einspänner. She sat behind her newspaper for a long time. She had opened the business section. Stared at the columns of stock exchange rates and the performance of stocks and shares. Helene read the Neue Züricher Zeitung because, among other reasons, there were hardly any photos in it.

On Friday, Helene picked the children up from school. She would have dropped them off and picked them up every day. But the children didn't want her to. They wanted to walk by themselves. Not even with each other. Helene had to let them. It was also more convenient this way. But she couldn't bear thinking how these two little girls would wander along the streets. With their satchels on their backs. Katharina not even tall enough to be visible behind parked cars. Helene was glad for every moment she knew the children close and safe. Even in her pregnancies she hadn't been able to get over the thought that the children she was going to give birth to would die. Would have to. One day. Mothers are murderers, she had thought. Helene stood in front of the school. She was leaning against the railing in front of the gate. The young woman who always picked up her son came with a baby carriage. Helene walked up to her. "Did everything go well. Congratulations," she said. She looked into the baby carriage. The child lay on its stomach. The face averted. Helene could only see the little white linen bonnet. And the hands. The child had clenched its hands into fists. While Helene was looking at the little fists beside the right and left of the head, she wished she had another little child like this one. She could remember very well how unhappy and alone she'd been with hers. But also what it felt like to hold such a little one in her arms. To watch it move its mouth. What it smelled like. "Well, what did it turn out to be?" Helene asked. The young woman looked at her child in the baby carriage. "Unfortunately, only a Julia," she said with a smile. Helene turned away. Barbara was coming out of the gate. "I have to run," Helene said hastily. She hugged Barbara. Held her hand. As if the "unfortunately" had been directed at Barbara and Helene had to protect her from it. Helene and the children went for lunch at the restaurant in the Türkenschanz Park. She had to get back to the office soon. Nestler intended to come to Vienna around noon and wanted to be briefed in detail.

Alex phoned. They should see each other. Helene agreed. She hadn't gone out for weeks. Alex picked her up. They went to the Heuriger. They sat under the great linden tree at the Welser in the Probusgasse. Alex was taciturn. Helene made an effort to carry on a conversation. How was he. What was he doing. Where did he live. Alex gave short answers and was already drinking his third white wine with soda water. "A year ago we were happier." Helene couldn't say anything. She looked at him. "I should have stayed with you," Alex said. He sounded bitter. "I can't understand myself anyway," he said. "Why I, at the time. I mean. With Gitta. She did. At the time. Well, that's not it." He drank and ordered his fourth Gespritzten. Helene pushed her glass of wine away. She couldn't swallow. Suddenly. He said. "Can't we. I mean. You. And I. I can't get a divorce. Can't

[201]

afford it. But I'll live by myself. I'm looking for an apartment in Vienna. We could, couldn't we. Together." Helene watched Alex as he was talking. He was looking at the tablecloth and following the lines of the checkerboard with his index finger. He paused. "Helene. We are. I mean. We are attracted to each other. Don't you think." Helene looked at him. Alex looked up. Helene remembered Brixen. For a moment. A year ago. Trees in blossom on a steep slope. The balcony of a hotel room where they took all their meals. Because Alex couldn't be seen with her in the dining room. The taste of spinach dumplings with parmesan and melted butter. And driving. Sitting next to him. Helene got up. She grabbed her purse. She kissed Alex on the cheek and left. She couldn't say anything. She walked back down the Probusgasse and on to the Armbrustergasse. Along the Hohe Warte. She walked fast and with concentration. Helene arrived home. She was sweaty. She had the feeling she smelled sweaty. Her hands and feet were ice-cold. In spite of the long walk she was cold. She had a bath. She locked herself in the bathroom and had a bath. Sat in the tub and let more hot water run in. Until she was red from the heat, all over. Then she watched the end of a detective film on TV. Schimansky had hunted down a murderer. But he had to drink a lot. Afterwards.

Henryk had called. The phone had rung, and it had been him. Could she come into town. He was at Café Korb. It was a rainy day. The end of June, but cold and windy. Helene went into the bathroom and made herself up. She was slow doing it. And calm. To the children she said she'd bring some sweets back from town for them. They should watch TV. In this weather it'd be the most cozy thing to do anyway. Couldn't they come with her, the children asked. No. Helene was tired. It wasn't possible. Helene took the car to town. Found parking near the Salzgries, took her umbrella from the trunk and walked to Café Korb. She'd never been there. Knew it only from passing. Helene closed the umbrella and pushed the door open. People played cards. Table cloths made from green felt covered the tables. All the tables were taken. At the front, by the windows, were the only 3 coffee house tables. Henryk sat in the corner between windows and wall. Helene looked around for an umbrella stand. Suddenly shaky. She turned in all directions. Henryk got up. Walked up to her. Took her umbrella from her and put it into the umbrella stand, right next to the door. Henryk moved Helene to the table. Helene sat down on Henryk's chair. Henryk took the other one. Henryk looked awful. Pale. His cheeks were hollow. His hair thin. Sticky. Straggly. The jacket too big. His wrists stuck narrow and angular out of the sleeves. "Yes. I've been sick," Henryk said. Helene stared at him. Why hadn't he let her know. Why not have said anything. How could she have known. They could have done something. She'd thought Henryk had broken it off. That it was over. Henryk looked at the table. Stirred his short Braunen. Was this what she thought of him. Yes? Well. You couldn't expect any different. And he could understand Helene. Understand her very well. But he'd thought, also. Their shared history. It was something special, wasn't it. He'd thought. But now, well, it seemed he was mistaken. He loved her. Helene was looking out the window. She had thought she'd left all this behind. Wouldn't have to deal with Henryk anymore. At least not with the real Henryk. Only with her idea of him. Henryk bent more deeply over his coffee. Resigned. Helene saw the top of his head. His hair was too long. Thinner at the end of his part. Only a bit, but thinner. Even his neck looked thin. He really had lost weight. "I was so unhappy," she said. Henryk said nothing. He nodded. Helene thought she should leave. She stayed. She sat there. The murmuring of the players could be heard all around them. Sometimes a louder sentence. "Another Melange!" "Two Spritzer. Herr Ferdy." Or, "Why don't you deal. Finally!" Tinkling of glasses. So that's it, Helene thought. That's what it's been. What it had been. She continued to sit there. They were sitting in their corner, left to themselves. Not even the waiter paid any attention to them. Helene hadn't ordered anything. Outside, it rained more heavily now. Whenever the door was opened, a cold breeze blew in.

Henryk accompanied Helene to her car. He walked slowly. Held his arms away from his body, stiff. They didn't talk while they walked. Nor when they were at the car. Helene had unlocked the car door and was about to get in. Henryk had propped his elbow on the car roof. He held his head in his hands. Helene looked at him across the roof. Couldn't they see each other. Tomorrow. Now, he had to go back to bed. Where was he staying, Helene asked. In a small hotel. And how were the children. Fine, Helene said. They were fine. After all, school was almost over for the year. Shouldn't they have breakfast. Together. At the Landtmann? At 10 o'clock. Tomorrow? Henryk looked at Helene, pleading. Straight ahead of her, on the Schwedenplatz, Helene could see the memorial for the victims of the Gestapo. The wind was blowing into the treetops all around. And into the bushes in bloom. Helene thought, in a flash, how nature does not offer consolation. She'd come to the Landtmann. If she could arrange it. Helene got into her car. Henryk stepped back. She drove off. At the light down at the Schwedenplatz she had to stop. She turned around. Henryk was out of sight. She had forgotten her umbrella in Café Korb. She didn't drive back.

Saturday morning was beautiful. The wind was still fresh from last night's rain. Helene made breakfast for the children. If she wasn't going to eat with them, they'd rather have breakfast in bed, they said. Helene balanced a tray with cocoa and toast up to Barbara's bunk bed. Katharina ate butter biscuits with her hibiscus tea. "Like on TV," the children said. Helene was convinced she'd find the beds drenched with cocoa and tea afterwards. Then she asked what the children wanted for lunch and left. Helene sat on the terrace of the Landtmann. Only a few tables were taken. She ordered from the waiter who also played the part of a waiter in the TV show "Café Central." She had known him since university. He greeted her as if she were well known at the Landtmann. She ordered a big breakfast and got herself some papers. Helene felt at home. She found only the Standard and the Kronen-Zeitung. It was the only drawback of the Landtmann. They didn't have all the papers. And the few they had were always just being read by somebody else. Helene leafed through the Kronen-Zeitung. On page 17 she saw a photo of Sophie Mergentheim. Next to it the headline, "A Mother's Act of Desperation in Salzburg." It appeared that Sophie had mixed sleeping pills into her daughter's dinner. She then had taken pills herself. In the morning, the mother was found still alive. But the 7-year-old daughter was beyond help. The mother was accused of murder. For the time being, she remained in the Psychiatric Ward of Salzburg Provincial Hospital. Helene was looking at the trees in City Hall Park. They were bursting with every shade of green. City Hall was behind them. Towering. Dirty. The Burgtheater squatted across from City Hall. Helene sat there. Staring. The coffee in front of her. She knew exactly what the days had looked like. The days that had led there. How one had followed the other. How during the days the pain would be locked inside. And locked from the outside at night. How the decision from the beginning. Its execution still an absurdity. But each day and each night, decision and execution that much closer. Until it became possible. How she'd wished a love existed. And one would take the other's hand. And never let go again. And how the wish to protect the children from life. How this wish could drown out everything else. And how terrible life was. How fragmented. How dirty. How small. And nobody'd ever told you. Helene at first didn't see Henryk. Henryk sat down at the table. Helene looked at him. She told Henryk the story of Sophie. While talking, Helene found it curious how much she knew about the woman. She'd never talked to her. Only the one time on the phone. In Püppi's bathroom. She'd once seen her. And somebody had mentioned that it was the Sophie Mergentheim from Salzburg. That was before the children were born. Sophie's child was the same age as Barbara. Henryk had ordered a short Braunen. He asked if he might have one of Helene's Butterkipferl. Helene pushed a sweet crescent roll over to him and carried on talking. About Püppi. And Niemeyer. What had been going on there. And Alex. What did he have to do with the story. In mid-sentence Helene realized Henryk was hungry. She continued to talk. She buttered a bun for Henryk. Put ham on it. And cheese. She couldn't eat. What was really going on with him. Could he go shopping with her. He could tell her everything on the way. Afterwards, she would have to go home. The children. Yes. It was one of those ice ages with the grandmother. Helene had shown her the lawyer's letter and asked what she'd done to Gregor. How he'd been as a child. If as an adult he couldn't help being so cruel. And so irresponsible. "Yes," Helene said to the waiter. "Yes. Put it all on my bill."

Again Helene had to go to the Meinl in the Krottenbachstrasse. She needed detergent and toilet paper. And she didn't want to go to a whole lot of stores. During the drive she found out where Henryk had been. He said the arguments with his girlfriend from Munich had been horrible. And then he'd had to take her to Munich. Because of a myoma. And he no longer had anything to do with any of it. The girlfriend had gone through Gestalt therapy, and then the therapist had moved in. Two concerts had been canceled. The Commune di Milano didn't have the money. Although everything had been agreed to. Later in Munich he had fallen ill. Fever. Very high fever. He now had the apartment in Milan. The rent was paid up to September. What he'd do after that he didn't know. There was only his practice piano in the apartment. But then it would have to go back too. If he didn't have the money by September, it'd have to be returned. Other than that, there was only a mattress in the apartment. Henryk laughed.

Helene did the shopping. The store was full, and there were long lineups at the cashiers. Henryk helped Helene. He lined up at the deli counter. They'd pulled number 95. Number 83 was being served. Helene got fruit and vegetables. Milk. Yogurts. Cheese. She saw Henryk stand there. Patiently. He'd even started a conversation with an elderly woman. They were both smiling about something. She got pork schnitzels for lunch. Then she lined up with Henryk. Helene bought farmer's ham, veal liver paté and frankfurters. Henryk said good-bye to the woman when they moved on. She smiled at him in a friendly way. She did not acknowledge Helene. Henryk put his arm around Helene's shoulders. When it was their turn at the cashier, Helene had to free herself from his embrace. The sudden coolness showed her how intimately they had nestled into each other.

They had been talking the whole time. Chatting. Smiling. It was as if Henryk had been away only for a few days. And not for weeks. Helene had to hurry piling her groceries onto the conveyor belt. Henryk packed it all into two big shopping bags. He did it slowly. But he packed the less fragile things first. Eggs and yogurts he stacked on top. Helene paid. She suddenly liked Henryk again. He had stood there so seriously as he was filling the bags.

Henryk stayed for lunch. He helped Helene. The children came into the kitchen. They set the table. Henryk tried to teach the children an old English folk song. It started with words like "Summarisi Kummarisi" and was to be sung as a canon. They didn't get beyond the first line. Katharina couldn't sing. She droned a deep tone. Barbara made mistakes on purpose. They all had to laugh. And start all over.

For coffee, Helene sat down with Henryk in the living room. The children wanted to stay with the adults. Katharina sat on Helene's lap. Barbara climbed on the back of the couch and balanced on Helene's shoulders. Helene tried to persuade the children to go into their room. Didn't they have homework to do. Shouldn't they read a bit. Or draw. Or play a computer game. Or tidy up. Perhaps? To everything the children responded with "No, thank you" and laughed. Helene wanted to order them to leave. But she knew what an effort it would have been. And they would no longer be able to talk at all. She got up and said it looked as though they'd better go and get ice creams. They drove to the Ruckenbauer. At the bottom of the Sieveringer Strasse. The children got ice-cream cones. Helene had nothing. She always finished Katharina's ice cream. Katharina was never able to finish her ice cream. Henryk walked beside them. He had chosen chocolate ice cream. They walked for a bit down the Obkirchergasse. Looked at the shop displays. Licked their ice creams. Then Helene got Katharina's warmed, squeezed wrapper with some leftover lemon ice cream. They were standing in front of a shoe store window. Helene noticed their reflection in the glass. Like a family, she thought. Is that how it should have worked out? Maybe she was at fault, after all. Could she have done anything differently? Should she? "You know what," Helene said to Henryk, "I'll take you to Milan." Henryk had told her in the car he had to go back in the evening. And he would have to ride without a ticket. He had no money for a train ticket. But it wouldn't be a big problem. In Milan maybe one of his projects would work out. And he'd have to practice too. Henryk laughed and took a bite of his ice cream.

Helene had been serious about her offer. She took the children home. Went next door to the grandmother. Told her she had to go away. Would the old woman take care of the children. Everything was arranged. She wouldn't have to do a thing. Just be there. In case something happened. The old woman was immediately prepared to go to the children. But of course she'd be happy to make herself useful. And she loved them all. Helene held the old woman in her arms. She felt the loose, aged skin of the woman. It was silky and soft. The old woman leaned against her. Helene tore herself away. She didn't understand either how everything could have worked out the way it had, she said. She explained to the woman what there was for the children to eat. She kissed the old woman on the cheek and went back to her own apartment. She told the children again where they'd find the food. She packed a nightgown and her toiletries into a small bag. "Okay. I'm ready. We can leave," she said to Henryk.

They still had to pick up Henryk's travel bag from the hotel. He had asked Helene if she really wanted to drive that far. Helene had nodded. Henryk hadn't wanted to believe her. Helene sensed how he'd much rather have asked her to lend him the money for the ticket. She wondered whether to drive via Innsbruck and Bozen. Or through the Canal Valley. Henryk thought both routes equally long. Roughly. Helene decided to take the West autobahn. And then go back via the Canal Valley. In the end, she'd have driven a big ellipse through central Europe.

They drove in silence. For a long time. Henryk was asleep. Near Linz, they started talking again. About the many unexplained details that had in the meantime occurred to Helene. Where had the travel bag been. She'd had to buy sweaters and underwear for Henryk because he'd lost the key to the locker. In which supposedly his bag was. Where had he stayed when he hadn't come home all night. Where had he been when he'd gone on trips. Where had he been when he was in Vienna. Why had the phone bill amounted to 7000 schillings. Who had he been phoning. What did it mean to have found a tailor's bill for a suit in the trash can. Where had Henryk got the money for the suit. Was he even able to play the piano. Helene had never heard him play. Why hadn't he phoned. Why had he kept her waiting. Why had he declared his love for her. Did he think these promises were necessary. She would have gone to bed with him anyway. Did he feel great about himself now. At least she'd almost gone crazy with longing for him. Felt as if she were going to die. From the longing. He was welcome to smirk. Henryk sat staring at the autobahn. At first, Helene had only meant to ask about the travel bag. All the other questions had just poured out. Helene couldn't have stopped herself. She started chewing gum. She no longer understood why she'd started this trip. There was nothing she could do about it now. Henryk said everything was okay now, wasn't it. He'd made everything up to her, hadn't he. He was sorry. But she had to understand his situation. He was an artist. It wasn't his style. Had never gotten into the habit. Of staying in touch. He'd thought his declarations of love had been clear enough. Had simply been enough. Helene no longer understood why she'd been longing for this man. Maybe Püppi was right. It was all about having a man. Any man.

Helene drove all the way to Milan. She'd wondered in Innsbruck whether to take Henryk to the station. But by then it no longer mattered. They arrived in the middle of the night. Henryk gave her directions through streets that went on forever. Through alleys. Then she had to look for a place to park. Cars had been left in every conceivable spot. In the end, she parked her Renault 5 on the sidewalk. Henryk took her past a few houses. He unlocked a little door that was part of a huge wooden gate. They stepped into a high passageway that opened into a courtyard. Henryk switched on a light. Thin, it lit their way across the yard to another passageway and staircase in the poorer quarters at the back. The staircase rose up, square and narrow. Helene followed Henryk. At the top, she could no longer tell how many floors they'd climbed. They hadn't walked past a single door. High up. At the end of the staircase they reached a metal door. The door led into a long passage. This passage had doors on the left, evenly spaced. 2 lights lit the passage. The last paint job had been a long time ago. The paint had peeled off. One could see the masonry. It was hot and smelled dry and dusty, like sweltering roof joists. Henryk unlocked the first door. Helene followed him into a huge room. In the corner on the right was a mattress. The piano stood below a small round window at the other end of the room. A wooden-frame hammer piano. A valuable piece. Miniature blackamoors held up the case. The gold decorations glittered. The wood gleamed. On the wall to the left was a sink. And a shower stall. Helene could see where against the wall pieces of furniture had stood and where pictures had hung. The floorboards were painted white. In the center, a light bulb hung from the ceiling. Henryk stood there. Put his travel bag down. Helene put hers next to it. The bags sat in the middle of the room. Under the light bulb. Helene turned to Henryk. Henryk took a key from a hook, to the right of the door. He walked down the hallway with her. Then he unlocked a door. He tore it open with pizzazz and stepped aside with a bow. He remained in this position. Helene stared into the room. "This is truly the tiniest bathroom I've ever seen," she said. Astonished. Henryk nodded in agreement. Still bowing deeply. Twitching. Helene thought he was crying. Sobbing. Because everything was so terrible. Too exhausting. She being so awful. And so relentless. But Henryk was laughing. He struggled to get out "in the world." "The tiniest bathroom in the world." He was wheezing. Shaking with laughter. Stuck in his bow. And laughing. Gasping for breath. Helene pushed him aside and locked herself in. She had trouble pulling her jeans down without peeing her pants. She had needed to go to the bathroom since Brixen. But hadn't wanted to mention it. She carefully sat down on the tiny toilet seat. She wanted to flush. She didn't want Henryk to listen. He was puffing on the other side of the door. Helene looked around. The chain hung high up on the wall. Behind her. Unreachable while she was sitting. She couldn't get up. She let it pour out. Heard it rush. Felt it jetting out of her. Heard Henryk sobbing with laughter. Then she flushed. Pulled the chain. There was no handle. While pulling up her pants, she had to laugh. She went into the hallway to

Henryk. Then she stood in front of the door. She must have gone a few steps down the hallway. Towards his room. But Henryk had the key to the room. And he had locked it. When leaving. Helene felt as if she were alone. Up here. She stood there and giggled to herself. Henryk came out of the bathroom. The flush was roaring behind him. They looked at each other and giggled. Started to laugh again. Clinging to each other, they walked back to the room. Still laughing, Henryk unlocked the door. Locked it again behind them. Laughing still, they undressed. Each movement triggering another outburst of laughter. They lay down on the bed. Without brushing their teeth or washing. Henryk had no bedding. No sheets. No covers. There was a yellow sofa cushion and a green and blue checkered blanket. They were pushing against each other. There was barely enough room on the mattress. They continued to laugh. Helene could feel Henryk's diaphragm. It was throbbing against her belly. Hers against his chest. Whenever one of them tried to say something. Or moved. The laughing would immediately start again. They clung to each other, convulsing. Had to take a deep breath. And laugh about that too. Helene woke up. With a dull thud, Henryk had fallen off the mattress. Now it was 10 in the morning. Helene felt dirty. Sticky. She had a shower. There was only cold water. Henryk crawled back onto the mattress. He went on sleeping.

Helene woke Henryk. It was almost noon. She had sat down on the piano chair and looked out the window. You could see nothing but roofs. Roofs. Domes. Little turrets in the self-congratulatory bourgeois style of the 1870's industrial expansion. Flat roofs in between. And everywhere TV antennas. The sun had been beating on the roof. The room had gotten hotter and hotter. The air drier. And dustier.

Helene had opened the window. But the air hadn't moved. The piano had creaked. Henryk hadn't woken up. Helene shook him. She had to go. Henryk was heavy with sleep. Understood nothing at first, not even who she was. He went for a shower. Helene paced up and down. Until he was done. She took her travel bag down to the car. She was glad to be in the street. In the room under the roof she'd felt like the only human being in the world. They went to a bar. Had coffee. Ate Brioches and Tramezzini. Helene paid. Then they walked back to the car. Helene had to leave. They stopped at every window display. In front of a jeweler's, Henryk said she shouldn't leave him. She was all he had left. She had seen now how things were, hadn't she. Helene couldn't say anything. She had to go. She would have liked to go back up with him. Would have lain down on the mattress. In the heat. But there was no time. And he didn't seem to be interested. Helene felt heat rising into her cheeks. She had to look at the ground. She couldn't possibly beg. For it. At the car, she said she wouldn't leave him. He said nothing. She got in. Drove off. That moment when she was standing at the open car door and he wasn't responding. In that moment, she would have liked to hurt him. Cut him with a knife. In his arm. Or his cheeks. Because he was letting her drive off that way. Because he hadn't even tried. She hadn't even been given the opportunity to say no.

Helene took the long road through the Po valley. The heat lay heavy and hazy over the fields. The entire time she tried to figure out a way to do it. She thought she might go to the bathroom at one of the rest stations and do it there. As in the past, at university. She tried it in the car. But she was afraid the truck drivers would watch. Or the people in the buses might catch her. Doing it. She felt hot and swollen between her legs. Ready to burst. Her jeans rubbed her.

For hours, she was on the verge of an orgasm. But in agony. She was scorching along the autobahn. Through the Canal Valley. Already quite far beyond Udine, Helene ran out of gas. She hadn't paid attention to anything. Had only been driving. When the accelerator suddenly felt limp under her foot and she couldn't hear the motor anymore, she immediately realized what had happened. She let the car coast onto the shoulder. For a moment she was filled with blind rage. Then she told herself that at least it hadn't happened in one of the long tunnels. She got out. After a long time, an Italian gave her a ride to a gas station. The man even drove off the autobahn to help out. It was Sunday afternoon, and no gas station was open in the area. There were none on the autobahn. At the gas station along a small, steep road Helene had to buy a jerry can. The man didn't believe she'd return the can. Helene paid. A man in a red VW Golf gave her a ride back. He was a member of the Klagenfurt police, on his way to his boat in Grado. He wished Helene all the best. Helene had to sprint across the autobahn. She poured the gas. Spilled it. Got angry. Drove back to the gas station. Got gas. Returned the can. Drove on. Late at night, she arrived in Vienna. Everything was fine. The children were asleep in their beds. Helene tucked them in neatly. For a while, she listened to their breathing.

Helene went to a lawyer. She had read in the paper the lawyer had won a case against a painter. Who hadn't wanted to pay maintenance for his first wife. The first wife had supported the painter before he became famous. Now he was famous. And a younger wife had appeared. In the trial, the painter had argued. That the first wife, with her jealousy and her histrionics. That she had ruined him artistically. Had murdered his inspiration. That therefore she deserved no money. Dr. Loibl, the lawyer, had managed to make him cough up quite a substantial settlement for the first wife. And several paintings. Inspired by the new wife. At the moment, they were very valuable. Helene had immediately looked up the phone number of the law firm and made an appointment. Dr. Loibl. Dr. Otto Loibl was old. He was tall. Wore a pin-striped suit. Was tanned. Had a snow-white mane which he would flip out of his face with a toss of his head. He looked like the heroic mountaineer Luis Trenker. He invited Helene to have a seat on his black leather couch. He dropped into a leather armchair. He lit a cigar. And began to ask questions. It took him no time at all to get the whole story. The husband who had left. The wife who didn't know where he lived. "Outrageous!" Dr. Loibl said. Two years had passed since? "Unbelievable!" And had paid nothing? "Of course not!" Did she at least get the child allowance payments? No? For 2 years, that alone would add up to quite something. Helene only had to write a letter to the Child Welfare Office at the Department of Revenue. It could be informal. Yes. And next. Helene passed him the letter. "Oh well. Colleague Kopriva." Helene said the letter had arrived because Gregor. That is to say, her husband. Well. Because he'd seen another man with her. In the apartment. That is, in his former apartment. Their joint apartment. But it had been a misunderstanding. The man had only come for breakfast. Dr. Loibl smiled. This wasn't the issue. "My dear," he said. The man had to pay. After 2 years a woman, too, had a right to. Well. She understood, didn't she. Dr. Loibl smiled at Helene. In addition, Gregor had an affair with her best friend. Dr. Loibl shook his head. "How often do I have to hear that," he said. "You have no idea. But now. My dear." Dr. Loibl got up and started pacing up and down. "We must agree on one thing. You must trust me. Completely and without any reservation. Trust! Do you understand. It's the most important thing. If you trust me, I can get everything for you. Absolutely." Dr. Loibl was standing behind Helene. He put his hands on the back of the couch on either side of her head and bent over her. "Absolute trust. That's the condition. Then I can work." Helene felt his breath on her left ear. Dr. Loibl walked around the couch. He sat down on the coffee table. Perched there opposite Helene. He took her hands. Held them. He had dry, strong hands. Helene's hands disappeared in his. He didn't want to find a client stabbing him in the back. Because she started to feel sorry for her husband. Or allowed herself to be put under pressure. "Number one rule," Dr. Loibl said. He put Helene's hands back on her thighs. "Not a word to him. From now on, he must talk to me. Leave your address with my secretary. And his. His work address if necessary. And leave me this letter. Good. And if something comes up. Call. Just call!" He slapped Helene on the shoulder. Helene went straight to the Prückl and had a Campari Soda.

Helene only found the letter in the evening. She'd been alone at the office all day. Frau Sprecher had stayed home with a bad case of gastritis. She had become very thin, in the last little while. She had pressed her lips together and not spoken. Helene had asked once if there were no other tomcats. Couldn't she get another one. Frau Sprecher then said quite calmly that Helene evidently didn't understand a thing. Helene had to agree with Frau Sprecher. But Frau Sprecher did not want to jest. She could not be deterred from her mood. The next day, Frau Sprecher hadn't come to work. Helene had been glad about it. There was nothing to do. She read the paper at work. Henryk's letter was on the floor inside the door. Aunt Mimi had taken the children to a friend's place on Lake Atter. Helene bent down to pick up the letter. She had to sit down. She sat on the floor and began to cry. She'd been waiting for so long. Several times she'd wanted to take off and look for Henryk in his attic room, to pack a big picnic basket and drive to Milan, enter the house, run up the back stairs. The metal door would have slowed her. Helene would have had to sit on the stairs and wait. Wait. Until Henryk came up the stairs or wanted to go down. On weekends, Helene would have had time. She had sold her collection of gold coins, gold coins her grandfather received for his achievements when he retired as a civil servant. Gold medals of honor which the bank had studied with curiosity before buying them. Collector's items, the man in the Ögussa shop in the Kaiserstrasse had told her. She should sell them to a bank. He could only pay her for the value of the gold. Which would be a pity. She would lose. That was why once more Helene had a bit of money. Helene tore the letter open. Sobbing. During the sobbing she wondered why it all had to be this way. What was she doing wrong. Why had she to take it so seriously. Henryk wrote about a concert in Stresa. The second one. Again, everything had gone well. The piano had had to be shipped to the island by ferry. He'd been very worried about the safety of the instrument. He loved her. She should know that. He'd come back to Vienna soon. Helene was reading the letter, sitting on the floor. She had thought she would never hear from Henryk again. If only he had a phone. And if it had been possible to talk with him. His voice. At least.

Helene met Gregor in Café Bräuner Hof. Gregor had phoned her. Helene hadn't talked to him in weeks. It was a hot day. At the end of July. The Bräuner Hof was almost empty. The waiter leaned in the doorway, bored. Helene sat down by the window. Ordered the set menu, minestrone and cream cheese dumplings filled with apricots. She got herself some papers. As she ate the minestrone, Helene realized how nervous she was. She spilled some soup. Considerable effort was needed to steady the spoon. She ate the soup. Pulled herself together. The apricot dumplings were served. Gregor arrived at the same time and stood impatiently at the table until the waiter had put down the food and poured the beer. Gregor ordered a tall coffee with a dash of milk. He dropped himself onto the bench opposite Helene. He tossed a letter on the table. What was the meaning of this, he asked. Helene began to eat the apricot dumplings. She pricked them open, cut them up, sprinkled sugar on them and cut them up some more. Actually, she thought, she should be the one to ask this question. Helene held the letter for a moment. It was still unopened. Helene laughed. The dumplings tasted very good. The dough was airy and light, the apricots sweet and soft, the crumbs toasted golden-brown. Gregor leaned over the table. "If you stay with this swine, there'll be war," he said. "What swine?" Helene asked. "This swine!" Gregor pointed at the letter. "Loibl is known for his methods." "Well. You see. That suits me just fine," Helene said. And what did he mean: war? "War means I'll take the children from you." Helene laughed out loud. High. "There are enough stories about you." He said. "You know that. You sit around bars, entire nights. For which there are witnesses. You're a drunk. And probably taking drugs. Your companions are more than questionable. You take men to the apartment. Indiscriminately. And don't forget. Katharina's accident. How you let her fall off the changing table. It's on record. There won't be much to laugh about pretty soon. Even the teachers think the children should be sent to therapy. You'll see. I'll succeed. You always leave them with my mother anyway. I can do that too. Even though my mother is way too old and just can't cope anymore, you've left her to bring up the children almost entirely by herself." Helene took another bite of her dumplings. Say nothing, she told herself. Say nothing. He's trying to provoke you, she told herself and let the sweet dough melt in her mouth. But the fear rose, gripped her around the throat, made swallowing difficult and everything hazy before her eyes. "Charming," she said. Her voice failed. She was unable to speak. Helene had been staring at her plate during Gregor's speech. Now she looked at him. Gregor was filled with rage. Contorted with rage. The corners of his mouth were twisted into a furious grin. Helene was sure he'd hit her. The next moment. Here. Now. In the Bräuner Hof. Take a swing and thrash her. "Do it," she said. "Just do it. It would really impress the court." Gregor stared at her. For a moment it was possible. His rage caused the air around him to vibrate. He got up. He wanted to say something. Bent over the table. Hung above her. Helene shrunk back. She lifted her arm to fend off the blow. Gregor saw the movement. His rage dissolved into a contemptuous grin. "You see, I'm not your father!" he hissed at her, turned and charged off. He hadn't taken a single sip of his coffee. The letter lay on the table. Helene put it into her purse. She finished her meal, slowly, picked all the crumbs off her plate. She went back to the office. She would have liked to sleep. She had the need to lie down, right then. To curl up. Pull up the blanket and sleep.

Henryk wrote he'd be able to come soon. To Vienna. Maybe, after all, something could be achieved in Vienna. At the Conservatory. Henryk was fighting against the music establishment. Against the Vienna Philharmonic's version of A 440, excessively high in pitch. And against the fixed pitch of the iron frame piano. He was doing battle with the entire musical machinery of the second half of the 19th century. Helene couldn't understand all of his arguments. And at times his vehemence seemed a bit exaggerated to her. But Henryk had always been able to explain plausibly the conspiracies and commercial interests of the music business to her. It was solely about maintaining the market for castrated, canned music, he'd told her. Muzak becoming part of the serious music scene. No proper musician would want to be a part of that. Taking risks, such as varying the pitch of instruments. Taking risks of this kind that made music sound less pleasing. That's what the music industry was afraid of. Because they wanted the death of music. Because the corpse was better. Was easiest to sell. Like Jesus Christ. Another who could be marketed only as a mangled corpse. The iron frame piano had been the death sentence. And no Glenn Gould in the world could save the music now.

Helene had her period. After a pause of several months. It was hot. The hottest summer in 43 years, they said. She decided to see a gynecologist to get an IUD. She no longer wanted to have to think about whether or not she could do it. Or if she should use one of those contraceptive ovules. She didn't like condoms. Henryk had shown her an AIDS test. And she wasn't sleeping with anybody else. It probably wasn't what the brochures called a long-term relationship. But most women she knew didn't do it at all. Particularly the married ones. Helene made an appointment with a Dr. A. Drimmel. His practice was on the Gymnasiumstrasse. Just around the corner. At first she had to sit in Dr. Drimmel's waiting room. An older nurse came out of his office and asked her to wait a bit longer. Helene sat there. A window to the garden was open. It was quiet. Hardly a bird to be heard. Traffic hum from far away only. Helene felt how sweat gathered under her breasts and trickled down her belly. The nurse accompanied her into the examination room. She should take a seat, she said. The doctor would be with her in a moment. Helene sat down on a small art nouveau chair in front of an art nouveau desk. The doctor arrived. He was about 35. Looked fresh. Vivacious. Sporty. What was the problem. Helene told him she wanted to get an IUD. That she'd already mentioned it on the phone. And that she was having her period right now. So it should work. "Yes. Yes," Dr. Drimmel said. He looked at Helene. "There she is, on her first visit, and already wants an IUD." He said it sadly to the nurse, who stood next to the screen in front of the examination chair. The woman shrugged. Helene was annoyed. Why had she come to this doctor? She looked at him with hostility. "Do you know everything you need to know?" the man asked. Helene nodded. "Then let's do it," the doctor said. "Which one do you want," the nurse asked. "Well, Mom, let's have a look," the doctor answered. Helene was led behind the screen. She undressed and lay on the examination table. Her legs high. In the stirrups, way up. What a brain dead situation, Helene thought. Mother and son put their heads together between her legs. Something cold slid into her vagina. Making slurping sounds. The two of them talked quietly. The woman went to get something. The son waited. He held up his hands in their rubber gloves. Helene could hear a plastic package being ripped open. He pushed something thin into her vagina. A sharp pain deep in her belly. Helene started. "Done," the doctor said. He walked over to the sink. Pulled off the rubber gloves and washed his hands. Helene stood up and got dressed. When she came out from behind the screen, he was sitting at his desk leafing through a magazine. His mother would take care of everything else, he said to her. Absentminded, friendly. He didn't shake her hand. Was absorbed in his magazine. Helene left the room. The mother stood behind the reception desk. She was writing the bill. 2500 schillings said the piece of paper she handed to Helene. Helene took the money from her purse and put it down. The woman stamped the bill. Helene left. The A in front of Dr. Drimmel stood for Augustin. Dr. Drimmel's name was Augustin. Helene found it fitting.

Helene and the children returned from a swim. She found the mother-in-law sitting in her living room. Which was against all their agreements. Helene sent the children to the bathroom. To rinse out their bathing suits. Every day they either went to the Klosterneuburger beach on the Danube. Or to the beach on the Old Danube. Or else sometimes to the Schafberg Pool. Or they drove to Bad Vöslau. Helene was on vacation. Until September 10. 4 weeks. One of them without pay. Because the magnetic foil hadn't progressed as quickly as Nadolny and Nestler had expected. The older Frau Gebhardt looked at Helene for a long time. She said nothing. Helene leaned back in her sofa. The sun had made her pleasantly weary. The children splashed around in the bathroom. Henryk would come in 2 weeks. After dinner, she'd go for a walk with the children. And then, maybe, read something. She wouldn't drive to her parents. The car made a strange sound, on the right front side. And she couldn't get it fixed. In two weeks, maybe. When the child allowance payments would be transferred. And eventually Gregor's back payments would have to arrive. And then she'd be able to pay off her debts at the bank. Helene had almost dozed off. Had almost forgotten her anger at the old woman's intrusion. The old woman said, "So now it's come to this." She spoke calmly. "To what?" Helene asked. All her life she'd gotten along with everybody, the old woman said. It couldn't be her. But Helene, it was impossible with her. And it was Helene. Not her. And such a disgrace. She'd never experienced. The bailiff had come. She'd never thought she'd have to go through that. Helene might think it amusing. After all, she seemed to look on life as one big entertainment. But it wasn't. Bills were to be paid, after all. In real life. Afterwards. But. Helene would see. And. Under the circumstances it would be better if Gregor took the children. She was too irresponsible. Debts! The children would learn it from her. All of it. No order. There was no order in Helene's life. For children, that was the worst. And it had probably all happened for a reason. Gregor would know why he'd left her. No one could have expected it. Everyone had thought, the daughter of a Chief Justice of the Court. You'd have thought she'd be something decent. But they'd been wrong. All of them. The bailiff had put a lien on 3 Persian carpets and the TV set. And just how did Helene think she was going to pay her debts? She had, by the way, phoned Helene's parents and told them everything. And didn't it show that Helene had a guilty conscience. Her parents not even knowing that Gregor had moved out. Or of her lovers. Foreigners! Helene would see. Gregor would come back. After all, it was his apartment. And as for herself, she didn't see why she should have to do without so much. The flat had been divided to help the young family. If there was no more family, there was no longer any need to divide it up. Helene would have to leave. People had rights. And she was determined to get hers. And Gregor's. And his children's. And it was a pity that it all had turned out to be such a mistake. Helene didn't say anything. She didn't move during the lecture. She kept her eyes half closed and listened. "Please go now," Helene said. The old woman got up. "You can't tell me that. My dear!" She stressed the "you." And went. The children stood in the door to the living room. The grandmother walked past them. Walked out. The children ran up to Helene. They didn't want to leave. Did they have to leave? What was happening? They didn't want to be with Gregor. Katharina cried. Barbara threw herself onto the sofa, furious. Helene was afraid. What if Gregor came back? Helene grabbed the phone. Reached a recording at Dr. Loibl's. His office would reopen for business on September 3. Helene phoned locksmiths. But it was too late. She couldn't reach anybody anywhere. Various emergency lock and security services told her that it was possible to change locks. Only, she'd have to provide evidence that she was the owner of the apartment. But it would be very expensive. Would cost three times the normal rate. At least. Helene couldn't have afforded it. And what could she have done to prove her ownership. Helene allowed the children to sleep in her bed. She tried to explain everything to them. The debts weren't that bad. They had enough money. Their father would only have to pay what he was obliged to pay. Then everything would work out. And nobody could take them away from her. It was impossible. Grandma had gotten a scare. Grandma was from a different time when bailiffs in the house meant a terrible disgrace. Although even then most people had debts. And were dirt poor. She, Helene, would much rather have debts than brothers who were SS officers. As had been the case with Grandma. What was an SS officer? Helene told the children over again not to worry. She'd do everything for them. Hadn't she always? And at some point things would get better. They'd see. In the end, the children fell asleep. Helene had to stay in the room. Only when the children were asleep, was she able to go to the living room and think.

Helene checked once more that the key was in the lock. Then she sat on the window sill and looked down into the street. She had to talk to her father. He'd have to give her some advice. Helene was thinking. She tried to think systematically. She was afraid. She didn't want to talk to her father. But because of the children she'd have to do it. She felt caught. Caged. Helpless. One big case of blackmail, she thought. My life has turned into one big case of blackmail. She started to pace up and down the room. She would have liked to leave the apartment. Under the sky. And breathe. But she couldn't. Not because of the children, though. Suddenly she was convinced Gregor was lying in wait in his mother's apartment. Waiting for her to leave her apartment. Then he'd install himself in the apartment. Change the lock. Gregor was a skilled handyman. The children would be in the apartment which she wouldn't be able to enter again. And she'd have to sue for the children. And Henryk was so far. Nobody close to talk to. "It's too much to bear," Helene whispered to herself. "It's impossible. Nobody could. Nobody possibly could." She walked along the patterned edges of the carpet. Right around. Over and over. She had clasped her crossed hands behind her back. Repeated the sentences to herself. Over and over again. Helene was glad not to have sleeping pills in the house. She'd taken the Valium from Dr. Stadlmann back to the pharmacy, for recycling. Helene had a bourbon. Then she took the bottles and emptied everything alcoholic into the toilet. Even the cooking rum. She couldn't afford to make a mistake. She could not even be seen with a glass in her hand. For a moment Helene was tempted to behave the way she'd been painted. Then she sat down. They should not be proved right.

Helene was waiting for the locksmith. On the phone the man had said he could be there by 8 o'clock. She had asked him to be on time. At 8 her mother-in-law was at morning mass. The change of the lock could pass unnoticed. The man had said he'd only need half an hour. Then he'd be all done. The locksmith wasn't coming. Because of him, Helene had gotten up early. At 9, he phoned to let her know he'd make it by 11. Would she still be there at that time. "Yes," Helene said. She'd wait. The children were sleeping in. Helene sat in the living room. Nothing could be heard in the apartment. From the street, sometimes a car. It would be another hot day. Helene had already closed the windows and drawn the curtains to keep out the heat. She sat in the dim room, waiting. At first, she had been sleepy still. She sipped her breakfast coffee. She didn't want to eat anything. She didn't want to eat anything at all. She'd have liked to get out of the apartment. Escape. Somewhere. Where it was spacious. Open. The trees in front of the window crowded her. She wanted to have a view. Helene didn't know the legal implications of changing the lock. She'd have to say she had lost the key. And she was getting it done for safety reasons. In fact, there was no way to do things right. In her situation, there was no way one could get it right. She just wanted to be safe. At least. She was afraid of Gregor. The way he'd looked at her in the Bräuner Hof showed that he'd beat her. Nobody would believe it, of him. But he would do it. The children should not see this. Gregor had the reputation of being a real gentleman. Well brought up, polite, cool. And gifted. Everyone would say she was only trying to badmouth him. To take revenge. Or that she'd provoked it. There is only so much patience in a man. And that she'd always been difficult. Helene sat there. Time passed. Once the lock was changed, there was no returning. That was it. Once and for all. Each time she glanced at her watch, again 2 mere minutes had passed. Helene wondered why it was she who had to bring about the end. At least he could have taken on that much himself. He could have called it off at least. But he was waiting. Waiting for her to make a mistake. So that the whole business would cost him less. Helene felt helpless. A flood of decisions lay ahead of her. Lots of running around. Legal stuff. Appointments. And swearing affidavits in front of complete strangers. Helene said to herself that if he phones. If he phones before the locksmith arrives, we'll look for a way. Out of this. The locksmith arrived at 1 p.m. Gregor hadn't phoned. Helene pulled the phone jack. She crammed her shopping basket full of books. The locksmith didn't take more than 30 minutes. The mother-in-law didn't appear at the door. She was having her nap. Probably. Helene received the new keys. She had to sign two security cards. One she kept. In case new keys had to be made, they'd be handed to nobody but the owner of the card. Helene signed with her maiden name. Awkwardly. The signature read Helene Wolffen. And looked like the writing on an exercise book label. Helene called the children. Now they could go to the pool again. Helene hadn't dared leave the apartment until the lock was changed. She had imagined they would come back. And find Gregor sitting there pretending the past 2 years had never happened. The idea had been so monstrous. So dreadful. And so possible. Helene and the children had lived for 2 days on cornflakes and UHT milk. It was difficult to find a locksmith during summer vacations. Helene carried the books away. She threw them into a recycling container near the beach on the Old Danube. She removed all the books from the house the same way. On each trip from the apartment she would take a pile. Until the shelves were empty. She threw the art books out as well. And the scholarly books. The ones on art history. And those on math. Helene kept only the crime novels. Nobody lied in crime novels. By the end of August, the shelves were empty.

Helene played the lottery. She took the children to the tobacconist in the Krottenbachstrasse. Next to the post office. They each filled out two sections. Barbara slipped with her pen beyond the edges of the little boxes when she marked the numbers. She had to fill out several forms. Until it was right. Katharina always marked the same numbers, Barbara always different ones. On Sunday night they sat in front of the TV and watched the drawing of the numbers. Should they win, each one of them wanted to go away. For starters. To America. Preferably.

Helene's mother came. Helene hadn't plugged the phone back in. Had been unavailable. The door bell rang. Helene opened the door. There was her mother. Helene assumed she'd first dropped in on her mother-in-law. Otherwise she'd have rung the front door bell. Helene didn't ask her mother in. Her mother waited in the hallway. Helene eyed her. She hadn't seen her for some time. She's put on weight again, Helene thought. Her mother wore a green linen suit. With a long jacket, to conceal her broad hips. She wore green shoes. Her small feet jammed in the shoes. The heels very high. The feet swollen from the heat and slightly bulging over the edges. "So what is going on?" the mother asked. She sounded gentle. And sad. And reproachful. "I doubt you'll be interested," Helene said. She was imitating her mother's tone. She had to control herself not to giggle. It sounded so charming. After a long pause. During which the mother had stared at her. Full of reproach and entreaty. After a long pause the mother asked why Helene hadn't come to her. To them. "Do you have 50 000 schillings?" Helene asked. "Yes. Take it," the mother said. She fished an envelope out of her handbag and offered it to Helene. "But your father wants a receipt," she said. Helene had the envelope already in her hand. She handed it back to her mother. Very politely. Automatically, the mother took it back. Stood there with the envelope. Looked at the floor, resigned. Could she find her way out, Helene asked. Or would she rather go and visit the mother-in-law again? Then Helene closed the door. She leaned against it on the inside. Her mother shouted at the closed door, "You're sick. You need help." Helene let herself slide down the door. Squatted on the floor. Whispered to her knees, "Assholes. Damn assholes." She stayed there. Listened to her mother leaving. The high heels were clicking. Her mother took fast little steps. Mincing. Ladylike. Helene couldn't help laughing.

Helene drove to the Sonnberg market. To buy fruit and vegetables. The Leonhards' produce stall had reopened. The Leonhards were back from their vacation. They'd been in the mountains, they said. And that they'd only ever go to the mountains. Frau Leonhard couldn't stand the heat. It didn't agree with her. Helene looked around. There were edible boletuses. Looking at them, Helene could taste the baked choice mushrooms. But since Chernobyl they were no longer eating mushrooms. Spinach. Fresh Spinach. "There's a good housewife," Frau Leonhard commented and stuffed spinach into a big plastic bag. Helene would unpack it right away, wouldn't she, Frau Leonhard asked. Helene bought grapes, plums, lemons, lettuce, apples, onions. Where did she go for the summer, Frau Leonhard asked Helene. Herr Leonhard had disappeared for a cigarette. Behind the stall. Helene had given the children some money. They had gone ahead to the Ruckenbauer. To buy ice cream. Helene intended to meet them there. She told Frau Leonhard that the children had been at Lake Atter. "And what about you?" Frau Leonhard asked. "Aren't you getting about at all these days?" Immediately Helene's eyes filled with tears. She was grateful. She could have hugged Frau Leonhard. Somebody showed an interest in her. But the sympathy in Frau Leonhard's voice hurt her. Hurt her pride. Made her realize how far things had gone. Everybody could see it. She saw it herself, of course. Every morning. She saw in the mirror how she was looking more and more haggard. Faded. Just thinking about the apartment triggered the feeling that everything was unstable. Nothing solid. Nothing orderly. The old woman next door. Reproachful. Mute. But present, always. And always the fear of Gregor showing up. And not being able to get into the apartment. And yelling. In the stairwell. How much pleasure would that give Frau Bamberger from the first floor. Fear for her children again overcame Helene. She said she'd also take an eggplant. And that's all. Thank you. Helene paid and drove along the Obkirchergasse. She found the children sitting on a bench. They sat opposite the ice-cream parlor and licked their ice creams. Helene honked, and the children came running to the car. They properly looked right and left before they crossed the street. Helene let them get in. They licked their ice creams and chatted. There were certain sneakers that Barbara wanted. Katharina finished off all of her ice cream. No, Mom wouldn't get any. She was big enough to finish an ice cream, Katharina said cheerfully. She bit off the tip of the cone and sucked the ice cream through. Helene drove home with them along the Höhenstrasse. She thought it best that way. Driving along, with the children in the back of the car. They rolled over the cobblestones of the Höhenstrasse. Nobody knew where they were. Where she was. She would have liked to drive on like this. Forever.

Helene had rented a deck chair. She had carried it beneath the willows. At the "Old Danube" beach pool Helene and the children went to the left hand corner. Under the big trees there was always some shade. Then the children ran to the water. Helene could only just see them from her chair. She didn't always go in the water. Getting wet was an effort for her. She lay on the deck chair. She had closed her eyes. The hot air was still around her. From time to time a cooler breeze off the water enveloped her. Yet the heat immediately drove the fresher air away again. Helene could have embraced the heat. For a moment, everything was right. The warm air on her naked skin. The children were jumping and squealing in the shallow water. Soon they would come running back. Would splash water over everything and tear the food out of the bag. In the morning, Helene had prepared rissoles. Which were still warm inside the buns. They would go and buy cold Cokes. Then they'd lie on the blanket and read. Nobody knew where they were. That was very important to Helene. From her affair with Alex, Helene had learned two things. Private investigators did exist. And people really did give them jobs. And you wouldn't notice if they followed you. Helene immediately had this threatening, spiraling feeling in her stomach again. She had been shocked. Speechless. When Gitta showed her the photos the private investigator had taken of her and Alex. Helene kept an eye out for pursuers. She walked along the cars in the Lannerstrasse. To see if anybody sat there waiting. She checked her rear-view mirror to see if a car followed her. Or if someone's face popped up repeatedly. She hadn't noticed anything. Helene sometimes didn't believe Gregor would go to all that trouble. Neither did she believe he seriously wanted the children. But then it wasn't clear how far he would go. Helene didn't want to have to think that far ahead. And she couldn't imagine what it would mean for the children. Gregor didn't even know what the children had for breakfast. But she had to be careful. After all, she'd never thought, either, that Gregor would leave her. One day. Leave her. Or the children. Helene lay on the deck chair. The buzzing around her made her sleepy. The water splashed against the landing, and the reeds behind her rustled in the light breeze. She was thinking. Telling herself how wonderful it all was. Just like in her classes on

Relaxation Through Self-Hypnosis. She told herself how calm and relaxed she was. And no fear. She felt no fear. Very briefly she succeeded. The body responded to the words. Helene was floating. She floated above the murmuring and the high-pitched yelling of the children in the water. Above the smell of grilled sausages. Above the waves that were dancing darkly and would light up weakly from time to time. Above the rich green of the grass and the treetops against the sky, a maze of glittering golden-green against the thin blue of the hazy hot day. For a moment nothing existed but her. She didn't succeed for long. Below the calm, a longing arose. Expanded from the center and filled her. Henryk. The wish to kill herself had arisen the same way. Earlier. A year ago. Exactly in such moments. And then the wish had been there. Helene wished she had the desire again to kill herself. Because it'd had to do with nobody but her. The waiting for Henryk. That was humiliating. Dependency. Almost cutting her apart. In the middle. Helene lay on her deck chair, exhausted. Abandoned. Tired. "Why're you laughing?" Barbara asked and wrapped her arms around Helene. The slender body of the child, cold and wet against her. Helene felt so big. "Have you been laughing?" the child asked. "You have, haven't you. Just then!" "Yes, I have. Because we're such a terrific bunch," Helene said. "Aren't we?" Barbara flung herself on the blanket. "Can I get a Coke?" Barbara had rolled on her back. Had spread her arms wide. Her small chest was rising and falling quickly. She lay there. With her eyes closed. Helene could see her sense of well-being. It would give way to the next wave of pleasure. Or would be cut short by some disappointment. In which case she would complain about it. Loudly. Helene rummaged in her bag for her wallet. When had this "forever" been implanted in her. The one she couldn't help longing for. And from which there was no relief. Self-pity flooded Helene. "Get one for me as well. Get some for all of us. We'll eat when you come back," she said to Barbara. Barbara lay still. Smiled. Then she jumped up. Snapped the wallet and raced off across the lawn. Disappeared among the people lying on the grass and the crowd around the restaurant. Helene realized. For weeks she hadn't felt like it. Hadn't had the vague burning sensation between her legs. Or felt her breasts hard against the material of a blouse. The singing pressure in her throat. Tickling. Helene leaned back. What was the point in getting herself the IUD. If she'd never again anyway. With a man. Maybe people should age faster, she thought.

Helene drove up the Währinger Strasse past the Folk Opera. She turned onto the Gürtel. She crossed lanes to get into the one for left turns. Behind her, a police cruiser came to a stop. Its light was flashing. Helene tried to move to the left to let it pass. But there wasn't enough room. Then the traffic light changed to yellow. Helene started. Turned left. The police car behind her. She moved into the right lane. She noticed a police officer eating a sausage at a sausage stand. The cruiser stayed behind her. Could have passed on the left. Helene had driven off as soon as possible. She thought the police would pass her sooner or later. She looked straight ahead. The siren was turned on. She looked to the left. The police were right next to her. The officer signaled her to stop. Helene took the next parking spot. The police car parked in front of her. He got out. The light continued to flash. The officer from the sausage stand came running. The officer from the car put on his hat. He stood next to her car. Looked down at Helene. Demanded her ownership and insurance papers and her license. Helene searched for them. Her hands trembled. Katharina reminded her that she kept them in the door, didn't she. Generally. Helene found them there. She got out. She didn't want the man to hang halfway into her car. And she didn't want to talk to him in front of her children. The officer checked her papers. He made her show him the traffic warning reflector. And the first aid kit. Why had she been stopped? Helene asked. What was wrong? Helene asked the officer who had come from the sausage stand. He was still chewing on a bit of bun. He didn't react. Watched his colleague. The other officer made Helene give her address. And. He was not obliged to inform her of the reason. He could stop her as often as he liked. Helene put her hands into the pockets of her linen pants. Did she want to pay. Or did she want a ticket. Helene said she couldn't pay if she didn't know what for. "Well then. A ticket," the officer said. She wasn't aware of any offense. The officers grinned at each other. That's interesting, they suggested. Helene took her license and ownership papers from the man's hand. The officer only caught on when she was already putting the papers back into her purse. "That's not going to help you either," he said. He looked at her, challenging. He was very young. Much younger than Helene. Helene felt like knocking him down. With one smack. Then he'd lie there. And she could look down at him from above. And leave. Helene said, "You'd better quit biting your nails if you want to be an official." She gave his hands a look, replete with meaning. The man blushed. His fingers white as he held his pen and pad. "Good bye," Helene said and got back in her car. For a moment she thought the man was about to pounce on her. "What's it about?" the children asked. "We've won," Helene said and started the car. She had to turn left to drive around the cruiser. For a long time, she couldn't merge with the moving traffic. She watched the officers. How they got in their car and talked. How the light flashed. Then Helene could drive past them. She didn't even look to the right.

That'll be expensive, she thought. She wanted to take the children to get ice creams. The children were tired. They wanted to go straight home.

On September 3 Helene phoned Dr. Loibl's office. After several attempts. A secretary kept telling her to try again in 20 minutes. Then she said she'd phone Helene back. Helene couldn't very well say she wasn't picking up her phone. That she wasn't answering calls. Didn't open her door. Had changed the lock. Was afraid her husband might show up and make demands she wouldn't know how to respond to. Felt pursued. She repeated to the woman on the other end how urgent it was for her to speak to Dr. Loibl. Helene sat next to the phone and waited. The children were whiny. They wanted to go outside. They wanted to go by themselves. They had really enjoyed the times when Helene hadn't let them out of her sight. But it had lasted long enough. Now they felt reassured by their mother and wanted to have their freedom back. They prowled around the apartment. Listened if they could hear anything at their grandmother's. Asked innocently if they could go and see Grandma. The phone rang. Helene sent the children away. They wouldn't leave. Helene yelled at them. Reluctantly, they started toward the door. Helene picked up the phone. It was Püppi. Helene couldn't say anything. Was unable to utter a sound. Püppi said they had to see each other. She understood everything, of course. But they had to talk. Helene had trouble finding words. She didn't see the need. And. Moreover. Gregor was going nuts. She had to be very careful . . . "Gregor?" Püppi asked. "But he's in Taormina. He's going to be in Taormina until September 17." Helene sat there. The receiver in her hand. She was paralyzed. With rage. He was at a fancy resort in Sicily. She was in the Lannerstrasse. Or at the beach on the Old Danube. And so were the children. If it hadn't been for her sister, the children wouldn't have had a trip at all. And. All this fear for nothing. Gregor hadn't had any intention of acting out his threats. They weren't even worth that much. She wasn't worth it. Püppi asked if she'd come to the Santo Spirito in the evening. Or to the Kalb. Helene said nothing. Couldn't say anything. Püppi said, "Well then. 10 o'clock in the Old Vienna. Okay?" and hung up. Helene kept sitting by the phone. When Dr. Loibl called, she didn't know what to say. She couldn't very well tell the lawyer she'd been afraid her husband might abduct the children. But that he'd preferred to go to Taormina. And that she might have known from the beginning. Now. In hindsight she knew she should have realized. She told the lawyer she felt threatened by her husband. She started to cry. Dr. Loibl said in a fatherly tone, "Don't worry, Ma'am. I'm taking care of it. And best regards to your honorable father. You hadn't told me, had you, that your father is Herr Wolffen, Chief Justice of the Court. I'm very honored of course. I kiss your hand. My regards to the family. I'll be in touch as soon as things develop." Helene sank back into the couch. She sent the children shopping. They took off cheerfully. They were to bring back a big block of chocolate ice cream. Helene remained sitting.

In the evening Helene went to the mirror and looked at herself. The skin on her cheekbones was taut. She had rings under her eyes. The corners of her mouth were pulled. Into a kind of grin. Her eyebrows pointed steeply upwards. She could see exactly where one day lines would run across her forehead. She decided to drive into town. She wanted to know everything. She took special care to make herself up. The children would have to look after themselves. They'd have to get used to it anyway. If anything out of the ordinary came up, they'd be able to ring the grandmother's bell. Or phone her. Helene drove into town. She felt as if she was up again for the first time after a long illness. It seemed a long way from the Dominican Bastion to the Old Vienna. In front of the Kalb she ran into Haimowicz who was just beginning his daily pub crawl. He greeted her. Hugged her. Pressed her against his belly. Asked what she was up to. Turned toward 2 young girls who were coming out of the Kalb. Helene didn't have to reply. She walked on. She wondered if she really should go to the Old Vienna. What was there to discuss with Püppi. She blamed herself for being spineless. She created an oracle for herself. If at the next street corner. Just across from the Old Vienna. If at that spot she were to step with her left foot from the sidewalk onto the street, she wouldn't have to go into the Old Vienna. Would be allowed to turn around and leave. If she were to step down with her right foot, she'd have to enter. She stepped down with her left foot and went into the Old Vienna. It was almost empty. Still too early. Too early for most people. Püppi was sitting in the left corner by the window. Helene sat down opposite her. Püppi looked the way she always did. Her hair shorter. Less of a perm. It suited her. She looked gentler. Not as flaky as with the long Medusa curls. Tanned. Freckled. Younger. Helene ordered white wine with soda water. Püppi had a mineral water in front of her. No. She'd given up drinking. She was healed. She was starting over. Completely. And a precondition to her new life was Helene's forgiveness. Püppi said "forgiveness." Like in church. And Helene should accept Püppi's gratitude. Püppi talked quickly and hurriedly. Without pausing. Helene wouldn't have been able to get a word in. And about the requests for forgiveness and so on. Püppi had never talked like that. Never talked such sentimental crap before. Püppi put her hand on Helene's. Her therapist. The one in Switzerland. There. Where she'd been. He'd given her that as a task. She had a whole list of such tasks. And these two things. The gratitude and the forgiveness. They were particularly important. Helene didn't have any idea how much they'd talked about her. About her. The white deer. The therapist had asked her to describe everybody she'd been involved with as an animal. Helene pulled her hand away from underneath Püppi's. How had she described Gregor, she asked. "As a green lion. Of course," Püppi said. Then she put her hands around Helene's. Enclosed Helene's hands, which clasped the glass. "It was only once," Püppi said. "Honestly!" Helene could not feel her throat. Was only aware that it hurt. Was afraid she would no longer be able to breathe. Püppi was prattling on. Quickly. Cheerfully. She said that Helene had always been right. That she, Püppi, would concentrate now. Work. Take her painting seriously. And the conditions were favorable. She now had somebody who was also involved with the arts. Not the visual arts. But. Music and painting. There was so much they had in common. And he was a very special person. Helene didn't know him. Probably. Or maybe she did. She'd once seen him in the Santo Spirito. But that was a long time ago. She'd only again, by sheer luck. "But I have another chance. You understand? I'm just going to start all over. If I waste this chance. You understand. Then there'll be nothing left. I have to make it this time. But you have to say that you're not upset with me. And that everything will be just like before. And that we'll be able again to talk about every-thing. You'll get along well with him. I know that for sure. And we'll find a man for you. And then we'll all go out. And everything. What do you think. Don't you think it all incredibly exciting too. I can really start all over. But first you have to say that you're no longer angry with me. With-out the boozing. And you know. Everything else. That's what really caused it. I wouldn't have done it. Otherwise. Really. Trust me. Helene. You really have to trust me." Helene sat there. Tried to pull her hands away from beneath Püppi's. Püppi squeezed her hands tight. She should say that everything was fine. Püppi stared into Helene's eyes. Held her hands tightly. In an iron grip. On a TV show, he would enter at this moment. Or maybe not, it flashed through Helene's mind. Did Püppi refer to Henryk. Or to somebody else. Why wasn't she asking her? "You. Konstanze," Helene started. "Please!" Püppi said. "Please!" She squeezed Helene's hands even more tightly. Beseechingly. The thin sides of the cheap water glass in which the Gespritzte was served shattered. The fragments drove into Helene's palms, the balls of her thumbs and her fingers. Where her fingertips were interlocked, they remained unhurt. Helene whispered, "Püppi. Let go." Püppi almost yelled, "Please!" Helene said calmly, "Okay then. But now let go." She pushed Püppi away. Helene held her hands outstretched. Above the table. Blood, fragments of glass and the watered down wine. Blood dripped. Wine ran over the side of the table. The blood began to run. Püppi shrieked. Helene felt nothing. She started to pull the thin glass splinters out of her skin. She did it methodically. At first, with her right hand those in her left. Then with her left hand those in her right. The waiter just stood there. Püppi had jumped up and now stared at the table. Other patrons were stepping closer. Helene heard somebody ask for a doctor. Helene took the napkin off the waiter. Did he have a second one? The man rushed away and brought back another one. Helene wrapped the napkins around her hands. Her blood had started to flow seriously by now. Light red. Helene got up. Put her purse over her shoulder. She left. With her hands wrapped in the napkins. Walked along the Bäckerstrasse to the Jesuit Church. To the Bastion.

Haimowicz came chugging up from the Kalb toward the Old Vienna. He greeted her again. Exuberantly. Püppi stood in front of the Old Vienna. She called out, "Helene." Again and again. Helene walked away. She could still hear Püppi when she passed the Academy of Sciences. Helene walked mechanically. Driving the car was difficult. She could only steer with her fingertips. The napkins unraveled repeatedly, and blood was dripping everywhere. Helene drove in second gear. Changing gears was impossible. She dragged herself home in her car. She unplugged the phone jack. Tore the intercom off the wall. The wires dangled. But nobody would be able to ring. Helene poured disinfectant over her hands. The pain was unbearable. Sharp and throbbing. She didn't recognize her own hands. Laboriously, she wrapped gauze pads and bandages around them. Barbara had woken up. She came tiptoeing to the bathroom door. Peeked around the corner through the slightly open door. Helene asked her to help. Barbara finished putting on the bandages. Helene told her what to do. Barbara did a very good job. But she was white in the face. Helene asked her to help her. Undressing. The child didn't ask questions. She opened zippers. Buttons. Pulled the sleeves carefully over the hands. Helped Helene into a nightgown. Barbara brought aspirin and water. Helene would have liked to drink something stronger. But obviously there was nothing left in the house. Barbara should go back to bed now. And thanks so much for all the help. She wouldn't have known what to do. Without her, Helene said. And they had to tell Katharina very gently. She got frightened so easily. Barbara tucked Helene in. Helene put her hands back. Next to her head. Like a baby. So that the hands would rest on their backs. Palms up.

For the next few days Helene couldn't do anything. She existed only as screamingly painful hands. She would break into tears over anything. Most of all she cried when she heard the children discuss what else there was to do. For her.

Helene's left hand wasn't healing properly. She was forced to see a doctor. Her family doctor sent her to Emergency Surgery at the General Hospital. Her doctor shook her head. The doctor at Emergency Surgery shook his head. Why hadn't she come earlier. Helene didn't respond. Should she tell the doctor how Gulla in the novel for young girls Gulla at the Manor House. How, at least, Gulla had been nursed back to health by a charcoal burner. But that for her, no charcoal burner had been found. Helene tried to explain to the doctor how the accident had happened. He said something about her thenar. Extracted bits of glass from the ball of her thumb. The numbness in her left ring finger. It might disappear. One would have to decide later on. Normally one could only repair that sort of thing right away. Helene was off sick. But she drove to the office anyway. The photo shoot for the packaging of magnetic foil was coming up. Organized by Helene. Everybody was back from the summer. Nadolny had been hunting in Africa. He was in a jolly mood. Sparkling wine was taken in the morning.

The shots were to be taken in a photographer's studio in Hietzing. A star photographer. He was married to a former model. She would do the makeup for the nude shots. In this case it meant covering the young woman's entire body with gold paint. The photographer would then have thirty minutes to take his shots. The paint wasn't to stay on the skin much longer. There was danger of suffocation. Nadolny had repeated this sentence over and over. And lifted his champagne flute. The photographer had selected the model. After a movie director had recommended the young woman. Or so it was said. She was called Karin. Helene knew all about her measurements. And how sensitive Karin supposedly was. Requiring the utmost quiet. In the studio. Helene was to take care of that. Helene hadn't wanted to come to the shoot. Her hands were still in bandages. The left one big. With only her fingertips sticking out. On her right hand, only Band-Aids were left. Nadolny had asked her to come. For the atmosphere. She'd create a good atmosphere. A professional one. Helene drove to the studio. She was on time. 10 o'clock in the morning. She found parking in front of the house. The gate to the garden stood open. She went to the front door. An arrow on a bronze sign pointed to the studio. Helene followed the arrow. She didn't find a door. She walked on. Attached to the one-family home was a concrete building. Helene walked beside the concrete wall. She turned around the corner and faced a set of large French doors. Helene stopped, irresolute. Through the glass doors she looked into the room. So far, she hadn't seen anybody. Inside stood a woman. Naked. She propped herself up on a vanity. She was looking into a mirror. The man stood behind her. Looking past her into the mirror. The young woman turned away. Wriggled to the side. The man said something. His cock was jiggling out of his pants. The woman laughed and ran to the back of the room. The man went after her. He had taken his cock in his hand and was holding it up to the woman. Helene couldn't hear a sound. She went back along the path. She got in her car and drove up to the corner. She stayed in her seat. Had she gotten the date mixed up? Had she come the wrong day? She got out and walked to a phone box. She called the office. The appointment had been postponed by two hours. Hadn't she been aware of it. Frau Sprecher pretended to be dismayed.

Yes. The change had been necessary because the model's underwear had left lines. Now they had to wait until the lines had disappeared. It takes time. Frau Sprecher sounded satisfied. Well then. It'll all be at noon. Helene sat down in the Dommayer. The scene hadn't excited her. She could recall how the man had held up his erect cock for the woman. The woman should do something, he'd probably said. It was all her fault. Now she'd have to put it right again. That's what he had looked like. Sulking and accusatory. The way he'd been following the woman showed he was convinced he'd get it all. It was a game. Helene tried to put herself into the woman's role. She had no success. No part of her, inside or out, responded to the fantasy. Helene sat in the café. She had no more desire. Not even for it. It made her sad. Worn down, she thought. So you've finally been worn down, haven't you.

At 11 o'clock everybody was already there. A door stood open. Helene hadn't seen it before. Steps led downstairs. In the studio was a platform on top of scaffolding. Photo floods were aimed at the platform. The studio was deep below the ground. Or so it seemed to Helene. Nadolny and Nestler lingered next to the photographer. They weren't allowed to smoke. Big signs ruled it out. Nadolny and Nestler asked the man if he'd make an exception. They stood around. Shifted from one foot to the other. Adjusted their ties. 2 assistants were arranging the flood lights. They climbed up and down the balcony. And the scaffolding. The photographer yelled instructions up to them. Nadolny and Nestler talked quietly. As if they were in the waiting room. At the dentist. The photographer had been the man behind the glass door. He kept repeating to Nadolny, "Just be quiet, will you. All right? We're working, don't you see." And Nadolny nodded. Eager. After half an hour a woman came through a door on the balcony. "We're coming now," she called. The photographer stepped behind his camera. Upstairs, the model came through the door. She wore nothing. Without the lights, the gold paint looked dirty. She walked behind the woman who'd called down. The two women had been arguing. The older one walked full of reproach and disapproval. But she had won. She pulled her shoulders back and her chin up. She walked fast. The model seemed defiant. Didn't look up. Dragged her feet. Shuffled more than walked. She came down the steps and climbed up on the platform. She didn't look at anybody in the room. The men stared at the climbing woman. She positioned herself in the light. She lifted her arms. Put one leg slightly ahead of the other. She was beautiful. She'd been the young woman behind the glass door. The photographer gave instructions. The lighting was changed. The model Karin was to lift her head. Good. Good. As if looking at the sun. Or some other beautiful thing. Nadolny asked timidly if she could smile perhaps. A bit. Enraptured. She wasn't paid for it, the young woman called down. And the photographer should hurry up. She wasn't keen on dying. Not for some shitty photos. Helene saw Nestler staring up at the young woman. He stood holding his hands behind his back. He was rocking. He let himself roll on his bunions. And then tilted back on his heels. Helene's hands hurt. Her left hand throbbed slightly. She wanted to leave. The photographer was taking shots of the young woman's back. Again he gave instructions to adjust a flood light. The young woman dropped her arms. She wasn't going to continue. What was the time anyway. It had only been 25 minutes, the photographer said. And she shouldn't make such a fuss. One could manage for an hour. With the paint on her skin. The idea of having one's skin completely gummed up made Helene nervous. The mere thought made her struggle for air. The sticky air in the studio. The heat. No light. Helene wanted to get out. Karin had once more lifted her arms heavenwards and pushed forward her right hip. The camera buzzed and clicked. The model clutched her head. Helene heard the photographer whisper "hysterical bitch." The camera continued to buzz and click. Then the photographer said he thought he had what he needed. And Karin should go and have a shower. The young woman climbed off the platform. Walked past Nadolny and Nestler. Who tried to smile at her. Embarrassed. Karin looked angrily ahead. Walked to the balcony stairs. Went upstairs and disappeared. The other woman behind her. Helene left too. She wanted to go outside. She had to press down the handle of the heavy metal door to the studio with her elbow. Her hands were hurting.

Helene drove back to the office. Nadolny and Nestler had arrived ahead of her. Nestler sat on the black leather couch in Nadolny's office. Nadolny was pouring drinks from a bottle of sparkling wine. Helene had to walk past the open door. Nestler called cheers and drank to her health. Nadolny was just saying to Nestler, "He always does it. Has to have her. Before. Can't take photos otherwise." At "photos," Nadolny burst into laughter. Snorted. Helene walked to her desk. Walked back and closed her door. She sat down. Leaned back. Her left palm throbbed. She propped her left arm on the desk and held her hand up. The throbbing turned into an aching. She tried to move her ring finger. She had to support it with her right hand. The movement needed to be triggered from the outside. Then she was able to bend her finger further. Or use the Vulcan greeting. The children had laughed a lot at her. Because she'd been unable to imitate the Star Trek greeting. The unresponsiveness of her ring finger gave Helene butterflies. Nadolny jerked her door open. Was the handout for the news conference ready. Could he have it. Helene handed him the file. Nadolny took it and left. He left the door open. Helene heard him bolt into his office. Slam the door. After that, murmuring. Frau Sprecher talked to somebody on the phone. Helene took her purse. She went to Frau Sprecher. Wanted to say good-bye. The conversation seemed to take longer. Helene held her left hand up. Pulled a face. Signaled she was leaving. Frau Sprecher nodded and waved. Helene left. She pressed the button for the elevator. Got in. Saw herself in the mirror on the back wall of the elevator. Got out. Walked out of the building. She paused for a moment in the narrow entrance hall. The afternoon sun shone into the street. There was no shade outside. It smelled of dust and heat. Helene pushed the door open. Let it swing. Her car was on the left. By the Federal Insurance Office. She took her sunglasses from the glove compartment. There was no way she could continue. Not at this office. Helene was surprised how little the thought frightened her. She drove home. Driving was still difficult. When she changed gears, she could hold the steering wheel only with her left thumb and index finger.

At home Helene found the children reading. They had warmed up their meal. She had cooked in advance. These days, noodles with frozen sauces were the only option anyway. Helene couldn't have chopped anything. There was no mail. She hardly ever got mail now. Nothing anymore for Gregor. Not even bank statements. The woman at the Credit Union in the Schottengasse obviously had his address. Invitations had become increasingly rare. Hardly any over the summer. There was an invitation on the little table in the hallway. A company "All Around the Household" was inviting guests to a most interesting lecture at the

Steirerbeisl on the topic of "Nature's Most Important Treasures to Benefit your Health." Right afterwards you would be given to take home a ten-piece set of kitchen knives with serrated edges and safety handles, and, in addition, a mirror with lights, batteries and bag included. And you should bring your friends too. Helene asked the children if they'd like to go for a walk. She'd just get herself some coffee. They'd go for a drive. To the Long Path. Or somewhere. The children wanted to come. But only if they'd also go to the playground. Helene agreed and went to make the coffee. The children should start putting on their shoes. And grab their coats. It would get cool toward the evening. Katharina brought the Kurier for Helene into the kitchen. Grandma had sent it over. She had marked what she thought was of interest to Helene. Helene took her coffee to the table and leafed through the paper. The article was marked with blue pen. Her mother-in-law had drawn a big exclamation mark in the margin next to the article. And underlined Püppi's name. Helene was surprised. How come the old woman knew Püppi's name. Püppi. Konstanze Storntberg was dead. She'd been found dead. In her apartment in the 4th district. She must have been dead a few days. Other tenants in the building had called the police. The cause of death hadn't yet been determined. There was an inquest. The article was short. One paragraph. On the local news page. Helene tore the page out of the Kurier and folded it. She put it in G. K. Chesterton's The Man Who Was Thursday and put the book in one of the empty shelves in the book case. The children shouldn't read it. She would tell them. Some time. The children were bouncing in the hallway. Helene put on a different pair of shoes. Then they drove off.

Helene left the children behind on the playground. She walked ahead. They were to catch up with her. The playground was beneath a huge linden tree in the middle of the Keller district of Obermalebarn. Helene walked through the Kellergasse. Onto the Long Path. At the wayside shrine with the crucifix. On the first hill. Right at the bottom of the path, the Madonna picture had been replaced. Before, a reproduction of a Madonna icon had hung behind the glass. Now an image of Our Lady of Fatima had been put up. New and shiny. Asters bloomed all around the stone pedestal. The fields had been harvested. The rutabagas and potatoes, too, had been pulled. Clover grew on some of the fields. The soil was a shining dark-brown. The hills on the right rose into the sky, as before. On the left, the hills rolled into the distance. The trees in the little forest hadn't changed color yet. But the light was an autumn light. Clear. Shining. As if everything was quite close. Helene walked down the hill. She propped her left arm up with her right one. Held her left hand up. Diagonally across her chest. She walked slowly. She went to the crossroads where she always turned around. When she was by herself. Up to that point, no road and no transmission tower could be seen. There she turned and walked back. If she'd left her phone plugged in. Would Püppi have called her? And would she have driven to her? And would Püppi still be alive in that case? And Sophie? What was now to become of Sophie? She would never see Sophie again either. Helene found the children, who were still on the playground. Helene called the girls. They wanted to stay longer. Helene wanted to leave. After some reluctance, they finally came. Helene drove with them all the way to the Czech border. Her hands hurt. But Helene wanted to have open country around her. And sky. The thought of sitting in the apartment made her chest heavy. And frightened her. Then they had to drive back. The children still had homework to do. They might want to stay home. The next day. Helene suggested. The children didn't want to. Then they'd have to make up for it. It'd be too dull, they thought.

Helene sat in her living room deep into the night. Again and again she had taken the newspaper clipping from the book and read it over. She'd wondered whom to call. To find out more. Wondered whether to call anybody. She didn't plug her phone in. Long after midnight she went into the kitchen. She pulled the big casserole for making jam out of her cupboard. She filled it with water and put it on the gas. In the past, Helene had made her own jam. Gregor used to like it. Then he'd given up eating sweets. And the jars just sat there. Helene didn't like jam. There were still two jars of cherry jam left that were the same age as Barbara. The casserole was big. It took a long time for the water to boil. Helene hadn't wiped it. Dust and threads of spider web floated on top. When the water bubbled, Helene got all the CDs, tapes and records. She threw them into the boiling water. This way they'd surely be wrecked. She broke the LPs. Unwound the cassette tapes. Poked the CDs in between. She watched the water. How it was bubbling up. Between the shining silver disks. Pushing up the tapes. How the water was changing color. How it started to stink. Then she turned off the flame. Poured the water off and put the casserole back on the stove. To let it cool. She put a dish towel over the casserole. Somewhere there had to be a lid. She was too tired to look. Helene went back to the living room. Paced up and down. Looked out the window. Lay on her bed. Threw herself on the couch. Hung about in the armchairs. Poured herself a bath. Drained the water. Everything was wrong. Helene searched for the Valium pills from Dr. Stadlmann. Didn't find them. She was no longer able to cry either. Scream. She could have screamed. But the children. Between her sobbing fits. When she regained her breath, she stood still. Or leaned against the wall. She couldn't grasp it. This was supposed to be life. And yet she knew at the same time that she had been dealt an easy one. That the horror could be way worse. How alone Püppi must have been. Helene had to bend over to endure the pain in her middle and her chest.

In the morning Helene put the casserole with the boiled CDs, records and tapes back into the cupboard. She had found the lid. All the CDs, records and tapes had belonged to Gregor. If he wanted his music back, he could have it. Boiled. Gregor had mostly listened to opera. There was a hideous lumpy mass in the casserole in the morning. In which the CDs stuck. And the tapes wriggled. Helene prepared breakfast for the children. Sent them to school and went back to bed. When she woke up again, it was almost noon. She phoned the office. Asked to be connected with Nadolny. Frau Sprecher wanted to chat. How was she doing. Helene asked her to connect her quickly. With a peeved "It's for you. Frau Gebhardt," Helene got Nadolny on the phone. She would apologize to Frau Sprecher. Another time. Helene told Nadolny she would no longer come to work. And could he fire her. Because of the unemployment money. Nadolny said immediately he'd do that. If she wished. Of course. Nadolny was very friendly. He obviously had somebody with him he wanted to impress. Had Helene really given it enough thought? "Yes," Helene said. Yes, she had. She'd thought about it very carefully. Then she phoned Dr. Loibl. He wasn't in, she was told by his office. Could he call her back. As soon as possible. It was urgent.

Helene didn't find a seat right away. She stood in the doorway. Leaning against the door frame. Opened her paper and started reading. Whenever Helene went to the unemployment office in the Herbertstrasse, she would first drive to the Franz Joseph's Station and buy papers. The Neue Züricher. The Guardian. At the unemployment office she then dropped off her forms at the counter for the letters F - I and read the papers. People came. And went. Children ran around. A baby cried. Another one slept. After half an hour, a seat became available. Helene sat down. She started reading again. All the papers were dominated by the unification of Germany. Helene let her paper drop. Folded it. Stared into space. In the corridor, outside. Near the elevator, smokers paced up and down. Inhaled hastily. Stubbed out their cigarettes and returned to their seats. People entered offices. New people arrived. Pulled numbers. Waited. Others left. It never took very long. Helene would have to take some courses, they had told her. Computers. Accounting. Something of this sort. The way it was, she was unemployable. Helene sat up. Names were called out through a microphone. It had happened that Helene had missed her name. At first, she would take a computer course. The family court had sentenced Gregor to backpay and payment of maintenance. Yet the money had to be collected. Dr. Loibl thought Gregor wouldn't let it come to a notification of his employer and seizure of his salary. So the money should arrive soon. Helene leaned her head against the wall. At first, she would take the computer course. Then it would be Christmas. And next year, everything would be better. Helene heard her name called.